# E.S. BARRISON

# THOSE COBALT CURRENTS

Dedicated to anyone who has sought out a new home.

And to everyone who has found such peace.

Kainan
Knoll's Gully
Chelidae's Mark
The Capital
Rosada
Hutch's Creek
Rosadi Gulf
Newbird Mountain Range
Newbird's Arm
Siren's Bay
Grover's Marsh
Volfium
L'Perle

The Schanifeld

Merton

The Blood Sea

ian
f

# A Rabbit in Port

The pirates arrived on an unsuspecting summer day. I saw them from my perch atop a roof I'd been repairing. With two nails hanging from my mouth and a hammer in hand, I froze, unable to take my eyes off the navy-blue sails moving into port from a distance. On the largest sail, the emblem of a white rabbit marked their arrival.

"Lyam!" my father shouted from the ground. "What's the holdup there, boy?"

I shook off the trance from the ship, removing the nails from my mouth and returning to work. "You cannot rush perfection, Père! I'm cherishing the timber."

"Well, cherish it tomorrow. The day is growing weary. I would like to tell Monsieur Aubert that his roof is repaired before nightfall."

"I know, Père! It won't be long!" I resumed my work on the roof, hammering away at the wooden shingles, my attention drifting every few moments to the sails. As I lined a nail with a shingle, I glanced again toward the harbor. There was something haunting about the way the ship moved, approaching like a monster with skin painted obsidian.

My attention torn, I raised my hammer.

Rather than hitting the nail, I hit my finger.

"Merde!" I cursed.

"Lyam! What are you doing!?" my father shouted again.

I shook out my hand. "Sorry! There's a strange ship in the harbor."

"We get ships every day. What'cha mean?"

"It's painted…black."

"Black?"

"With navy sails…and a white emblem of a rabbit," I glanced down at my father.

He furrowed his brow so the wrinkles on his forehead became more defined.

I glanced one last time at the ominous ship, then slid down the ladder to where my father waited. "What's wrong, Père?"

He adjusted his smudged glasses and shook his head. "Not sure. Just remembered a rumor I heard down at the docks 'bout a couple ships down in the Malva Straits. Pirates, someone told me. Said it was an obsidian ship with a tortoise on its sails."

"This is a rabbit, though."

"Yeah…not sure, really. Could mean anything." He eyed me. "Go home to your mother, Lyam. She'll want to know."

"Are you sure you don't want me to finish up here? The roof will be done soon."

"You mean, in three days."

"I'm a bit faster than that, don't'cha think?"

"Monsieur Aubert needs his roof done today. Your jobs are always done perfectly, but sometimes we need a bit of speed."

I scoffed but didn't argue. My father waved me off and ascended the ladder. Halfway up, he paused to catch his breath before continuing.

I waited until he was on the roof before leaving. After setting my hammer on my belt, I turned down the road.

A monstrous storm had struck our little island of L'Perle only a week earlier. With torrential rains, winds that uprooted the trees, and flooding that invaded the harbor for a week, it was only now that life had started to return to normal. My father and I had set out to work at once, repairing homes and structures around the island. It was good, honest work; mundane, but reliable.

But the idea of a pirate ship in port filled me with bubbling excitement. What stories could they tell me? What treasures had they uncovered? But for the storms, life on

L'Perle was as smooth as an actual pearl. Things didn't change.

As I climbed the hill away from port, I continued to steal glances at the ship. It was quite the vessel; not only did its navy-blue sails cast a shadow, but its obsidian body stained the entire harbor. Could it really be pirates right here in L'Perle? What could they want?

If pirates were here, my mother would want to be the first to know.

While my father had worked as a carpenter, my mother became a seasoned importer for the local government. She negotiated deals too complex for even the wealthiest of men. Ever since I was a little boy, she took me down to the ports to assist with trades. I spent countless hours playing with children who sailed across the seas. In our countless games, I learned their languages and their stories, and at night I would go home and imagine life at sea.

But instead, I stayed here on the island, helping my mother with her trades and my father with his repairs. I had resolved to be content with that, letting the stories of voyagers and adventurers carry me away like the tune of my flute-pipe.

I stopped at the top of the hill overlooking the harbor. A few gray birds flew above, their flight reminiscent of smoke. I whistled in their direction. One gray bird with yellow and orange tail feathers broke off from the flock. It circled me for a moment, then landed on my shoulder.

"Lee-Yam!" the bird exclaimed.

"Hi, Cheddar-bird. Good flight today?" I asked.

The bird clicked her beak and mimicked the sound of thunder.

I smiled and bobbed her on the beak. "Thunderous excitement today then?"

The bird produced a similar noise once again.

With Cheddar on my arm, I continued down the narrow path toward my family home. With my mother's work and my father's skill, our home was certainly one to be admired. It sat perched on a stone base, with winding stairs that reached its carved door. Sitting two stories high, even its smallest windows could see the sea in the distance. Unlike many other homes on L'Perle, my parents made sure to commission a fresh coat of paint on the wood after each storm season, ensuring that the home glistened like a jewel on a necklace.

As I approached the door, I ushered Cheddar to step onto a nearby branch. "I'll be back out soon, okay?"

Cheddar bobbed her head.

I reached into my tool belt and removed a seed. Cheddar took it with excitement.

"Good bird," I whispered, then pushed open the door to the home.

While our home did indeed loom in size, once inside, it shrank. With its eclectic assortment of goods, every day I scrambled over the collection of crates in the entranceway. As I entered, it was no different, tripping over one of the boxes and hitting my head on a nearby beam. The wood clunked, yelling at me for my clumsiness.

I uttered a curse under my breath, then shouted, "Mère! You home!?"

"Upstairs!" my mother called back, her strong voice loud enough that the bottles clattered on a nearby shelf.

I navigated through the piles of books and knick-knacks, hopped over a blanket-covered couch, and found my way to the stairs.

A pile of clothes sat on the steps. As I reached the landing, I grabbed one of the disheveled piles of tunics and placed them under my arm before turning to the ajar door to my mother's study.

"Mère?" I peeked inside the room. Like the rest of the house, my mother's study comprised a vast array of unique items, disorganized and strewn about in random locations across the room. From books to model ships to the twenty-or-so globes, the room was a disorganized museum. Even the walls, decorated with scribbled maps, had no empty space.

My mother stood in front of a map, her hair pinned in a disheveled bun, her glasses riding down the tip of her thin nose. A smile filled her face as she turned. "Lyam! You are home early! Wonderful… that means you can help me. There's a Rosadian book downstairs with updated maps. It should be on the kitchen table… or the sofa… or perhaps under the boot rack. I was looking at it, I know I was…but it has updated maps. One of my traders wants to know a good place to trade for ore, and I know a few cities in Rosada, but I need to check. Could you go find it?"

I nodded, trying to keep track of my mother's slew of thoughts. "Yes, of course, Mère, but one thing—"

"Oh, and if you could help me later, there was this trader in town who speaks Vernnes. I'll need you to join me tomorrow, if your father can spare—"

"Mère!" I interjected.

She stared at me, wide-eyed.

"Sorry. It's—I have important news."

"Oh?"

I motioned toward the window, covered in maps. "A pirate ship pulled into port. Thought you'd want to know about that."

"Are you sure?"

"It's an obsidian ship—"

"That sounds like the Commeant's Obsidian Fleet to me."

"It's not. They have a skeletal flag of a rabbit."

"Oh…really?" My mother's face lit up like the sky, and a smile raced across her face. "Fantastic! If I hurry, I might be able to corner them. I haven't had a good pirate trade in years…not since Venom Mouth got themselves killed at least. You know, they might cause terror across the sea, but pirates are damn good trade partners."

I smirked. My mother had gone on tirades about pirates on more than one occasion. When I was a boy, she used to trade regularly with the infamous Venom Mouth, a ruthless pirate known for disrupting trades and claiming the sea. Once word spread that Venom Mouth had passed, no other pirate visited our little island.

"Would you like me to come with you in case they need translating?" I asked.

"No. No… stay here. Find that book for me. I need to get that information to my buyer before they leave in two days."

"Of course, Mère."

She patted my cheek. With a smile laced on her lips, she hurried downstairs, nearly tripping over one of the boxes on her way out.

I watched for a moment, but rather than following her downstairs, I continued along the hallway and retired to my room. Unlike the rest of the house, my room maintained a rather bland interior. My father handmade all my furniture, and sitting on my dresser was the first thing he ever taught me to carve: a wooden flute, one that did not produce a sound as clean as the performers in town, but a flute nonetheless.

After putting my clothes in a drawer, I took the flute and sat on my bed. Carefully, from under my pillow, I removed the very book of maps my mother had asked me to find. I flipped through the pages. This, and the stories from sailors in port, provided the only escape from life on this island. It wasn't a terrible life by any means, but the sight of the sea and the hillsides only provided so much enjoyment.

Especially when the world was far more intriguing.

I brought the book to my door and placed it in the hall for my mother to find later. With my door shut, I reached for my flute and opened my window. The blue edge of the sea waved at me. A flock of birds took to the clouds.

Except for Cheddar, who flew up to my windowsill as soon as I opened it.

I held out a finger, which she pecked once.

"Why don't you go flying far away, huh, Cheddar?" I asked the bird.

She tilted her head to the side.

"Yeah, I get it…it's a little scary."

She whistled once.

And with a slight smile, I raised my flute to my lips to play a gentle song that Cheddar might someday carry to the sky and set free.

# CHAPTER TWO

# Aquamarine

My father and I ate at our cluttered kitchen table. The glow of sunset cast an orange light over us from the open window. My mother had yet to come home. She often spent long nights at the docks, dealing with sailors, her tongue sharp and mind quick. So, we ate our seafood bisque, sharing a few anecdotes and our company, as we always did.

"Did you finish Monsieur Aubert's roof?" I asked my father.

He chuckled. "Of course I did. I might be old, but I still got my speed."

"But was it as perfect as my work?"

"Perfect? Pfft. That's a little pretentious, don't'cha think? No one is *that* talented."

"Then why do you keep me around?"

"Because I'm old," my father chuckled.

I grinned. With my mother's success in port, my father could probably rest easy now. Money was no issue. But once when I brought it up to my father, he simply said, "It's not about the money. The wood speaks to me like the sea speaks to a sailor… or the trees speak to a forest queen. Don't you understand?"

In part, I did. Some days, when working on a house or carving a piece of furniture, I thought that the wood whispered my name, instructing me where to best hammer a nail or remove a shaving.

It was hard to ignore the way the wood spoke to me… and I knew my father felt the same.

I picked up the bowls after we finished and carried them over to the basin. From the window, I stole a glance at the tree line. Cheddar, as usual, had taken her nighttime perch outside my home. The orange feathers on her tail blended in with the sky.

"I am going to retire early for the night," my father said. "Will you be staying in tonight?"

I shrugged. "I may go into town. New sailors are in, and you know I like their tales."

"As I expect," my father patted my arm. "Now, don't go stirring up trouble."

"When do I ever?"

"There was that lad a few weeks ago… the one you brought home…"

"How was I s'posed to know that he was the son of some important Rosadian official? We were having some fun, y'know."

"Still, remember to ask questions. Especially since there're pirates about."

"I'll try, but no promises, Père."

"Very well. Good night, Lyam."

"Night."

My nighttime excursions into town were nothing new. I'd been sneaking out since I was fourteen or fifteen. Now, five years later, I didn't have to worry about sneaking, but my desire to find something new had grown. Night brought out a different world, repainting the town in a way that daylight failed.

With night as a guise, fresh faces appeared on the docks. Colorful personalities occupied the tavern. Liquor tasted more exciting. Even the music tore through the air, like on the back of comets.

These new personalities drew me. On more than one occasion, I'd found comfort in visitors from abroad, bringing an odd man home every now and again, granting me a momentary reprieve from monotony.

But it was only for a moment. All of these visitors left.

An experience. Gone.

A memory.

But that was my life, and I'd come to accept it.

I'd found a home at one specific place on the docks. A small saloon, hidden between a boarding house and the Postal Bureau, with its door painted blue. While it had no signage, we all knew its name: the *Aquamarine*.

Unassuming in the daylight, it was easy to miss. But at night, with a glow over its door from a single lantern, it attracted the most interesting visitors, as well as those of the locals who wanted an escape. I'd been frequenting it for years, finding comfort in its colorful walls and multicolored gas lamps. The patrons were like paintings, arriving in eccentric outfits, towering hairstyles, and variegated cosmetics. When I first came, I felt out of place in my boring tunics and worn pants. But they welcomed me like all the others.

Stories brought the *Aquamarine* to life. It was there that I learned the tales of the seas, from the rumors of serpents and seagrips shifting through purple-painted waters, to stories of sirens and their fear of daylight, and to legends of pirates who lived for a thousand years with a blessing from the Gods. Here, people were unafraid to be themselves, to tell stories wild and untampered by disbelief.

At the *Aquamarine*, people not only visited…they lived.

As I entered, a server with a tall pink pompadour and a face caked with powder greeted me. "Lyam! How are you, mon amour?"

"Bonsoir Ora," I said to them, taking their hand and planting a kiss on it. "You ready for a pretty bit of coin to-night?"

"With pirates in port? I'm expecting a fortune."

"You'll be the talk of the seas for years to come."

Ora placed her hand on my arm and lowered her voice. "By the way, at the end of the bar, there's a handsome fella with blue eyes waiting for someone to whisk 'em away."

"I care about more than *just* blue eyes, you know."

"Yes, but you always chase after those blue-eyed lads."

I flushed, stifling a laugh as I slipped Ora a single doubloon. "Well, thank you, pépée."

"It is but my job, mon amour." They slipped the coin into their blouse and then sauntered off to greet another patron.

I brushed back my hair and straightened my tunic, reciting a few different greetings to myself, before heading to the back of the saloon. As Ora said, a slim fellow with bright blue eyes sat at the bar counter, his gaze distant. An uncombed mop of red hair glowed like fire on his head. Freckles dotted his nose.

My stomach leapt. Not only did his blue eyes pull me in, but something else. There was an odd allure to him. I was a mosquito drawn in by his fire.

I gulped, then approached him. Sweat dotted my brow. "'Scusez-moi?"

He stared at me.

*Must not speak Volfi.* I changed to Vernnes. "Sorry—is this seat taken?"

The fellow shook his head. He was about my age, but something in his eyes said he'd lived the life of someone far older.

I took a seat next to him. "If you haven't ordered yet, I recommend the Twist. Made with local rum, and will send your troubles on an adventure."

The fellow half-smirked. "Sounds like something I need."

I snapped my fingers to get the barkeep's attention. "Oi! Willy! Two Twists. Put it on my tab."

The barkeep acknowledged me with a grunt and turned to his liquor cabinet.

While he worked on the drink, I returned to the new fellow. "Guessing you got into port today? Haven't seen you around here before."

"Just passing through," he replied, his voice low and warm.

"Well, you found your way to the *Aquamarine*, so I'm guessing you've got some troubles you want to forget for a bit."

"A bit is an understatement."

"I won't ask—if you're here to forget, then let's forget."

The barkeep interrupted with two drinks, with blue and red colors twisting in the glass.

I picked one up and raised it ever so slightly. "Name's Lyam by the way."

My neighbor raised his own glass. "Tristan."

We clinked our glasses. Tristan downed his at once.

I followed suit. The liquor warmed my insides, and I smiled to myself.

"Few more of those might just do the trick," Tristan muttered.

"Careful now, they leave their mark in the morning."

"The ship already rocks enough. Can't make it much worse." He closed his eyes and sighed, "What I would do for one night on shore."

I licked my bottom lip, pulling out my pathetic attempt to flirt. "Well, I can certainly provide you with a…night on shore."

"Hm?" He opened one eye.

"Only if you want, of course. But you are here at the *Aquamarine*, looking for an escape. I'm here…if only for the night." I tapped my fingers on the counter as I waited for Tristan to reply. These foolish nights did not always end in success, and the moments between the "yes" and "no" seemed to last forever.

Tristan raised his brow, cocking his head to the side as he analyzed me. He raised one of his hands, covered in a leather glove, and brought it to my bottom lip. From beneath his glove, a strange warmth radiated.

Our eyes locked. My heart thumped in my ears.

But before Tristan pursued me further, his eyes darted to the far end of the room. His face grew hard, and he dropped his hand to the side.

I turned to follow his gaze.

A woman had entered the tavern. In the *Aquamarine*'s glow, I couldn't make out much of her, but her presence commanded attention.

As did the sword on her hip.

Tristan cursed under his breath. Without saying another word to me, he rose from his place and approached the woman.

I could not hear the two from my spot, but I knew then that my chances with Tristan had passed. The woman placed a hand on Tristan's shoulder. He stiffened but followed her out of the saloon without another drink.

I groaned to myself and turned back to the bar. *So much for that.* Tristan's face remained vivid, but it would fade. A night of fun was not meant to last. It was just a way to escape the ongoing monotony.

"Need another one, boy?" the barkeep asked me.

"Please. And make it the strong stuff this time."

He obliged, pouring out another drink that would pick me up and take me on a boat through my dreams.

# Negotiations

My head pounded the next morning. I lost track of how many Twists I had, but somehow in my drunken stupor, I still made my way home. If it weren't for the incessant knocking on my door, I might have slept the entire day.

But my mother's voice pulled me from such a sleep. "Lyam! Are you in?"

I groaned, covering my eyes with my arm. "Yeah…"

"I need you at the docks with me today. The pirate captain doesn't speak Volfi, and I'm fearful I'll flub the trade if I try to speak Vernnes."

The room spun as I swung my legs out of bed. "Can I get a cup of coffee first?"

"There's a mug outside your door already."

I rubbed my eyes and climbed to my feet. Cheddar sat on my windowsill, watching, her head tilted to the side.

"Don't look at me like that, bird," I grunted.

Cheddar laughed, a shrill laugh that sounded like my mother's laughter. This wasn't the first time I had to go down to the docks with my mother hungover…and frankly, I'd rather do that than climb a roof with my father.

Although if my mother had taken the time to learn Vernnes, I'd still be asleep.

I picked up the cup of coffee outside my door, and nursing the warmth of the beverage, took each step slowly down the stairs. My father sat on one of the couches amidst a few piles of boxes, sorting through his toolbox on his lap.

"Morning, Père."

"Late night?" He grinned.

"It was…a night."

"No visitors though?"

"Père…" I groaned.

He chuckled. "Well, you'd better get your head in order. Your mother is waiting."

I grunted and placed my empty coffee cup on the side table. After slipping on my boots and a wide-brimmed hat, I stepped out into the blinding morning light.

"Yam!" Cheddar greeted me with another guffaw. I held out my arm, letting her land.

My mother waited for me down the steps.

"Ah, hello, Cheddar," she said to the bird as we approached her.

"Hello!" the bird chirped.

My mother laughed and offered Cheddar a couple of seeds from her hand. Once Cheddar finished her morning snack, my mother motioned me to follow her down the hill and into town, where the sea continued its beckoning. As we trudged down, I once again saw the dark sails of the pirate ship. The night before, they had blended with the sky, one with land and sea, like a ghost in the night.

While I'd met plenty of sailors before, I'd never met a pirate. After Venom Mouth vanished, only rumors ever entered our port. Most recently, talk of a young pirate captain seizing ships and laying claim to the sea had passed through the mouths of sailors. Was this the very captain? Or someone else?

I wrung my hands together as we approached the pier. While I'd spoken to countless sailors, the prospect of pirates sent my nerves tumbling.

My mother placed a hand on my arm. "Lyam, do not fret. They are merely traders by a different name."

I nodded.

She smiled. When she smiled, I saw myself in her. We had the same dark eyes, the same wide jaw, and a similar smile that stretched from cheek to cheek. My height and strength, coupled with my mousey brown hair, came from my father.

"Come along. I promised we'd meet Captain Davies and his crew as soon as the sun climbed over their tallest sail. It is not wise to keep a pirate waiting." My mother beckoned me to follow.

Cheddar jumped from my shoulder as I stepped onto the boardwalk, circling once before landing on the roof of the boathouse guarding the dock. She whistled once as if to say she'd be watching me.

I waved, then followed my mother to the end of the dock, where the pirate ship bobbed up and down with the waves.

I swallowed my nerves and joined her outside the ship. Waiting by the gangway, a woman with long black hair falling down her back greeted us.

"Captain Davies and his quartermaster will be out shortly. They have an artifact that they believe will be of interest," she said in broken Volfi, then motioned to a nearby crate. "Please take a seat."

My mother took a seat with little protest. I glanced between her and the woman. Instinctively, I reached for my belt, but my tools had stayed home today.

Although what good would a hammer do against a pirate?

I took a hesitant seat next to my mother. We sat there waiting as the sun climbed above the sails.

Right as it passed the tallest sail, on cue, heavy footsteps came from the gangway.

My stomach dropped upon seeing the ship's captain walking off the ship.

*Tristan?*

Decorated in a navy coat, with bright orange hair and those gorgeous blue eyes, his presence commanded my attention. He stood stiff and emotionless, his face turning pale as he locked eyes with me.

Beside him, a woman in a long black coat stood, wearing a sword across her belt. Around her neck, she wore a large golden pendant with indecipherable words inscribed on it. Her dark eyes followed Tristan's gaze, locking onto me for a moment and raising a single eyebrow.

The first woman who greeted us approached Tristan. "Captain Davies, Madame Beaumont and her son are here to discuss the trade."

Tristan's attention snapped back to the job at hand. "Thank you, Hari."

I couldn't keep my eyes off Tristan. This frail boy from the *Aquamarine* was the captain of the pirate ship? He couldn't be a day older than me!

The woman called Hari strode back into the ship, her hands laced behind her back, head bowed.

Tristan and the other woman in the black coat approached my mother. "Madame Beaumont?"

My mother rose, fumbling through her broken Vernnes. "Yes. Hello, Captain."

"You spoke with Sybyl yesterday, correct?" He motioned to the woman beside him.

My mother glanced at me. I joined her side to translate.

"If that's your quartermaster, then yes. I ran into her at the Postal Bureau, and we spoke ever so briefly about a trade opportunity. Luckily, Madame Augustin was there to help translate because otherwise I would have been lost!"

I translated most of what my mother said, keeping the statements succinct and in place.

"Well, I am hoping you might be able to help us offload a… unique good. Many traders have already denied us assistance."

"And what might that be?"

Tristan glanced at his quartermaster. The woman removed a vial from her front pocket and handed it to my mother.

I joined my mother's side as she held it up to the sun. Inside, a strange silver liquid glistened. At first, there was nothing unique about it, reminiscent of an odd concoction I drank once at the *Aquamarine*. But the longer I stared at it, the more it pulled me in, as if someone was in there, staring right back at me. Bumps rose on my skin, and my fingers pricked.

"Is this magic?" My mother asked, speaking my exact thoughts as I translated.

"That is my understanding," Tristan said. "Our sister ship found it and provided us with a barrel, in hopes we might find a trader."

"And…what magical properties does it have?"

Tristan frowned, then said in a low whisper. "It seems to have many capabilities. In some instances, it heightens magic, while in others…I've heard rumors that people see the future. All I know for certain is that there is something unique about it…and in all my travels, I have never seen anything quite like it."

My mother shook the vial once, her brow furrowed. "It is quite fascinating…but here on L'Perle…it's hard to offload something like this. We don't have the resources…"

As I translated, Tristan frowned, but my mother continued.

"But I do know of a trader in the far north who would happily take your unit. They have knowledge of all things magic, and I am sure they would be interested in this…artifact. In fact, I'd say they'd make a valuable trade partner for any… king of the sea."

As I finished translating, the quartermaster's face scrunched in frustration. She opened her mouth to speak, but Tristan interjected.

"I suppose you require payment for such information?"

My mother's lip twitched. "Unfortunately, it is hard to put a number on what I desire. What you have here may be worth a fortune…" She rolled the vial in her hands.

"We can offer you a twenty percent interest," Tristan said, almost at once. This was not his first negotiation by any means.

Another twitch crossed my mother's lips. "Thirty."

"Twenty-five."

"Deal… but…" she eyed Tristan, "I have worked with pirates. How can I be certain that I can trust you to return?"

He did not reply.

Now, my mother ran the negotiation. This was her place to rule, and honestly, if Tristan wasn't scared yet… he should be now.

"I say you leave behind something that you cannot live without. Something that will force your return," my mother leaned forward on her toes, "what that is, well, that is up to you."

Tristan's face fell.

And finally, the quartermaster spoke, her voice like the deep rumbling of a storm. "Why would we, a cohort of *pirates*, leave something behind? We could easily take this information from you."

"Sybyl, don't," Tristan muttered.

But she continued, not pausing for me to translate, as she reached for her sword. "I believe you have things more valuable on shore than we have on our little ship. So I'd say you cough up that information."

My mother held her ground. "You wouldn't be able to verify it."

Sybyl glowered at me as I translated.

I held up my hands, "I am but the messenger."

She spat at my shoes.

Beside her, Tristan shook his head.

Locked in a stalemate, my mother continued her glare. My attention, though, fell on the boathouse, where Cheddar flew in a circle over the shallow waters of the sea.

*The sea.*

The one thing that kept me from escaping monotony.

I loved my family. L'Perle was a gorgeous home. The work was good. What more could I want?

But the maps, the sea… the stories at the *Aquamarine*…it was all that ever filled my dreams.

I turned to my mother. The words that followed exited my mouth like a waterspout. "What if I go?"

My mother stared at me. "What?"

"You tell me the details. I travel with them and guard the knowledge until we conduct the trade."

"What stops them from killing you once the trade is over?" My mother hissed.

*Point.* My mind raced as I chose a reason. "Because… I'll offer services to their ship. Services they need to navigate home. Carpentry, translation, entertainment…you name it. My skills will be valuable to them."

"But Lyam—"

"Mère, it's not like I haven't thought of leaving for years."

"I know."

"Please. If I go…everyone wins."

She pondered my idea for a moment, then nodded. "Very well. Tell them the offer… and inform them that you'll need a few days to prepare. Understood?"

"Thank you, Mère."

"No. Thank you."

I gulped, then turned back to Tristan and his quartermaster, and offered myself to their ship.

# CHAPTER FOUR

# A Puzzle for the Seas

I placed my wooden flute into my satchel and pulled the drawstring closed. This was it. All my possessions packed away in one bag, ready for me to set sail. This was no dream. But the moment had come…and I was going to seize it.

With my satchel over my shoulder, I opened the door to my bedroom. My father waited there silently, looking rather small in the doorframe.

"Père," I said.

He didn't meet my eyes, shifting a poorly wrapped parcel in his hands. "Always knew you'd leave this island. It's in your blood. I left Janis, your mother left Rosada…so of course you would leave L'Perle. But…I didn't think it would be so soon."

"I know, Père. But the opportunity was right."

"Always seems to come at the wrong time, though," he sighed, then held out the parcel to me. "I want you to have this."

I took the parcel from my father. It weighed heavy in my hands.

"Go on. Open it."

Even before I pulled away the paper, I knew what lay beneath the wrapping. Even so, as I unwound the parcel, a smile crawled from ear to ear across my face.

There, with a freshly smithed head and a carved handle that matched my grip, was a hammer.

"Père…this is gorgeous," I marveled.

"Worked with the help of Mademoiselle De Grace. I carved the handle, she welded the head. You know, it's a small thing…so you remember where you came from," my father said.

"I'll never forget where I came from."

"Eh, you'd be surprised what the sea might do."

I placed a hand on my father's arm. He looked older standing before me, his graying hair draping around his face, the wrinkles beneath his eyes like baggage. But he still smiled at me. The same smile he gave me as a boy when I learned to build a birdhouse. Or when I repaired my first leak.

I equipped the hammer on my belt, and we walked downstairs to where my mother waited.

She had already reorganized the entire state of the sitting room. Books and papers lay scattered across the table before my mother, who sat cross-legged on the sofa. Her eyes lit up as I entered, marred with a sleepless night.

"Lyam, you do not need to go—we can forget about this silly trade," she said at once.

I took a seat next to her. "Mère, I want to go. I can't stay on L'Perle forever."

She sighed, "I know, but…with them? Pirates? They're great traders, Lyam, but…they're *pirates*. You're too kind to affiliate with them."

"Isn't being a pirate but a name?"

"It is…but not one I ever saw you taking."

"I know. But now's my chance." I glanced at her and then at my father across the room. He grimaced.

My mother shuffled the papers on the table. "Well, since there is no changing your mind…I have put together a set of maps for you from that book you *stole* from me."

I scoffed.

She spread the papers out on the table. "Each of these show a piece of the map based on what I know of this trader. I never met them in person, but I met one of their colleagues years ago. They were searching for magical artifacts and asked me to send it their way if I ever come across one,."

I scanned the papers. Each piece only showed a part of a map. Disorganized, they were a puzzle waiting to be put together.

"I have put a different word on each map's corner…in Volfi, of course. They won't make sense to anyone but you." She pointed a word at the corner of one of the pages.

*Timber.*

My lip twitched, and I said softly, "Treasure every moment like a flame cherishes its timber."

From the other side of the room, my father spoke. "Just as I told you the first day you picked up a hammer and nearly nailed your hand to the wall."

My throat tightened. Yes, this was one statement that had sunk deep into my heart. It guided my work as a carpenter.

Now, on this new adventure, I wouldn't let a moment pass me by.

I know, you probably think I am overdoing this…but it is the best way to secure the map and ensure that the pirates don't harm you." My mother placed her hand over my hand.

"I know, Mère."

"Yes, of course. Now…one last thing…the name of the trader. I am going to tell you it now. Do not speak their name until you arrive at the last spot on the map."

She leaned forward and whispered a name to me. A unique name. One I'd never heard in L'Perle.

*Tarek Kek.*

I recited it to myself, committing it to my memory, promising my mother that I would never speak it aloud until needed.

Even to Cheddar.

"I understand," I said as I picked up the papers, glancing at the disorganized words in each corner.

"Remember, Lyam, you can never trust a pirate. Not in full. They have no laws, only obeying the ocean's currents." My mother punctuated her statement.

I nodded, securing the pages in the deepest pocket of my satchel.

My mother continued. "Now promise, when you arrive in that last port, you will write to me. If the waters are co-operative, it should take you three to four months to arrive at your destination…so I should expect a letter no later than eight months from now," she paused, calculating the distance in her head. "Yes, that's right. Eight months. And if I don't receive anything, well… I have connections."

"I know Mère," I replied. There was no doubt in my mind that my mother would burn the ocean looking for me. When I was a child, one evening I got lost on my way home. My mother rallied the whole town to find me, deep in the forest and well into the night.

She would slaughter pirates to protect me. That much I knew.

"And if you get scared, there is no harm in stealing a lifeboat and heading to safety. I promise Lyam—"

"Alice," my father interjected, "he'll be fine. He's not a little lad anymore."

My mother frowned.

I took her hands. "I promise, Mère. I can handle these pirates. Besides… they need me."

"They do…" she whispered.

"I'm not scared. Really…. I'm excited. This is my chance to go on an adventure. I'll be okay, Mère. I promise."

My mother and father coddled me for another thirty minutes, then, after a few shared tears, I headed down the hill, glancing back once at my parents standing in the doorway. *Be well. I'll miss you.* I recanted to myself, adjusting the bag over my shoulder.

Cheddar landed on a branch at the bottom of the staircase. She chirped, tilting her head to the side.

"Yam!" she exclaimed.

"Hey, Cheddar-bird." I removed a few seeds and held them out to her. She snatched one in her beak and cracked it open.

I continued, "I'm setting sail today, Cheddar. But you should stay here with your friends."

She stared at me.

"I know you're a bird. You probably don't understand."

She jumped from the perch and landed on my head.

"The sea isn't a place for a bird like you," I had her step off my head onto my hand. "You won't be happy."

She clicked her beak and bobbed her head.

"You want to come? Are you sure?"

Another head bob.

"Well, if you change your mind, you have until you leave port, okay?"

She chimed five times, the same sound that came from the bell tower each day at sundown.

"Right. Five bells," I replied. It was enough for me to know that she understood.

So with Cheddar on my shoulder, my satchel on my back, and my newly minted hammer on my belt, I headed into town.

An air of silence hung over the town. While I said goodbye to Ora and other familiar faces at the *Aquamarine*, I hadn't paraded about town to announce my departure. I would leave that to my mother, who would, as soon as I boarded that ship, be telling everyone who might listen.

Yet, it felt like the town was still watching me, with a silent judgment that followed anyone who left L'Perle. I had no shame in my decision, but I knew people would talk. Why leave L'Perle? It was quiet, undisturbed, and peaceful. We were often spared from the political antics of Gonvernnes in the south, or even of our mother country, Volfium. We were but a haven for traders, travelers, and pirates.

Why leave behind all that?

My heart thudded as I reached the dock. The pirate ship, with its obsidian glaze that reflected the blue sky, bobbed at the end of the dock. It wasn't the largest ship, but compared to the fishing and trade boats in port, it was as menacing as a storm cloud.

Outside the ship, the same crewmember with long black hair waited. She glanced my way as I approached, her dark eyes worn by days at sea. She smiled without showing her teeth.

"Hello," I said as I approached. "Um, Lyam Beaumont, at your service."

"Yes, Captain Davies said to expect you. I'm the boatswain, Haritha Sharma. You can call me Hari."

"Nice to meet you." I adjusted the bag on my back. Cheddar fluttered once. "Oh, and this is Cheddar... she'll be joining us."

Hari grimaced. "Well...that might not please Sybyl."

"Oh?"

"She doesn't like birds."

My mother's voice echoed in my head; the voice of a negotiator. "Well, then I guess I won't be going. Where I go, Cheddar goes."

Hari's grimace transformed into a full smile. "No matter. It is not like Sybyl is the captain. Cheddar is welcome to join us."

"Hallo?" Cheddar squawked.

Hari laughed. "Yes, hello. And let me be the first to welcome you both aboard your new home: *the Cobalt Hare.*"

Hari set me up in a private cabin. To my surprise, everyone on board had their own room, with only fourteen occupants on the entire ship, including me. This brigantine very well could have housed up to fifty crewmates, and as I walked along the corridors, the echoes of a previous crew scarred the wooden planks. Having worked with my father for years, it was easy to tell how much wood had been worn down by boots or weather. This ship, with its obsidian exterior, had once known greatness, but now…it was merely a skeleton of its former self.

After dropping off my bags, Hari showed me around the ship. With only five levels, the ship was not expansive, but its woodwork showed its transformative journey. Quarters had been redesigned for privacy. Cheap steel reinforced the doors. The narrow corridors wove through the ship, lit by gas lamps swaying above us.

In the lower decks, the cargo hold contained unassuming barrels of food and water. Amongst them, I was positive the magical liquid they had shown my mother waited. Where? I hadn't a clue. All the barrels look the same.

That was probably for the best.

From there, Hari led me back through the decks, pointing out the heads, the brig, and the mess hall. She then led me up through the galley and onto the main deck, where the midday sun cast a shimmering glow across the deck. A few crewmates worked to prepare the ship for sailing.

On my shoulder, Cheddar laughed, taking a leap into the air, before nesting in my hair.

Hari placed her hands on her hips and peered around the deck. "And, here we are. The Captain's Quarters are at the stern, but otherwise…I think that's it."

"Thank you, Hari," I said as I guided Cheddar onto my fingers.

"We'll be setting sail soon…which means I need to find Rémy." Hari glanced around the deck, then, with a quiet exclamation, walked across the deck to a tall woman adjusting one of the sails. I failed to hear them as they spoke, except for a shared laugh.

This laughter seemed to dominate the ship. It was hard to ignore the jovial undertones that filled the young crew. There was freedom, joy…and so much more.

Hari returned with the woman at her side. She was taller than me, with bright green eyes and short brown hair.

"Lyam, this is Rémy Allard, our navigator."

"Nice to meet you," I said.

"Hullo!" Cheddar chirped on my shoulder.

Rémy beamed at the bird, "Oh, what a beaut. Reminds me of a bird I saw back home."

"Yes, she's a fumeux parro. They're common on L'Perle."

"Ah, right! They used to make their way down south."

"For the winter migration?

"That's right!" Rémy held her finger out to the bird. Cheddar hopped onto it, chirping again. "Do you know the legend about them?"

"No, I don't think they ever made their way to L'Perle."

"Well, back where I come from, there was a legend that said how these birds carry the souls of the dead."

"I cannot imagine Cheddar doing anything so morbid," I chuckled.

"Well, not with a name like Cheddar," Rémy responded with a grin. She let Cheddar step back onto my shoulder and turned to Hari. "Does Sybyl know?"

"Sybyl isn't the captain," Hari grumbled.

"She sure acts like one."

"But she isn't."

I had only seen the quartermaster briefly, with her determined gaze and stern voice on the dock. For now, her presence was defined by a whisper from the few crewmates to whom I had spoken.

But my gut feeling said I should do well not to cross her path.

"Still, be careful around Sybyl," Rémy continued, "She doesn't like birds."

I reached for a seed in my tool belt and handed it to Cheddar. "Can I inquire why?"

"From what I've heard, she's been the receiver of bird excrement on more than one occasion," Rémy withheld a laugh.

"Well…I guess that is a reason. But maybe Cheddar here can change her mind."

"I suppose we'll see."

Hari cleared her throat. "Rémy?"

"Hm?"

"Don't you need something from Mr. Beaumont?"

Rémy clapped her hands together. "Right, my apologies. I will require the maps, of course."

"Oh, right, of course. I have them in my quarters…I can retrieve them, if you'd like."

"Yes, please. We leave soon."

I nodded once, then with Hari's permitting smile, I left the main deck and headed back down into the crew quarters.

On my shoulder, Cheddar calmed and observed her new surroundings. She seemed undisturbed as I navigated the ship, trying to remember where my room was located. While the ship wasn't large, each corridor looked the same.

*Three floors down. Second to last room toward the aft.* I recited to myself as I climbed the ladder to the third floor. The corridor consisted of two lanterns, with an uneven floorboard two doors from the ladder.

My cabin was nothing special. I had only dropped off my bag before Hari led me around the rest of the ship. Now, alone at last, I took in my new home. It was empty. A clean slate. Without the scattered belongings of my mother, or the sanded wood smell of my father. This was my place, ready for me to carve.

I helped Cheddar onto the bedpost and placed a thin blanket on the ground beneath where she slept. *Tomorrow I'll set her up a proper perch.* I stroked back her feathers. She slept without disturbance. It was a big day for this bird; I hoped she understood in her little head what this meant.

After removing my clothes and putting them under the bed, I found the pages of maps my mother gave me. I sorted through them, looking for the Volfi word for "treasure" written in my mother's curly handwriting. I unfolded the page, but to my untrained eye, the map looked like a set of squiggles and lines.

I turned it upside down and frowned. Even when I managed to locate L'Perle, the coastline made no difference.

My fingers clenched the page. Once I handed it over to Rémy, this would begin our voyage. But would they continue to trust me with each page of the map? Or would they force me to hand each page over before sending me to the brig? Or, worse, throwing me to the sea?

But they didn't have the trader's name. *Tarek Kek.*

Plus, with all the faults in the ship that needed repairs, I had my own way to prove my worth.

I pocketed that first map and returned to the corridor, leaving Cheddar to rest on the bedframe.

As I exited my room, the door across the hall opened.

It wasn't just any crewmate who exited that cabin, but Captain Tristan Davies himself.

He stared at me, brow furrowed. His eyes darkened.

"Oh! Tris—Captain Davies! Hello, sorry, I—"

He interrupted. "Listen, you're here as a crewmate and to help us secure a deal. That is all."

"I was—"

"What happened was a fluke. I'm trying not to eat where I sleep, Mr. Beaumont."

Before I could say anything else, Captain Davies strode away, adjusting the gloves on his hands and not paying me a second glance.

# CHAPTER FIVE

# Stories of a New Home

I sat alone in the crow's nest as we pulled away from L'Perle. The island glimmered with a smattering of white light as we departed. Except for the *Aquamarine*, twinkling with its iridescent colors. While my heart did not sink for L'Perle, my excitement masking any sensation of regret, a feeling of melancholy washed over me. Someday, I'd return with stories of adventure. But until then, would they remember me? Or was I but another person, passing through their doors, and vanishing to the sea?

I gripped my flute tight as the *Aquamarine* disappeared into the blurred collection of lights. Did Ora know that Tristan was the captain of this ship? In those dim lights, he was mysterious and merely a moment of my life. Now, while I had only seen him once, he was a different person; a captain, strict and commanding, even with his young age.

It fascinated me, but now…I knew my place. At the *Aquamarine*, I was like a bird, flying free, unhindered. Flirting with a mysterious sailor? That belonged to that version of me. Now, I was here for a job, and the captain was but a trade partner.

And that was how we would stay.

*I don't eat where I sleep.* Tristan had said to me.

"Well, neither do I, Captain Davies," I grunted, then placed the flute to my lips. The notes danced with the gentle winds, trailing up the sails. I took pause, noting a few cracks in the ship's mast. It was one of many imperfections that needed fixing.

*Show your worth. Earn your keep.* My mother's voice echoed in my head.

*Tomorrow, Mère. I can't work in the dark.* I clutched my flute as I descended from the crow's nest and onto the main deck.

A few crewmates sat amongst the crates, watching as I had as L'Perle became nothing more but a twinkling star on our horizon. Rémy stood at the helm, issuing navigation orders to a few other crewmates. Hari bustled about the ship, tossing different tools and items to each working crewmate. It was like watching a bird's flock together, setting off from our island as winter ended.

Yet, while everyone worked, Captain Davies did not show his face.

"Excuse me, Mr. Beaumont?"

I turned. Sybyl approached me, a kind smile on her face, her dark eyes alight. She was tall and curvy, with long brown hair that gathered in the wind. When she smiled, dimples pressed into her cheek. There was an aura of maturity about her, at least a few years older than most of the crew, that commanded attention.

She placed a hand to her chest. "My name is Sybyl, the quartermaster aboard this ship. I want to welcome you aboard the *Cobalt Hare*."

"Nice to meet you."

"Pleasure is all mine." She crossed her arms. "So you're here to fix up this ship of ours while we travel north?"

"Yes, ma'am."

"Good…good. This old ship has seen better days. I thought it would fall apart in our last storm."

"Yeah, I'll fix her up real good."

"Good," Sybyl smiled again, her eyes flickering bright. "I hope these trade details your mother gave us pan out."

"If not, then I guess you're getting free labor.

"That is true. It's a win-win situation, I suppose," she chuckled to herself. "Well, I have other duties to attend to, so I look forward to seeing your work. Once again, welcome aboard."

She strode toward the captain's cabin, confident in her steps, as if she herself were the captain.

As she left, I took a seat on one of the crates beside a short young woman with misshapen glasses.

"At least you're on Sybyl's good side," she said as I sat beside her.

"Huh?"

"She can be intense. But she seems content with you. Which is good, all things considered."

"Oh?"

The young woman beside me was like an open book. "She's skeptical of a lot of things…and she has the captain's ear, so you want to not get her attention."

"Although I heard she hates birds."

"Oh, right. Rémy told me about your little friend."

"Yeah, she's sleeping now."

"Well, keep her on the downlow. Not sure why Sybyl hates birds, but she sure does."

"Hm." I watched as Sybyl approached the captain's cabin. The door opened, and Tristan stepped out. His eyes locked with Sybyl, and she reached for his shoulder, caressing the side of his neck with her fingers.

My stomach fell.

"I thought—" I shook my head.

The woman next to me tilted her head to the side. "Huh?"

"Nothing."

"No…no…you cannot leave me hanging. What is it?"

"Are…Sybyl and Captain Davies…well, you know?"

"Oh…well, they're not together, but they're not apart…if you understand me right."

"I think so…" My throat tightened. There was no reason for me to feel like this—I had flirted with Tristan once! I could move on like I had with everyone else.

"Why?" The woman asked.

"It's nothing."

"You cannot go saying it's nothing when you react like that!"

"Well, it is!"

"No, it's not!" She narrowed her eyes, glancing at me once over. Then she guffawed. "Oh! I know!"

"What?"

"I know! I know!" she leaned forward, "You fancy the Captain!"

"Wha—what!? No! I—no!"

"You do. I can tell!"

"No—it was just a moment. It's really nothing that serious!"

"Oh, this is great!" She turned to the helm where Rémy continued to give directions. "Oi! Rem!"

"What now, Veta!?" Rémy shouted back.

"Gotta tell you something great—real great! You're gonna love this!" Veta replied.

I covered Veta's mouth and hissed, "Please. Don't."

She shoved me, "Oi! Don't touch me!"

"Then don't go sharing my personal affairs!"

"Fine!" She brushed off her hands. "But I'm still telling Rémy. I tell her everything."

"Fine. But no one else," I snarled.

"Fine!"

"Good."

"Great!"

"Fantastic."

"Exuberant!"

Veta and I continued to eye each other. Then, in what seemed like unison, we both began to laugh.

Veta and I became fast friends. She spoke a lot, inundating me with constant tidbits about the *Cobalt Hare*. When morning arrived, she cornered Cheddar and me outside the mess hall and lured me to the main deck.

"I was gonna get a cup of coffee, y'know," I muttered.

"Do you honestly think we have good coffee on this ship?"

"Gotta have something."

"It's basically bean juice, a'ight?"

I grunted. *Another thing to fix, I suppose.*

"Besides, the best thing to wake you in the morning is the fresh sea air," she winked at me.

"Hmph."

"You'll get used to it. There's a lot to take in here on our little ship."

"I'm getting there," I held out my hand so Cheddar could step from my shoulder to my fingers. She bit at my thumb, then leapt into the air, taking flight above the ship.

"Well, you've met the crew, right?"

"Sorta."

"Well, you know me, Sybyl, my girl Rémy, Hari, and of course. you know *Captain Davies*." She smirked.

"Drop it," I hissed.

She chuckled. "Well, either way, there's a total of fourteen of us onboard. If my math is correct, then that means you know almost forty percent of us."

"Suppose so."

"And let's see now, we have Zo over there by the cannons. They're our Master-of-Arms." She pointed to a burly individual with long braids cascading down the left side of their half-shaven head. On their baldric belt, they wore three different swords, each of different lengths and curves. They approached Hari at the far end of the deck and leaned against the railing beside her. They moved their hands as if they were talking.

Veta continued, "Be careful not to startle Zo. They can't hear or speak, so if you catch them off guard, they might not hold back an attack."

"Understood," I continued watching Hari and Zo. With a smile on their face, Zo seemed to laugh at Hari. She threw an indistinguishable piece of fruit at Zo, then hurried off, leaving Zo still cackling.

Veta, of course, did not stop her rambling. "I'm so impressed by Hari. She only joined us a few months ago and attempted to speak with Zo. Most of us can understand them, but not with the same grace. Must be a distraction for her—she always seems quite sad after what happened with the *Tortuga*."

That caught my attention. "The *Tortuga*?"

"Oh! You must not know about our sister ship, huh? Or anything about our ship even, huh?"

I shook my head.

Veta clapped her hands and hopped to her feet. "Oh, this will be fun! Right, okay, so first let me give you some backstory. And I promise, it'll all come together, so bear with me."

I crossed my legs on top of the crate and leaned forward, awaiting the tale.

"So, the *Cobalt Hare* wasn't always a fun ship like this, a'ight? We used to belong to the Commeant. Do you know about them?"

I nodded. The Commeant had long visited L'Perle. While they brought riches from abroad, they were one of the few groups that my mother never traded with because of her own personal morals. I glanced at the floorboards of the ship and mumbled, "They're slave traders."

"Well, I've never heard anyone say it so directly…but yeah, basically. Most of us here were bought or acquired in some way via trade. I mean, I traded myself for medication for my mother. In exchange, I worked with our old physician…which is why I'm the physician now."

"*You're* the physician on board?"

"Eh, I learned what I needed in three years. Trust me, if you get sick, I'll mend you."

I scoffed.

"Everyone's got stories like that. Why do you think we're all so spry?"

She had a point. The crew was young, naïve, but also fit and excited. That meant something, right?

"Well, right, okay, so," Veta continued with her rambling story, "A couple years ago, our sister ship, the *Sanguine Tortuga*, was taken over by pirates. Not sure about the whole story there, but our old captain, Freda Platt, had a vendetta. So, she made it her mission to find the *Tortuga*. Too bad though, cause the *Tortuga* is way bigger and way stronger than us.

"A few months ago, we finally found the *Tortuga* down south in the Vapor Pits. They took control of our ship, killing a handful of the Commeant, without really losing much of their crew. I wasn't there for most of it, since I was busy caring for the injured and all, but from what I heard, it was a bloodbath…and pretty damn impressive too. That's what Rémy said at least." Veta blinked once, her attention locked on the floorboards. "I'm glad I didn't see it. While the Commeant was horrible…I knew these people. Some of them…this was all they knew, y'know?"

Cheddar landed on my shoulder and cocked her head to the side. I did not reply, letting Veta speak when ready.

It didn't take long for her to bounce back into the tale. "So, after the pirates took control of our ship here, they liberated all of us acquirees. The captain of the *Tortuga* selected Captain Davies to run this ship and assist with trading that silver goo…and well…here we are."

I eyed the captain's cabin across the deck. No one had entered or left the facility in the time since we'd arrived. "Why Tristan?"

Veta shrugged. "Not entirely sure. He's not the most charismatic leader or anything. Maybe it had to do with his magic."

"Magic?"

"Ah—I've said too much now! I'll leave that as a surprise."

"Really? You won't tell me *that*?"

"Gotta leave something to the imagination," she winked at me.

I rolled my eyes and leaned back, taking in the sea air and ocean waves. A few more crewmates had come aboard, branching off into their respective duties. I'd need to begin my job soon enough, but today was a chance to breathe.

Although my racing mind did little to bring that peace. Tristan had magic. That was something I did not expect. But then again, it wasn't like magic was visibly out in the open. There were stories of seers, of enchanters, and of illusionists, all of whom were nothing more than ordinary people. Tristan was no different.

But I supposed that the truth would come if needed.

"Well, this has been enlightening," I said as I climbed from the crate, "but I am going to get that *bean juice* so I don't get a migraine."

"Aw, c'mon, Lyam," Veta bemoaned.

"I'll be back."

Truthfully, I needed a moment alone to think. I climbed down the stairs that led into the belly of the ship, where the small, narrow mess hall waited. As I entered, the door to the galley opened. Captain Davies stood there, a steaming cup in hand, still dressed in uniform from boots to gloves.

"Good morning, Captain," I said.

He stared at me. Exhaustion amplified the dark circles beneath his eyes, even in the dim light of the nearby lantern.

"What're you doing mulling about?" he asked.

"Getting some coffee?"

"Oh, well, fine. Just…you better get to work soon. This ship needs maintenance," he grunted as he turned away from me.

"Aye aye, Captain." I restrained a laugh. Not at Tristan, but at the ridiculousness of the reply.

But Captain Davies did not relish my humor. He shot back around, "What is so funny, Mr. Beaumont?"

"What? Nothing! Just the statement—'aye aye.' It's amusing."

Captain Davies narrowed his eyes.

"Really, it is no qualm against you, Captain Davies."

"Aye," Cheddar chattered on my shoulder.

Captain Davies continued to glare. "Get to work."

Before I replied, Captain Davies stormed out of the mess hall.

# CHAPTER SIX

# Firewood

In the week that followed, I settled into a routine aboard the *Cobalt Hare*. With Veta and Rémy as my new confidantes, my comfort grew. We shared anecdotes and stories of fantastical magic and legends. I told them about my life on L'Perle, while they highlighted adventures at sea. Veta told each tale with gravitas, while Rémy tapered her lies.

During the day, after my morning coffee, I got to work fixing the ship. Or, well, attempting to fix it. I spent the first few days examining each deck and making notes of each crack and fault in the structure. With every discovery, my heart sank. The ship's faults, hidden by its glorious obsidian coat, were far more than cosmetics. The charred remains of old beams barely kept the ship afloat, while the sails hung on single nails, threatening to be cast away by one severe storm.

"I'm surprised these sails even function," I said to Rémy while noting the sails' condition.

"They're catching the wind, so they're doing their job," Rémy replied.

"But they're hardly attached!"

"Here, I'll show you."

Rémy taught me the basics of sailing the *Hare* that day, but it didn't change the fact that the ship was falling apart in plain sight.

No one else previously had the skills to complete these repairs.

At least I'd be earning my keep.

With Cheddar on my shoulder, I got to work, setting up shop each day, like I was back home on a roof.

While there was a small supply of materials in the cargo hold, it was not enough for the necessary repairs. The nails had rusted over, and rot settled into the spare boards, which seemed to groan at my touch. I spent hours sifting through the materials, placing them in different piles, using only a small lantern for light.

"Merde," I whispered as I finished sorting them. Not only had I gone through the piles four times, but I swore that throughout the process, the materials grew less fruitful with each pass. There was enough to fix the cracking pillars in the hull and possibly enough nails to secure one of the sails, but we were lacking in rope, small planks, and other necessary materials.

I cursed under my breath again. On my shoulder, Cheddar mimicked, "Merde! Merde!"

Her voice echoed around the dark hold.

A moment later, someone replied, "Who's down here!?"

I gulped, forcing Cheddar into my jacket. The bird flapped once, but after I poked her beak, she settled.

"It's me—Lyam!" I called into the darkness. "Was working on some inventory."

Footsteps approached, and Sybyl emerged from the crates, her arms crossed. She narrowed her eyes. "Did the Captain give you permission to be down here?"

"I was instructed to get to work on the ship. Need materials to do that."

"I see. Have you found what you need?"

I kicked the planks. "Honestly? Not really."

Sybyl's nose wrinkled. "Well, that's unfortunate. For now, prioritize the important things."

"I considered that already, ma'am, but we still don't have enough materials. It's all well and good for general maintenance, but this ship is sick."

Sybyl's arms loosened, and she chuckled, a soft noise that caught the air. "You're a funny fellow, Lyam."

"Pardon?"

"The ship is sick? Ha!" She placed a hand on my shoulder. Inside my coat, Cheddar fluttered, but I kept her hidden. Sybyl continued, "Listen, hun, the ship is just a vessel. Fix it up with what you have—get her to the next destination. We'll deal with the…*illness* later."

"But there's rot…she's in pain and—"

"We do not have time for pit stops, Mr. Beaumont. Work with what you have."

I frowned. Sybyl squeezed my shoulder, then, without another word, strode out of the cargo hold.

As she disappeared up the ladder, I let Cheddar out of my coat. She flew out with a loud chirp before landing on a nearby crate. She clicked her beak in distaste.

"Sorry, Cheddar-bird. Didn't want Sybyl to see you."

The bird clicked her beak again.

"Yeah, I know," I muttered as I turned back to the pile of rotting wood. I would have to be creative.

And creative I was.

I spent hours each day fixing sections of the ship. At night, I retired to my room, where I worked on sanding down the old wood and sorting through the nails that hadn't quite rusted. I swore, the wood mocked me in my sleep.

"We're screwed," I grumbled to Veta and Rémy as we sat on deck, like every evening, eating our rations of dried meat and hardtack bread. "How am I gonna fix this thing up if I have three pieces of wood and a rusty nail? I can't just *magic* the ship better!"

"Oh, relax, Lyam. You're working too hard," Veta said, leaning her head against Rémy's shoulder. "The only one who works this hard is Hari… and maybe the Captain. Not that we ever see his face."

"If we want to complete this trade, I have to get this ship fixed up," I replied, my mouth half-full.

"Is it really that bad?" Rémy asked.

"A few months without a carpenter can send a ship to its doom."

"Oh, don't be so dramatic!" Veta waved her hands above her head. "We've only had this ship for a few months!"

"And that's enough time. Whatever battle you had, there is burnt wood everywhere, and the nails are coated with rust. But no one seems to have stocked up on supplies…" I trailed off. Would this crew even know? Hadn't the ship been handed to them by the *Sanguine Tortuga* only months earlier, without any knowledge of what was left behind?

"Well, if you'd share more of that map with me, I could find us a port," Rémy grumbled, crossing her broad arms over her chest.

"Not happening," I replied. Thus far, I had only given Rémy two of the pages, keeping the others folded deep in the crevasses of my flimsy mattress.

"You don't trust us?"

"I trust you. It's others I don't trust…"

"Yeah, it's not like Cap really wants Lyam around," Veta chimed.

"Don't go calling him Cap to his face," Rémy responded.

"Why not? Maybe he'll actually smile."

"The day he smiles is the day that we survive a sea monster attack."

"Ooh, I hope we see a sea monster!" Veta exclaimed, gripping Rémy's arm.

"No, you don't!"

"Yes, I do! Wouldn't it add a bit of excitement to all of this?" Veta smiled at Rémy.

Rémy laughed, "We have plenty of excitement."

The two continued their flirtatious bickering. I grinned to myself and removed my flute from its holster on my belt. With Rémy and Veta encumbered by their little discussion, I fell back into my thoughts. Talks of sirens, tales of monsters, and stories of magic failed to tug my thoughts away from the ship. One wrong storm, one incorrect wave, or one hurried current might tear the ship apart…and the quartermaster didn't seem to care.

Did she tell Tristan?

Honestly, I hadn't seen Tristan in days. The captain was aloof as always, hiding in his rooms, doing who-knows-what. Sybyl emerged at times, giving orders and observing the sea. There was a commanding presence about her. She understood how to run the ship—but why not seek a way to repair it?

These thoughts followed me as I played my flute well into the night, until the moon rose high above us, casting a partial glow with its half smile. Once Veta and Rémy retired to their room, I let the notes lull me back to my quarters, where Cheddar snoozed undisturbed.

As my hand wrapped around the doorknob, I paused, a strange noise filling my ears.

A sizzling noise.

A crack.

A pop.

Next came the smell.

Like wood burning.

I inhaled and turned.

Smoke bubbled from the crack in the door across the hall.

I didn't even think. My hand went to the door handle.

Upon touching it, heat ripped through my palm.

"Merde!" I dropped my hand and bit my lip. How many times had I hit myself with a hammer? This was no different.

Swallow the pain and move forward, that's what I always told myself. Even if it stung. Even if it cut through my skin.

Even if there was blood.

I stepped back from the door. Smoke continued to rise. Coughing, I croaked out toward the door, "Captain? Are you alright?"

No reply.

"Captain!?"

Still nothing.

"Captain—aw, screw it," I readied myself, positioning my shoulder so it would hit the door just right.

Just as I was about to ram myself into the wood, the door flew open.

Tristan stood there in a loose tunic, wringing his glove-less hands together. Dark burns covered his fingers.

"Captain! Are you—I smelled smoke. I was worried." I exhaled.

"Don't be," Tristan stared at me with those wide blue eyes.

"Well," I chose my words carefully, "not about you. The ship. I'm doing all these repairs and—"

"Doesn't look like you'll be able to repair much more with that hand," he motioned his chin toward my burnt hand.

"Oh, it's fine—"

"Go to Veta so she can fix you up. Can't have you free-loading around here."

"I'm here with the maps you need… that's hardly free-loading."

"I am sure we could find a way to get rid of you…then the maps are ours."

"You wouldn't be able to read them."

"You're not the only person who knows Volfi. We could find someone to translate," Tristan started to walk away, his fire-red hair glowing in the lantern light. "Go get your hand fixed. That's an order."

"Aye aye, Captain," I grunted. If he heard me, he showed no signs of responding, disappearing as he always did up the stairwell.

Rather than following him, I approached his room. The door remained open a crack.

I pushed it open with my elbow.

My heart stammered.

The room was nothing like any of the other crew quarters. Inside, panels of thin sheet metal coated the walls and floor. A single bed sat against the wall, its blankets burned, and the cot was torn around the edges. Char marks covered the metal. In the crevasse where the floor and wall met, piles of ash steamed, glowing with the last pulse of fire.

"What the…" I gawked, unable to find my words.

The *Cobalt Hare* had far more secrets than a mutiny and a magical barrel of liquid.

No…there was something far more mysterious, and it started with Captain Tristan Davies.

# CHAPTER SEVEN

# Whispers of Monsters

Veta took care of my hand, applying bandages and a strange salve while grumbling about her beauty rest. Late at night, she didn't speak much, compared to her usual bubbly personality, and was quick to send me to bed.

But I couldn't sleep. Between that horrid salve that Veta used to coat my hand, which caused the entire room to smell like rotten fish, and the quarters across the hall still sizzling, my mind continued to race. What caused the fire? My rational mind told me it was tobacco. It would not surprise me if anyone on board this ship enjoyed a good pipe. But if that was the case, why the metal? It was easy enough to go on deck.

So, of course, with my rational side floundering, my imagination took hold.

It had to be magic. But…most magic I had seen was passive; a traveler from São Caméliosa who had a remarkable green thumb, a seer who saw the future in their sleep, or even an enchantress who could move the waves of the seas. But with charred burns? Fire? That felt, well, alive. It was rare to find magic that powerful nowadays. It only existed in legends from years past, slowly vanishing like the green of the trees.

I tossed and turned until the sun finally peeked through the porthole, and with Cheddar waking, I gave up my pursuit of sleep. After applying the greasy salve to my burn, I left my bunk with Cheddar on my shoulder.

In the early hours, the ship operated under a restful lull, humming with the thrashing waves. Only Zo and Rémy occupied the deck. Zo sat on one of the barrels, polishing their longsword, while Rémy stood at the stern of the ship, a spyglass to her eye as she gazed out at sea.

"Morning, Rem," I said, taking a place next to her. Cheddar leapt from my shoulder, taking flight in the morning sky.

"Hullo, Lyam." Rémy lowered the spyglass and smiled at me. "Veta told me you had a run-in with our captain then, hm?"

"Huh?"

"The burn."

"Right… the burn…" I rubbed the mark on my palm. "The Captain didn't really want to talk about it with me."

"That doesn't surprise me. He's private about his magic."

"I knew it was magic…" I muttered.

Rémy laughed. "Are you telling me that my lovely fiancée did not tell you about Captain Davies's magic?"

"She wanted it to be a surprise."

"Well, that's…shocking. Not sure why she wouldn't just blurt it out. But that's her game to play."

"You know her better than me."

"Right, but I'm not going to play her game. You should know the truth about our captain."

"And that is?"

"He's a pyromancer?"

"You mean he can control fire?"

"That's right," Rémy lifted the spyglass to her eye again.

"Is that why he's the captain then?"

Rémy shrugged. "Not sure. The agreement wasn't widely publicized—just that it was decided by Captain Lok of the *Sanguine Tortuga*."

"I see," I stared out at sea, watching as Cheddar swooped through the air. Her bright orange tail feathers flirted with the edge of the water, before she swooped upwards and landed back on my head.

Rémy raised her spyglass again and peered out at the water. Questions continued to bud on my lips, but I restrained my curiosity. As my mother always said, in any exchange, you had to play your pieces at the right time.

Besides, did I want to lose all my bargaining chips over this withdrawn captain?

Rémy frowned, then lowered the spyglass. "Listen, I know we have a deal with the maps, but can I peek at the next one?"

"What? Why?" I clenched my fists.

She pointed to a land mass in the distance. "Do you see that?"

I nodded.

"See how it looks like a sleeping lady?"

I tilted my head to the side and squinted. With its curved mountains, I could see the body of a sleeping woman. Barely.

"I suppose so," I remarked.

"I've seen it on countless maps. Always thought it was a rumor."

"What is it?"

Rémy turned to me, her short blonde hair catching the ocean breeze. "It means we're entering Siren's Bay."

After I gave Rémy the next map, inscribed with the Volfi word for 'moment' in the corner, she disappeared into the crow's nest with her spyglass. She did not return for mealtimes, leaving the rest of the crew to go about their business. I took my place on one of the beams, but the blisters on my palm cursed every time I dared attempt to work.

Struggling with the hammer, I turned my attention to the deck. Hari hurried about, adjusting ropes improperly secured and tossing instructions to crewmates. *Why is Hari doing all of this?* I wondered. From my own knowledge, the boatswain kept the ship in order, but the quartermaster dictated orders. Where was Sybyl in all of this? She was as elusive as the captain. But then again, I wasn't sure *what* Sybyl's job was. Sure, she bellowed the occasional order, but she was no captain. From my spot on the beams, I could see her leaning against the port-side railing, observing but not acting. Merely a passenger.

Zo approached her with an unpolished sword and motioned to it with their chin. Sybyl glowered at them, then shooed them away, her expression unchanging.

"Rude!" Cheddar chirped from her perch above me.

"Shhh," I hissed.

She cackled and then took flight, circling high above the ship. I couldn't keep her from flying, but every time she flew in daylight, my entire body froze. So far, Sybyl hadn't noticed her… but that could change with a mere—

"SHIT!" Sybyl shouted. She scowled toward the sky, where Cheddar had swooped upwards, still cackling. "Damn bird!"

I squinted down at her, then choked on a laugh. On her face, a visible white smattering of bird poop dripped from her forehead.

*Cheddar, you silly bird.*

She circled around the ship before returning to her perch.

Sybyl glowered in my direction.

"Get down here!" Sybyl ordered.

My smile fell, and my chest tightened. After securing my hammer, I climbed down the narrow ladder. Cheddar, that good bird, stayed on her perch, cocking her head to the side as she observed her surroundings.

The moment my feet hit the deck, Sybyl was in my face, breath hitting my skin, her voice a mere whisper. "Did you bring a bird aboard my ship?"

"Your ship?" I asked, raising my brows. "I didn't know you were the captain."

Sybyl's eyes narrowed. "Don't be a smartass."

"It's an honest question. I was never sure what you really did around here. But now I know you're the captain. Got it."

Sybyl grabbed the collar of my shirt. "Who are you to question me?"

"I'm just making an observation."

"I should have you thrown overboard."

"Not sure if the real captain would like that," I whispered.

"Why? 'Cause you think he's soft on you?"

I kept my face steady. "No. Because I have the map to your riches."

Sybyl's grip loosened. "If I see that bird again, I cannot promise I won't shoot it. Understood?"

"Aye."

Sybyl released me. I stumbled backwards, catching a glimpse of the crew around us, watching the altercation in awe. But Sybyl did not humor them, snarling in Zo and Hari's direction, before stomping away from me.

Before she reached the door to the captain's cabin, Rémy slid down from the crow's nest and cornered Sybyl. Rémy held out a map to her and gestured to the sea, but Sybyl was quick to push Rémy to the side.

"Stay the course! That's an order!" she shouted as she stormed into the captain's cabin, slamming the door behind her.

*Great. Another hinge I'll need to fix.*

Rémy stayed the course. She didn't join Veta and me for dinner, wasting away over the new map I had provided to her.

Veta rambled, mouth full of food. "Rem really thinks we're approaching sirens. Really would rather us go around the bay, but it'll add a week or so to our course. She tried convincing Sybyl a few more times, but she's got no bite."

"Guess the bay's too big to wait until daylight?" I asked.

"No clue. I'm excited though—we might actually see a siren!"

"You realize sirens lure sailors to certain doom, right?"

As I spoke, Hari took a seat beside Veta, a bowl of stew in his hands. She raised her brow. "What about sirens?"

Veta blurted, "Rem thinks we're heading into siren territory."

"I see…" Hari frowned. "Did she tell the captain?"

"She told Sybyl, who told her to stay the course."

"What!? Doesn't she know the risks?" Hari asked.

Veta shrugged.

"Sirens…by the Gods…I've never seen them, but it's hard to ignore the tales. Does she want us to die?" Hari's usual calm demeanor snapped, her face turning maroon in visible frustration. "We can't lose anyone because of stubbornness."

"So, what are we going to do? Ignore Sybyl?" Veta asked, leaning back with a smirk on her face.

Hari shook her head. "Trust me, I would love to ignore her. But whether or not we like it, she is the quartermaster."

"Could we talk to the captain?" I glanced over my shoulder, seeing if the captain had entered the mess hall. But, as usual, he haunted the ship like a ghost. Always there, but never seen.

"Good luck finding him," Veta muttered.

"It's not a big ship!"

"We don't have time. Nor do we know what he would do. It's best that we prepare for night before the sirens come out."

"And how do we do that?" Veta crossed her arms, eyeing Hari carefully.

Hari tapped the edge of her bowl. "These sirens, how do the legends go again?"

"Something about how they try to lure sailors to their doom with their seductive voices."

Hari laced her hands together and closed her eyes. It was a contemplative expression that made her look older. My mind raced as well. How did we stay safe from a foe that threatened everyone on board? Everyone had a desire, and if the siren's songs managed to lure even the firmest of sailors, then no one was safe.

But, sitting there, pondering the threat, a memory surfaced. I was a boy, no older than nine, and my mother took me to the docks to barter with merchants. While my mother argued with a Rosadian merchant, a fisher with an assortment of odd fish caught my attention. I wandered over to one of the barrels, where little silver fish darted about in the water. Their eyes bulged from their head, as if detonated by explosives. Smoke rose from their little bodies.

"Ah," the merchant said, "are you interested in my Blind Cavern Tetra?"

"What are Blind Cavern Tetra?" I responded, excited.

The merchant grinned, wide and ready to barter. "Well, these little fish might not look frightening now, but in the caves where I found 'em, they're the most frightening predator. They can see in the dark, and few can escape their grip. But, when I found 'em, I showed a light in the cave... and their eyes went and exploded."

Before I could ask more, my mother called to me. I told the merchant I would be back to learn more.

But...I never returned.

They were strange fish. Magical. But their weakness had been light.

So, sitting with Hari and Veta, I couldn't help but wonder...

And a grin crept over me as I turned to my crewmates. "I have a wild idea...just hear me out."

# Blinded

We got to work at once. With the sun setting and the siren's territory approaching, we knew we wouldn't have a lot of time. Hari sent instructions throughout the ship: bring out every lantern. We would be as bright as a comet.

I secured Cheddar in my room, shuddering my window tight so the light would not disturb her, then joined the crew on deck to assist. Everyone, except for Sybyl and the captain, worked on preparing the ship. Did the captain even know what was happening? Or was he locked away in his room, ignoring the world?

Despite the absence of our captain, the crew acted with cohesion. We gathered every mobile lantern on the ship, placing them on crates and barrels. I gathered any additional ones to hang on the strongest beams. We did not light them, waiting as the final stretch of sun cast its glow over the sea.

My heart thudded in my ears. What were these sirens like? Were they as alluring as the songs went? Some sailors claimed they took the form of women, but I heard other tales that they lured you with your greatest desire. How else would it capture the hearts and minds of sailors alike? Not everyone desired a woman. Some only wanted a cup of coffee.

Oh, what I would have done for a good cup of coffee right then.

While I stayed on the beams, the other crewmates took their places around the ship. Hari stood at the port-side of the bow, with Zo on the opposite side. Veta waited by the stairwell, carrying a satchel of makeshift medical supplies. Then, of course, there was Rémy at the helm of the ship, steering us carefully through the approaching sea.

And the last of the sun cast a thin orange glow along the horizon.

There, I saw it. It rose from the water, a mere shadow, and turned its head toward the ship. It was neither human nor animal. Smoke pulsed around it, etching across its outline but hiding any defining characteristics. The creature didn't swim, but crawled to the ship, leading the charge as more of these shadows emerged in the distance.

They moved in silence. The water did not even thrash, whistling along, calm as an empty breeze.

As they approached, the smoke wrapped around the ship. It washed over me, like a half-awake dream, transporting me back home, to my kitchen, where my mother finished pouring me a cup of coffee. The fumes lapped around me, and I settled into the chair, bringing the coffee to my lips. Before drinking, I said something that I could not hear, then turned to my companion sitting next to me.

A fiery redhead with enchanting blue eyes.

I opened my mouth to say his name.

Only to be pulled back to reality with Hari shouting, "NOW!"

I blinked, once again standing on deck, still encased in that thick smoke. But I was on the ship—not in my mother's kitchen. Home might have good coffee waiting for me, but it did not have adventure.

I shook off the lingering dream and jumped into action. After removing a piece of flint and steel from my tool belt, I flipped the small lever on the lantern to release the gas. Then, I struck the two rocks together, catching the lantern's wick beneath the sparks. The lantern caught light. I winced as the orange flames of the fire filled my dark field of vision.

Across the deck, additional lights flickered to life, casting their reach out to the sea.

The smoke started to hesitantly recede.

"It's working!" Hari shouted.

"We'll need more light! We're moving deeper into their territory!" Rémy shouted from the helm.

We took action at once. Everyone raced to another lantern, bringing it to life, so its light could shine across the obsidian coating of the ship.

"Is this actually going to work?" Veta asked as I walked past her.

"We can only hope," I replied.

I lost track of Veta amongst the hustle and bustle of the ship. The thrashing waves and crackling flames suffocated our voices. Each additional light polluted the sky, masking the stars. We were only a beacon on the horizon, bobbing up and down, slow and steady, letting the currents guide us.

Until Sybyl emerged from the captain's cabin in a long robe, a gold pendant around her neck, her hair frazzled, and a scowl plastered on her face.

"What the hell is going on out here?" she shouted, booming over the crackling fire.

Hari stepped forward. "Ma'am, we're merely trying to ward off the sirens."

"Sirens?"

Rémy slid down from her spot at the helm. "I told you—sirens loiter in these waters! But you insisted we stay the course."

Sybyl shook her head. "I don't recall this."

"It was this morning!"

"You must have told someone else…not me."

"But—"

The door to the captain's cabin opened again. The captain stood in the doorway, his uniform pressed and hair combed back, as though he'd been waiting on guard the whole night.

"Sybyl? What is going on?" the captain asked.

"They're going to catch the whole ship aflame!" Sybyl exclaimed, waving her hands in the air. "All over sirens."

"Sirens?"

"Ridiculous, right?"

But the captain brushed Sybyl's comment off, approaching Rémy and Hari. "Are you sure? Sirens are quite the story."

"We already saw them, Captain," Hari responded. "But they seem to have quieted with the light."

"Oh?"

"They're used to the dark. Light seems to blind them."

Rémy added, "But we need more. If the maps are correct, we're only going deeper into their territory."

The captain crossed his arms, taking in the complete explanation as he observed the lanterns around the ship. He then asked, "Who thought this was a good idea?"

Rémy and Hari glanced at each other.

Before they answered, I pushed my way forward, "I did, sir."

The captain eyed me. I couldn't read his expression, contemplative and alert, his blue eyes dark like the nighttime sea. His lips twitched a hint upwards. "Good thinking, Mr. Beaumont."

I restrained myself from smiling back. "Thank you, sir."

"Tristan! The entire ship is a fire hazard!" Sybyl shouted.

"By my observations, it's under control."

"But—"

Tristan waved her off and approached one of the lanterns. The flames flickered in his eyes, cradling his narrow-freckled face in its glow. "I can take it from here."

He removed his glove and placed his hand above the flame. Burn marks coated his fingers, leaving the nail beds of his smallest two fingers with permanent damage. He stretched out his fingers, and around them, the fire flickered. It wisped about his hand like he guided it with a paintbrush. As he closed his fist, it brightened, doubling its glow with a mere flicker.

While I didn't see her, I could hear Veta's excited clapping.

"Tristan! What're you doing!?" Sybyl cried, her body stiff.

The captain did not reply, sculpting the fire with his magic. It shifted in style, flickering with a stylistic glow, resembling flowers, trees, ships, and seas. Each image was brief, before being cast back into the flame, casting light into the dark waters and thick smoke.

Sybyl approached the captain, her entire body shaking as she neared him. She placed a hand on his shoulder, whispering too softly for me to hear.

It happened in mere seconds. Tristan's eyes widened at Sybyl's touch. He spun around, and with him, the fire rose from the nearby lantern. It lashed out, slamming against Sybyl's side.

Sybyl screamed and stumbled back, the flames riding up the side of her robe.

And that's when I noticed Veta. She'd been sitting on the ground near the jugs of water. Like a rabbit, she moved with dexterity, uncorking a jug and climbing onto a nearby barrel.

Where she dumped the water over Sybyl's head. The flame fizzled.

Yet, Sybyl did not show any gratitude. She glowered at Veta, then spun back to face Tristan. She wrinkled her nose and took a step toward him.

He stepped back, his face pale.

"See, love? The fire is not controlled. We need to put it out," Sybyl said to him.

Tristan bowed his head.

"It's best to use only when necessary."

The words slipped out of my mouth. "It is necessary!"

Fuming, Sybyl glowered at me. "You know nothing, Mr. Beaumont. I suggest you stick to your repairs."

"But the—"

She closed the gap between us and poked my chest. "You know nothing, you goddamn leech."

"Oi! Leave Lyam alone!" Veta jumped to my side. "Nothing bad happened. Your clothes are a little burnt, but otherwise you're fine."

"Fine? I am far from *fine*," Sybyl sneered.

"If you want, I can take a look—but the flame barely broke through your clothes."

"Why would you take a look?"

"I'm the ship's doctor!"

"You think knowing how to bandage a wound makes you a doctor?"

"Well, I'm the closest thing you have."

"Hmph. Whatever." Sybyl pushed past her and marched toward the captain's cabin. She shouted over her shoulder again, "I'm done! Put the goddamn fire out!"

Then slammed the door.

But for the crackling flame, no one spoke. Tristan remained standing there, eyes wide, hands opening and closing. In the distance, the whistling of sirens filled the emptiness, but their songs did little to lure us into their arms.

We still had our flame.

For now.

Hari took her place beside me, as determined and focused as ever.

"What do we do?" I asked her after a moment.

"I'll discuss with Rémy. Can you take the captain to his quarters?"

"Aye."

Hari left my side and approached Rémy. I watched them for a moment, then walked over to the captain. He remained in place. Still. But for his eyes, darting back and forth. His glove lay at his feet.

I picked it up and held it out to him, "Captain?"

No response.

"Captain?" I tried again, a bit louder.

He inhaled once, then glanced at me.

"Let's get you to your quarters, alright? Don't worry…we'll turn off the lights."

He stared at me, eyes locking with mine. My stomach flipped over. Even now, those blue eyes captured my heart.

"Here, c'mon," I wiggled the glove in front of him.

He took it carefully, slipped it back on, then followed me back down into the belly of the ship. We didn't speak. Only Tristan's exasperated breaths told me he still followed, one step at a time. It wasn't my place to prod at his thoughts; something had happened on deck, but it wasn't my place to inquire.

We arrived at the door to his room. He gripped the metal doorknob, then turned to me.

"Get some rest, Captain," I whispered.

He licked his lip, then replied, "Don't turn off the lights, Mr. Beaumont."

I raised my brow. "Pardon?"

"You heard me. That's an order." Tristan then entered his quarters and closed the door without looking back at me.

With the last turn of the lock, it was as though a shift happened on the *Cobalt Hare*. Captain Tristan Davies had given an order. And with it, the currents began to change.

# CHAPTER NINE

# Changing Course

We spent the night adjusting the lights. Every now and again, the smoky shadows of the sirens appeared near the ship, but at the touch of the light, they fizzled into the water, nothing more than sea foam. Their song was no stronger than the whistling wind, tickling my earlobe, and catching the loose strands of hair falling behind them.

No one spoke as we navigated Siren's Bay, focused on keeping the lights aglow and the ship moving toward its destination. Even Veta kept quiet, focused on filling jugs of water and keeping the flames contained.

The captain remained below deck, and Sybyl never reemerged from the cabin. She kept the shutters shut, allowing us to continue our journey without further altercation. Her reaction to the fire had been interesting to say the least. I couldn't quite wrap my head around it. If she was as close to Tristan as it seemed—although I still didn't know *what* that meant—would she not trust him?

Or had something else occurred?

When the dreary hours of the morning arrived, we let the flames sizzle to ash, so the sun might cast its warmth over the quiet waves. In those moments, the last signs of sirens dissipated into the depths of the sea, leaving behind those calm cobalt waters that sailors sing of back home.

Amongst the stench of ash, I collapsed on a nearby crate, the last remaining strands of adrenaline escaping my body. Exhaustion now found its place, cushioning my eyes and head. Sleep became my core thought, but I knew more work needed to be done.

And Cheddar would be less than thrilled if I did not let her out of the room soon.

Yet my body refused to rise. Sleep. I just wanted to sleep.

Veta sat on the crate next to me. Despite her visible exhaustion, a wide smile crossed her lips.

"Well, that was some good thinking you had there!" she exclaimed.

"It was worth a shot…" I rubbed my eyes. "Glad no one went overboard."

"Yeah, the worst casualty was Sybyl's robe."

"Right…"

Veta read my mind. "I am sure Hari will defuse the situation."

"She doesn't have to…the Captain gave an order." I leaned back on my elbows, watching as Hari strode across the deck. She paused at one of the beams and pressed her hand to it, mumbling under her breath before retreating down the stairwell.

"You think Sybyl cares?" Veta asked.

"If she cares as much for him as you say, then she should."

"Shagging the Captain doesn't mean she cares about him."

I frowned. "Still doesn't mean she should be giving orders."

"She is the quartermaster." Veta shrugged. "And she's one of the oldest on board. Probably thinks it's her right."

"Guess she wasn't too thrilled when Tristan got the ship then."

"Not sure, honestly. Tristan never really argued much with Sybyl on anything. Actually, this is the first time I heard him give a different order. No…wait…the second. There was one other time."

"Oh?"

"Yes…it was when you came aboard."

My throat tightened. "Wha—what do you mean?"

"Sybyl thought it was an intrusion for you to come aboard to babysit us. Demanded that we get rid of you once we left port."

"If they want the map—"

"Well, Tristan obviously disagreed and decided you were worth keeping."

"Why?"

"Not sure. But I think it's worth noting that something about you makes the captain speak."

The memory of the *Aquamarine* flashed over me. Tristan had dropped his defenses, if only for a moment, in our momentary interaction. But when Sybyl arrived, he closed in on himself, disappearing into his poised persona.

Veta nudged me, smirking. "Although I think the Captain has a soft spot for you."

"Perhaps."

I wanted the captain to have a soft spot. With every passing day, I couldn't deny the attraction I felt for him. But I didn't *know* him. He was nothing more than a few embers, flickering in my subconscious.

And occupying my dreams.

And as I drifted, leaning on that crate, it was hard to shake the image of the captain surrounded by fire. The little courage that rested in his core fueled his flame. Yet, without it, he was but a scared boy.

It infiltrated my sleep, where once again, I was on the docks, trading with my mother. Captain Davies approached us. In his hands, he carried a miniature version of himself. He begged us to take the tiny person, to free it of all responsibilities and worries, to nurture its flame until it was ready. In response, my mother offered a pretty doubloon and set Tristan free from the captain.

In my irrational state, it made sense. Why not separate the boy from the captain? Why not set him free from the world? Wasn't that my job as a trader? And as a carpenter, I could build him a home, layer it with a cushion of safety, and promise to keep little Tristan safe.

But it was nothing more than a ridiculous dream.

It fizzled away when someone shook my shoulder.

"Mr. Beaumont?"

I rubbed my eyes, then glanced up at who woke me.

Like in my dream, it was Tristan, standing before me. Cheddar sat perched on his shoulder.

"Oh…morning, Captain." I sat up slightly. "I must have dozed off."

"More like afternoon." The captain almost smiled as he spoke. "Your bird was not pleased…heard her screaming in your room," Tristan held his hand out to Cheddar, who hopped off his shoulder, then placed the bird on the crate beside me.

"Sorry, Cheddar-bird. Come step up." I offered my hand to her. She chirped and turned away from me. "Oh, I see…you're gonna hold a grudge. That's not going to last long…especially because I have this." I reached into my tool belt and removed a few pieces of rice from my pocket.

Cheddar tip-toed back in a circle before hopping into my hand to take the treat.

"Hmph." Tristan crossed his arms, still restraining that smile.

"What? Birds can be temperamental."

"Clearly." His face fell. "I…cannot thank you enough for your fast thinking yesterday. You saved this ship from a foe that few sailors survive."

"Oh, it was luck really."

"Nevertheless, we might not have survived the night without you. If there's anything you need, please, do not hesitate to ask."

"Thank you, Captain." I shifted slightly and glanced at my feet. "We went against Sybyl's orders, though."

"I will handle her." There was a twang in the statement, one that I could not identify. Sadness? Melancholy? Tristan did not open the door wide enough for me to comprehend it.

Tristan turned from me. "Have a good day, Mr. Beaumont. Please let me know if you need anything."

"Actually, Captain…" I hopped off the crate and adjusted my tool belt. "I do need one thing."

"Oh?"

"We need supplies to fix the boat. She's hurting, and I cannot mend her with what we have."

He fidgeted with one of his gloves and nodded. "Understood. I will consult with Rémy."

"Thank you, Captain."

With that, Tristan left, leaving me on deck with Cheddar and a day's work ahead of me.

Rémy navigated the *Cobalt Hare* to the west, slightly off course from our destination by a couple of days. The entire ship could hear Sybyl and the captain arguing about the change of course as we sat in the mess hall. No one spoke, their muffled shouts reverberating throughout the ship.

Well, we only really heard Sybyl's side. The captain did not yell.

But otherwise, we traveled to our new destination with no further hiccups, the oceans calm and the ship creaking along to its destination. I argued with the wood daily, willing it to stay in place until we received more supplies. It mocked me, really. I hammered it down, only for another piece to spring upwards and wave in my direction. How this ship kept running, I didn't have a clue.

But it did.

And we soon made it to a small port town off the coast of Rosada.

The drab grasses of the coastal marsh skimmed the distant edge of the horizon as our first signs of land. A thin mist danced over them.

I paused my arguments with one of the beams as the marsh approached. Cheddar leapt with joy, flittering through the air, before resting again on my shoulder.

Land. I hadn't realized how much I missed land. After weeks of seeing nothing more than blue, the mere sight of anything else caused me to jump from my spot, clutching the hammer in my hand.

I closed my toolbox and rushed over to the helm, where Rémy stood holding a map, frowning.

"How good is your Rosadian?" she asked as I joined her.

"My Rosadian?"

"We're docking on Grover's Marsh, a small town in south Rosada. I highly doubt they speak Vernnes…maybe some Volfi."

"It's not my strongest, but I can speak it." While I spoke Volfi and Vernnes regularly back home, my Rosadian did not expel the same confidence. "My mother knew it and taught it to me…but we didn't use it on the regular…so I'm a bit out of practice."

"That should be good enough." Rémy folded the map. "I am not too thrilled to be docking in Rosada, but based on the map you've given me, we'll be traveling along their coastline for quite some time."

"What's so bad about Rosada?" I asked Rémy. With traders few and far between in L'Perle, Rosada was merely a whisper. While it was a growing nation, most of its history remained hidden behind a veil of religion. To know Rosada was to know their god, and I barely knew the deities of L'Perle.

"Their government is quite strict about the use of magic. With our precious magical cargo, I doubt it would be wise to stay long."

My thoughts immediately went to the captain. But I didn't dare to verbalize my thoughts.

"By my calculations, we will arrive in port this evening," Rémy turned back to her map.

"Great. Thank you, Rémy."

She grunted and continued examining the map.

I returned to where I had been working and gathered my toolbox and supplies. Cheddar watched me from her perch, head bobbing with the ship, chirping once with excitement.

After gathering the supplies, I climbed below deck to the cargo hold. Cheddar flurried behind me, landing on my head as I opened the door. I returned the beams of wood to the shelves. Only eight beams, about as long as I was tall, remained. A small collection of rusted iron nails, brass hinges, and blunted screws filled the jars on the shelves.

I made a mental note of the supplies. As I turned to leave, I paused, glancing down at the rows of barrels. A figure stood over one of them, a vague silver glow capturing its shadow.

"Captain?" I called.

Tristan shut the barrel and turned to me. "Mr. Beaumont…what are you doing down here?"

"Sorry. Inventory, sir," I stretched my hands. "I did not know you would be down here."

"Neither did I…" Tristan turned back to the barrel, scowling.

I licked my bottom lip and asked, "Is…something wrong with the goods?"

"What? No," he pulled at the top of the barrel again. "It was…calling me."

"You mean the magic?" I took a step towards him.

"I guess."

The captain did not retreat as I joined his side. That strange silver liquid stared back at us, mirroring the glow of the nearby lantern.

Tristan held his hand over the liquid. It bubbled as his fingers grazed its surface.

"What's it doing?" I asked.

"I don't know. It does this whenever I visit…but not to anyone else."

"Does it have to do with your magic?"

"I think so."

I said nothing, watching as he continued to thumb its surface in silence. Tristan furrowed his brow, visibly lost in thought. While a slew of questions crossed my mind, I did not ask them. Why did it recognize his magic? What did Tristan think it could do?

And really…what was this artifact that we sailed across the world to deliver? Even my mother had no name for it.

I rested my hand on the edge of the barrel as I peered at the silver liquid. My thumb poked at its surface.

A few bubbles gathered at my fingertip.

Like with Tristan's touch.

Tristan removed his hand from the liquid. The bubbling continued around my finger.

"Lyam…do you have magic?" He asked.

"What? No."

"Then why is it reacting to you?"

"I don't know…" I lifted my hand. The surface calmed. "Maybe the treasure just likes me."

Tristan scoffed. I smirked at him.

His cheeks turned a slight hint of red as he turned away from me.

# CHAPTER TEN

# Alder, Mahogany, Oak

Tristan asked no more questions, leaving me alone with the barrel. Once he was gone, I slammed the barrel shut and retreated to my quarters. Cheddar followed behind me, landing on my bunk post, and proceeding to chirp a collection of nonsense.

I slid to the ground and stared at my hands. While I'd tossed a cocky smile and proclamation at Tristan, my mind raced. There was no way that I had…magic. Everything I had ever done required practice and talent; if I had magic, what did that mean? It wasn't like I ever waved my hand and conjured a ball of fire.

Perhaps the strange liquid was wrong. Tristan's presence probably confused it.

"I don't have magic," I recited to myself.

Sure, when I was a young boy, the idea of magic excited me. I used to pretend I could turn trees green or summon a hurricane with a flick of my fingers. But, as I grew older, I settled on more practical talents. Ones that could be taught. Learned.

Cheddar hit her beak against the bedframe. I turned.

"Sorry, Cheddar-bird. Talking to myself," I said.

She hit her beak against the bedframe again, then, with evident happiness, recited, "Wood."

"Yes, good bird. That is made of wood," I removed a few seeds from my pockets and placed them on the bed. "The bed frame is made of wood."

"Wood," she chirped again, then hopped over to her seeds.

Right. I need to focus on the wood and other supplies. What did I need again? I lay back on the bed, running my mental inventory. With my mind wandering, I did not even hear as we docked, nor did I feel the quelled rocking of the ship. It was a half-dreamlike state. Half of my mind focused on the inventory, but the rest replayed every essence of my childhood, searching for some sign of magic.

Back on L'Perle, it wasn't as though we had people searching for magic. While down in Gonvernnes, the Gardeniros sought those with earthen-born magic, L'Perle just existed. If magic appeared, it did so by chance; often, it left as soon as it was discovered.

A knock on the door finally returned me to the present.

"Lyam? It's Hari."

"Yes?" I called.

"We've arrived in port."

I slid off my bed and opened the door. Hari stood there, her long black hair woven behind her, and a bag slung across her body.

"The captain asked that I accompany you when in port," Hari said.

"Are we going now?" I asked.

"If you want. Night markets often have the best deals, don't they?"

"Sometimes, yes." Once again, I smiled. While civilians frequented the markets in the morning, the best merchants always appeared in the evening. Now was as good a time as any to make a deal.

I covered the window for Cheddar. As she took to her perch, I paused, glancing at the pages sticking out from beneath my cot. I'd placed them there when I first arrived to keep the map safe. Something in my gut compelled me to snatch them before I followed Hari from my room. I folded them carefully, sticking them into my tool belt, before shutting the door.

"We should have enough gold and silver for bartering," Hari said as we headed down the ladder.

"Is that what they use as currency?"

"Yes. Rosada has a primitive currency system; gold, silver, and copper coins are the primary means of trade. It doesn't matter what is embossed on its face."

"Guess you learned that aboard the *Sanguine Tortuga*?"

"Did Veta tell you about that?"

"In her way."

"I see." Sadness pinched her voice. But she continued walking forward, her posture standing tall.

"I suppose the captain is lucky to have you aboard now. Seems you have the right experience," I remarked.

"Yes, I suppose he is…" she trailed off, attention locked forward as we exited from the gangway and onto the docks.

The cool humidity greeted me upon leaving the ship. While L'Perle shared a similar humidity, it was always, well, warm. Instead, the humidity weighed here on my shoulders, while brushing my skin with a chilled gust. The hair on my arms rose, while sweat gathered in my armpits and on my forehead.

We walked along the boardwalk in silence. The brackish waters of the marsh lapped against the mangroves and marsh grasses. White birds took flight into the evening light. The buzzing of cicadas sliced open the otherwise peaceful waters.

"Here, put this on." Hari removed two silver emblems from her bag. She affixed one to her blouse and handed the other to me.

I recognized the emblem. It had appeared in port in L'Perle: two triangles, point-to-point, forming an hourglass. But I never knew what it meant.

"What is it?" I asked as I affixed it to my chest.

"Our badge of safety."

"And that means?"

"Prevents the Rosadian authorities from investigating us for magic. I snagged a couple from the *Sanguine Tortuga* before leaving…just in case." Hari spoke pointedly. With the mentions of her old ship, it was as though she was taken far away, lost in a different life.

"Does the Captain know?" The words slipped from my mouth. I sucked in my lips at once.

"I left a badge behind for him. Don't worry…he'll be okay."

"Oh…good." I flushed.

Hari's lips twitched.

Hiding my face, I changed the subject. "We're lucky to have you, Hari, really—you know more about what is going on than most."

"If you spend a long time on ships, you learn things…and meet people who can teach you…so much…" Once again, she trailed off, her voice catching in her throat.

"You mean when you were aboard the *Sanguine Tortuga?*"

She nodded.

My curiosity struck. "Why did you leave?"

She rubbed her hands together, eyes downcast. "When the *Tortuga* attacked the *Hare*, it was not without blood. People died…and I needed to find a way to move past that."

"Oh." I fidgeted with my sleeves and turned to the ground. A pirate's life was one masked by loss, that was a fact of the sea, but when the currents were calm, without carnage, it was easy to forget.

We walked in silence for a few minutes. The boardwalk ended abruptly, directing us to a muddy stone path leading into a small, brick-laden town. In the early evening light, the town bustled, with guards in silver uniforms bordering the walk. I adjusted the insignia on my chest and threw a quick smile in the guard's direction, only to receive a glower in return.

Like with many port towns, the main market did not wait far from the boardwalk. Many merchants had already packed for the day, the dim gas lamps casting shadows over their vacant stalls. Yet, a few stalls remained, offloading their remaining food and goods to those loitering.

"Do you know what you're looking for?" Hari asked.

I nodded and scanned the market. The lumber merchants usually loitered close to the docks on L'Perle. They stayed late, supplying wood to the ships before they set sail in the evening.

Here, in this dreary market, it was a similar story. In an erect pavilion, on the edge of where the cypress trees met the boardwalk, lumber lay in stacks across the ground. I approached the pavilion. A small woman with frizzy blonde hair sat in the corner, glowering in my general direction.

I smiled at her, but she had no interest in my formalities, so I turned my attention to the lumber. The stacks each contained a different type, ones I identified with a mere glance or touch. *Pine. Cypress. Oak.*

"Excuse me?" I said in clumsy Rosadian.

The merchant glanced my way.

"You have…" I fumbled through my translation until finding the correct word, "mahogany?"

"Yes, there," the merchant pointed to a pile in the far corner. "Ten silver a beam."

I approached the lumber. Yet, without even touching the wood, I caught the merchant's lie. There was something about the wood that was different; mahogany was dense and took up space, but alder was flimsy. From a distance, no one could tell the difference, but me? Well…I knew.

"This is…alder," I said to the merchant.

She continued glowering. "No. Mahogany."

"No. It's alder."

"Says who?"

"Me."

"How do you know?"

I opened my mouth to respond, but froze. What would my mother say? I knew it was alder…but how could I explain it? And what would my father do? He had passed this knowledge to me. Now, I just had to use it.

The merchant didn't stop as I approached the lumber. I knelt beside it and ran my finger over a beam. With slight pressure, I pressed my fingernail into the wood.

When I removed it, the red stain painted my finger like blood.

"The wood is stained," I held my finger up to the merchant.

The merchant smirked. "Very well. Three silver."

"No, I'll take the oak for three silver."

"That's six."

My Rosadian grew stronger as I spoke, "Listen, I need thirty full beams. Cut me a deal. At six, that's over one hundred gold. We both know the wood isn't worth that much."

"Well, I guess you're out of luck."

"No, I think you're out of luck. This wood is going to rot soon, right? It's been sitting in this humid marsh for weeks now. You already sold off what you could to locals, so you're relying on some naïve sailor to pick up the rest. What is obvious to me is that you have a product to move, and I have money." My assumptions were based solely on my own feelings. I could have been wrong, but in my core, I had a feeling I was right.

The merchant continued her glowering. I crossed my arms.

With a sigh, the merchant leaned back and said, "I can do four silver and deliver it to your ship in the morning."

"And you'll throw in some nails and tools at a discount?"

The merchant groaned but didn't object.

And that was the game my mother taught me.

Hari and I headed back to the ship after completing the trade. When all was said and done, we acquired thirty new beams, as well as a box of nails, tools, and other necessities, for under one hundred silver. While I knew the deal would make my mother proud, I think my father would have been exuberant. How many times had merchants tried to swindle us in port? Without my mother, we might have fallen victim to such schemes.

"How'd you know about the wood?" Hari asked after I told her what I discussed with the merchant.

"I just…did," I said. "Instinct, I guess."

"Without even touching it?"

"Yeah…it was obvious to me."

"It's your own type of magic." Hari lowered her voice on the last word.

"It's not magic," I replied.

"Not all magic is flashy."

"Yeah, but it's not magic. It's practice."

Hari grimaced before saying, "I used to think similarly."

"What do you mean?"

"I have always had perfect aim. Thought it was luck, or talent…but as time passed, I realized it might be something more."

I had never thought much of Hari tossing different objects to the crew, without even a second thought. All those perfect throws could have been mere luck.

Magic? It seemed absurd.

"Guess there's no real way to be certain…" I mumbled.

Hari shrugged. "Perhaps not. But remember, not everyone's magic is as flashy as fire."

I didn't respond, turning my attention ahead. As if on cue, Tristan marched up the path with Sybyl. My stomach sank. Sybyl rested her hand on Tristan's back.

Hari immediately fell in step. "Captain! Do you have your badge?"

Sybyl interjected before Tristan could respond, "Yes. We have it."

"Make sure not to lose it. Remember, Rosada is not friendly to magic and—"

"We'll be fine, Miss Sharma. I'll keep a good eye on the captain."

I locked eyes with Tristan. He did not say a word, his gaze drifting past my shoulders as Sybyl tugged on his hand to lead him into town.

Hari and I exchanged a glance. A rock formed in my throat.

*Stop. He's my captain. Nothing more.*

But Tristan occupied my thoughts far more than I cared to admit. I was far too old for such swooning.

No. There was work to be done.

# The Pillars of Fire

With first light, I ventured to the docks with Cheddar on my shoulder to supervise the unloading of the materials. Clouds masked the sky, smoke rising and falling over the marsh. From up the boardwalk, the lumber merchant watched, arms crossed, glowering in my direction. The other crewmates went about their day. As usual, there was no sign of the captain.

I counted each beam as the workers loaded them onto the ship, placing my hand on each one to ensure their authenticity. Oak was common enough, but after yesterday, I wouldn't put it past the merchant to slip in some alder or pine.

With the final beam loaded onboard, I paid the merchant the final few coins.

"I suggest you leave soon, pirate," the merchant said as she pocketed them. "The Guard is investigating some magic in town last night, and foreigners like you will always garner interest."

I grimaced. "Thank you. I'll let the captain know."

The merchant didn't say anything else, motioning for her workers to follow her down the boardwalk, vanishing like a ghost in the fog.

I reentered the ship, taking a moment to secure my supplies in the hull, before climbing up onto the deck. Veta and Rémy sat together on a crate, their heads pressed together as they whispered. Hari paraded around the deck, completing inventory. She waved me over upon seeing me.

"Did you get everything you needed? No further disagreements?" she asked.

"Everything's ready. The ship will be brand new in a matter of weeks."

"Excellent. We're just doing our final checks—we should be ready to leave in the evening."

"Actually, I was speaking to the merchant—she warned us that the Guard here is investigating some magic and might be a good idea for us to leave."

"I'll inform the Captain." She turned and marched toward the Captain's Cabin.

I joined Rémy and Veta at the far end of the deck. Veta tossed me an apple as I approached, nearly hitting me on the head.

"So you gonna turn this piece of junk into something extravagant with your fancy new materials?" Veta asked as I took a seat.

"I was thinking I'd knock out the wall of my room and expand it, actually," I chided as I took a bite of my apple.

"Not sure Zo would like that."

"There are other rooms."

"Personally, I think you should erect a giant statue of Cheddar," Veta motioned to the bird circling the deck.

"I am sure Sybyl would love that," Rémy added.

"Cheddar is a better crewmate than Sybyl will ever be."

"Just because Sybyl is…Sybyl…it doesn't mean she's a bad crewmate."

"Sorry…Cheddar is better all-around than Sybyl," Veta claimed.

"Cheddar is better than most people," I added.

"Very true," Rémy conceded.

I took another bite and leaned back, tapping my fingers on the surface of the ship. The rotting wood hissed beneath my touch, as if arguing with the very prospect of being replaced. But the wood wasn't talking. It didn't have emotions. The idea of saying otherwise was preposterous! Hari's comments on magic had gotten into my head—that was all.

Across the deck, I noticed Hari arguing with Sybyl outside the Captain's Cabin. Cheddar sat on the roof of the cabin, head cocked and listening.

114

"Oi Lyam—have another one!" Veta threw another apple at me. It flew past my face, rolling in the direction of the Hari and Sybyl.

I glowered at her.

"Go get it," she lowered her voice, "and find out what's going on with those two."

"If you're so nosey, why don't you do it?"

"I'm spending time with Rem," she leaned against Rémy.

Rémy shrugged. "Sorry. My hands are tied."

I hopped off the crates, yielding to Veta's demands. Granted, I was curious just as much, but I wasn't the most subtle person on board.

As I approached the apple, I ducked behind a few barrels, crawling to my knees. The apple lay a few paces away from where Hari and Sybyl stood.

"I don't understand," Hari hissed at Sybyl.

"What's there to understand? He was being an ass, so I let him have his fun last night and came back to the ship. He's a big boy and can take care of himself." Sybyl adjusted her golden necklace, playing with the pendant on the chain.

"Did you at least leave the badge with him?

"He's fine."

"You didn't give it to him!?"

"The Captain doesn't need a babysitter. Stop being overbearing, Miss Sharma."

"I actually care about the welfare of this crew! But that's beside the point...that badge would have protected him!"

"Not if he showed off his flame anyway. I always knew that magic was a bad idea. Rosada might have the right idea."

"How could you say that!?"

The two continued to bicker as I slipped back from the barrel. I glanced around the ship. No one else had heard the conversation. While I considered returning to Rémy and Veta, I was hesitant to let word get out to the rest of the crew. What panic might ensue?

If the Rosadian Guard were investigating magic, and if the captain was missing... Well...

I didn't want to think about what might have happened.

Cheddar fluttered over to me, landing on top of my head. She clicked her beak, as if mimicking the sound of a flame popping.

"Cheddar, go fly into town. I'll meet you there, okay?"

She clicked her beak again.

"See if you can find the captain, alright?"

Another click, and she lifted off my head and soared toward the boardwalk.

I took a bite of the new apple, then, after glancing back at Hari and Sybyl and tossing the remainder of my apple in the bin, climbed below deck.

116

Before heading to the gangway, I stopped on my floor to snag the badge and my work belt from my room. It felt heavy on my chest, its hourglass-shaped insignia unnatural on my clothes. Would it help me here? I wasn't sure. But at least I had it.

I paused in the doorway to my room and glanced across the hall. The door to the captain's room hung ajar, untouched from the previous night. Curiosity nipped me, and with a gentle push, I pushed the door open in its entirety.

I hadn't seen the inside since I first discovered Tristan's magic, but it was just as I remembered. Sheets of metal layered the wall. Char marks left a permanent signature on their surface. Other than that, the room was nothing special. A simple wire-framed cot and a chest sat against the far wall.

My legs carried me into the room. I approached the cot and placed my hand on its surface. It was like sleeping on stone. Why was this room like a jail cell? It had no heart, no warmth; nothing. There was so much I didn't know about our captain. Granted, I didn't expect him to tell me his life story… but it didn't hinder my inquisition.

It wasn't right for me to be snooping. It was time to head to town.

As I exited the room, I noticed a plaque hanging on the wall, its inscription embossed with pristine gold.

It read:

There was something haunting about that plaque that followed me out of the ship. I didn't tell anyone that I headed back into town. I hoped that I'd find the captain at some tavern, drinking, and I could guide him back to the ship without incident.

The rumor I had heard had to be a coincidence.

*You belong to us.* There was so much about Tristan that I did not know. Was he part of the Janis Militia? Was he still loyal to them? The *Hare* had belonged to the Commeant, according to Veta, but were there further ties? What did that mean for the future of the *Cobalt Hare*?

It shouldn't have mattered to me. I was merely a trader and a temporary hire. In the next year, I'd return to L'Perle. From there, my future was still as open as the murky sky above Grover's Marsh.

But that plaque remained in my mind's eye like the sun, rising over Grover's Marsh.

In contrast to the night before, daylight transformed the town. Civilians hurried about, not looking up from the ground, their drab clothes blending in with the lackluster trees. At night, the surrounding marsh held an invisible magic, brought to life by the nocturnal creatures croaking. But during the day, it might as well have been a pile of mud.

I entered the town square, where a grandiose tower stood. On its roof, an hourglass sat, grains of crystallized sand counting every passing minute. I stared, entranced. It would take a year to go through every grain.

Cheddar's squawking pulled me out of its gaze, though. She landed on my head and banged her beak on my forehead.

"Feu," she recited in Volfi

"Feu…Fire…" I lifted her off my head, "Did you find Captain Davies?"

She bobbed her head. "Feu."

"Show me."

Cheddar jumped from my hand and fluttered forward, her orange tail like a beacon through the sea of grays and browns. She darted through a few civilians, nearly knocking over a small child playing with a ball.

I mumbled an apology to the child's father as I rushed after the bird. She guided me around the back of the tower, where a bland, unassuming brick building stood. Guards stood out front like statues, and a line of civilians waited, heads bowed, locked in prayer.

Cheddar directed me around the building. She landed on the ground in front of a locked cellar door. In the brick-laden structure beside them, narrow windows allowed light into the basement below us.

"Feu," Cheddar remarked again.

I knelt beside the building and peered inside the window. In the dim light, I could vaguely make out a figure hunched over, hands trapped in metal casings linked with chains. Even in the dim light, I could make out the figure's red hair.

"Captain?" I whispered.

The figure raised its head.

"Captain, up here! It's me…uh…Lyam Beaumont."

He stared at me. Yes, it was definitely Tristan. I knew those blue eyes anywhere.

"What're you doing here?" He hissed back.

I stammered. Why was I there? What compelled me to sneak off the ship like this? I could have waited for Hari. She was far more seasoned in this sort of… diplomacy.

"We were concerned that you hadn't returned, so I sent Cheddar to look for you. Since I can speak Rosadian, it made sense for me to come." It wasn't a complete lie.

"Good, you can tell these Guards that it was an accident," Tristan replied.

"What was an accident?"

"The fire."

"Fire?"

"You didn't know?"

Before I responded, the door to his cell opened. A brooding figure stood in the entrance. Without a word, it lurched Tristan's chains, yanking him out of sight.

"Merde," I cursed and jumped to my feet. Sybyl hadn't mentioned any fire…but perhaps it happened after she abandoned Tristan.

I abandoned my spot and hurried back around the building. The line into the small building had transformed into a crowd, gathering at the entranceway. I pushed my way through, standing on my tiptoes to see past the threshold.

Rows of chairs filled the entrance hall, encircling a podium designed for prayer. A man in a red robe stood there, an hourglass hanging around his neck, a thick book of scripture before him.

His voice boomed as he spoke.

"Let it be known, let it be graced, the Effluvium has granted us this space. Where we can be untainted, unafraid, away from those that wish us ensnared. So, recite with me, loud and clear, we're cleansed of all that makes us fear. Because we say, we say it now, I am the Effluvium, loud and proud."

"Loud and proud!" the congregation chanted.

"Loud and proud," I whispered to not draw attention.

"And let it be so." The robed preacher pulled out of his sermon and turned his back on the congregation. "Last night, we had a plague rock our community. You may have already heard of this curse, guided by fire, beneath the watchful eye of the Effluvium. It threatened the very Year Glass that acts as the Effluvium's eyes and souls. This fire was born not of incessant malice but of magic…and I have proof."

Murmurs filled the room. My stomach tightened. I knew what happened without the speaker's explanation. So, while there was no surprise when the armed guards led Tristan into the room, his hands chained and guarded by metal, it didn't stop me from gasping.

I hadn't gotten a good look at him in his cell. While I'd seen his hair and blue eyes, the bruising on his face was less apparent. Now, I could visibly make out the black and blue blotches around his eyes, as well as the dried blood beneath his nose and painting his lips. His clothes, singed, hung from his body like wet feathers, weighing down his bony physique.

I bit my lip to keep myself from shouting Tristan's name.

The preacher continued, "We found this Magii beneath our Year Glass last night, dancing in the fire he wielded with his own hands! But we will not stand for such a plague. The hands of the Effluvium will cleanse his soul."

With that last word, he motioned to the guards on the other side of the room. They stepped to the side, revealing a porcelain basin filled with ice. Steam rose into the humid air.

The guards led Tristan to the basin. He did not flinch, his head bowed, any fight taken from him. Just like the plaque reminded him on the wall of his room.

*You belong to us. You deserve only the loyalty you give. Your freedom was sacrificed for peace.*

They lowered Tristan into the ice water. As it met his skin, it sizzled, ice meeting fire, boiling as one.

The preacher rested his hands on Tristan's shoulders and said, "Today, we cleanse another soul. Tomorrow, this soul faces the consequences decreed by the guard. Why do we do this? Because…we are the Effluvium's soul."

"We are the Effluvium's soul," the congregation chanted.

I couldn't even mumble along with the declaration.

Instead, I gawked as the preacher thrust Tristan under the water. He held him there as Tristan's legs thrashed. Was he going to kill him? How could I stop him?

But as the thirty-second mark passed, the preacher released Tristan's shoulders, allowing him to come up for air.

The fear in Tristan's eyes was palpable.

Before the preacher thrust him into the water again.

# CHAPTER TWELVE

# Jailbreak

I wish I could say I was a hero right then and there. But, as the preacher thrust Tristan into the water nine more times, paralysis washed over my entire body. I could not move. Even speech became foreign. All I could do was watch as my captain withered beneath the water, his fear growing each time the preacher dunked him in the water.

After the tenth "cleanse", for lack of a better word, the preacher finally lifted Tristan from the water. His clothes stuck to his frail body. I'd never considered Tristan frail; his layers of clothes always amplified his role as captain. But now, he was any other boy, shivering as the preacher turned him to the congregation.

"Now, boy, what do you have to say?" the preacher hissed.

Tristan responded in Vernnes, "I don't understand."

The crowd shouted in disdain. Someone threw a boot at Tristan's head.

"We will try again tomorrow," the preacher said, then motioned to the guards. They grabbed Tristan's chains and yanked him to follow. Tristan tripped, hitting the ground. Before he had a chance to climb to his feet, the guard pulled on the chains again and dragged him along the floor.

The congregation jeered as the guards dragged Tristan back down into the prison beneath us.

The preacher bowed one last time to his congregation, then followed behind the guards, leaving the congregation to go about their day.

I still didn't move as the crowd filed from the building. It never occurred to me that Rosada was like…*this*. What would happen to Tristan if he stayed here? And what could I do to help?

"Fire?"

I hadn't noticed Cheddar sitting on my shoulder. She touched her beak to my ear.

"Yeah, yeah, we'll free him. Don't worry, Cheddarbird."

I unclenched my fist and adjusted my tool belt. With my feet shaking, I exited the building, stopping outside to stare up at that giant hourglass. Should I go back to the ship and tell the crew? But if I did…in that time, what might happen to the captain?

My legs shook as I looped back around the building. A guard stood watch by the cellar door near the window from earlier.

*Well, that's no good.* I motioned for Cheddar to step onto my hand. She bobbed her head to the side.

"Feu," she recited again.

"Yes, I'm thinking." I bit my lip as I analyzed the building. From here, I noticed that the cellar door was weak. There was something about the way the wood behaved. Hari's voice echoed in my head about magic, but it was a mere observation…nothing more.

I reached for my hammer on my belt. If I found a way to distract the guard, then maybe I'd be able to break it.

Cheddar hopped back onto my head and chirped.

I grinned. "Well, Cheddar…you think you can distract the guard there?"

The bird danced on my head.

"I trust you've got a handle on this. Go for it."

That smart little bird launched from my head, and with a dramatic flap of her wings, launched at the guard. The guard cursed, waving her away, but it did not scare Cheddar. Instead, she stormed upwards, spiraling. As the guard unfurled his sword, she began her descent, shooting at the guard like a cannon bomb.

But rather than attacking, as the guard turned his attention to her, Cheddar let loose her bowels.

I covered my mouth, restraining a laugh as a smattering of white and black landed on the guard's face.

He cursed, hacking as he stumbled forward. Cheddar cackled, then flew off into the forest.

"Damn bird! Get back here!" The guard shouted as he chased after her.

*Cheddar, you silly bird.* I waited until the guard disappeared into the trees, then unhooked my hammer from the belt. My heart thudded as I approached the locked cellar door. To my disappointment, the metal bolt remained secure in place.

I took one last glance around, then placed my hand on the door. My fingers traced the old wood beams, finding a weak spot toward the upper right corner.

After weighing my hammer in my hand, I lined it up with the weak corner. I counted to ten and slammed it into the wood.

Once.

Twice.

Thrice.

Four times.

The right side of the door caved inwards, releasing its grip on the left side and allowing me to open the door.

A stairwell led me into the basement. It wasn't an intricate prison by any means, hidden only eight steps beneath the earth. Stones layered the walls, where a set of four doors lined the wall. One door, wood with no distinguishing factors, opened without contest, leading to another set of ascending stairs…most likely to the heart of worship above me.

The other three doors did not look much different, except for the thick metal bolts guarding their knobs.

I approached the first one and tapped on the wood. "Tristan?"

No response.

I moved to the next one. "Tristan? It's me, Lyam."

A weak gurgle replied.

I checked the other door, then returned to the second one. "I'm going to get you out of there, Captain. Don't worry."

The gurgle did not return.

I positioned my hammer in my hand. The door's wood was stronger, but it was not impossible to break. I pulled back my arm and flexed my back, then with a heavy thud, slammed the hammer into the wood.

And again.

And again.

Until an opening large enough for me to peek inside formed.

Tristan sat slumped against the wall, fresh blood pooling from his nose and mouth, his clothes still damp from the cleansing ritual. He locked his tired blue eyes with mine.

I clawed at the wood with my hand. It peeled back like burnt skin, allowing me passage into the room.

"Captain, c'mon…let's get outta here."

He stared ahead, unresponsive.

"Tristan…" I hooked my hammer back to my belt and knelt beside him. Metal covered his hands, chained together to block his magic.

In the dim light, I noticed a tear fall down his face.

"Okay, c'mon, I've got you." I hoisted him up and pulled him onto my back. He slumped over my shoulder, the loose chains around his hands hitting the back of my thighs. It surprised me how light he was; I had carried bundles of wood heavier than him.

I navigated out of the cellar in haste. To my relief, the guard hadn't returned. But I knew I couldn't parade Tristan through town. Everyone knew of him. Even the merchant I spoke with earlier mentioned the magic.

So, I went the only way that I could: into the trees.

I found us a secluded spot, bordering the tall marsh grasses, but still high enough that pine needles blanketed the ground. After double-checking no one followed us, I knelt beside

Tristan, tore a piece of my tunic, and used it to clean the blood from his face.

He stared into the forest. Other than that single tear, he showed no other emotion, his expression as blank as the cloudless sky.

"I'm sorry, I don't have any food, Captain. Or water. But we'll get back to the *Hare* soon," I finished cleaning his face.

He still didn't respond.

I glanced at the chains on his hands. "I…can try to break those with my hammer, if you'd like."

He shook his head.

"Are you positive? You cannot access your magic otherwise."

"Why would I want to?" He snapped. Tears once again formed in his eyes. "It only causes destruction."

"You told me it was an accident before."

"An accident can still destroy."

"Captain…" I refrained from touching him, but my questions did not cease. "What happened?"

He closed his eyes. "Too much to drink with Sybyl. Got frustrated. That's all."

"Wait…so Sybyl knew?" Hadn't she just said that he and Tristan went their separate ways in town?

"Of course she knew. We went to a pub, had some drinks, bickered, fooled around… My gloves must've come off during…all of that. Next thing I knew…fire." Tristan sighed. "Not the first time it happened."

While I knew it was inappropriate to inquire further, I spoke faster than I could bite my tongue. "Why were your gloves off?"

"I don't know. Sybyl must have taken them off. She likes to examine my scars."

"But in public?" I gawked.

"It's how she is," Tristan grunted.

"But she had to have known…if this has happened before."

"Doesn't matter. It's not like I can say no."

"Why not!?"

"Because it's all I've ever known!" Tristan's voice cracked, then his voice fell. "Sybyl is all I've ever known."

"It doesn't mean you have to…risk your own safety."

"What would you have me do?"

"You're the Captain." I punctuated the statement with no further explanation. There need not be one.

Tristan scoffed. But the sadness in his voice remained. There was more to his story, but it was his to tell when the opportunity arose. Perhaps I didn't understand his relationship with Sybyl because I'd never been in anything long-term. Only those flings at the *Aquamarine* with forgotten sailors and travelers.

We sat together in silence as the sun began its slow descent from high noon. Surely the crew would be looking for us soon, right? But if they were looking, then the guard would be too.

But the first one to find us was not our crew, nor was it the guard.

It was Cheddar, fluttering down from the trees, landing on my head.

"Yam. Feu," she proclaimed.

"Hi, Cheddar-bird," I motioned her onto my hand and brought her to my face. "You did well today, little bird."

If birds could smile, I'm sure she would have smiled at the compliment.

We sat there for a time, listening to the bubbling and croaking of the nearby marsh. The town was too far away for us to hear, but I remained alert. If the guard came to fight, I doubted that I could fend them off with my hammer.

"Stay here with Tristan, okay, Cheddar?" I said.

She squawked and hopped onto the log next to the captain.

I paced around the trees, finding a private corner to relieve myself. With my hand against a nearby tree, I exhaled. Exhaustion had caught up with me, and more than anything, I wanted a cup of coffee and a warm bed. Instead, I grounded myself in the bark of the trees. This tree was frail, rotted from the inside, struggling against the plumes of smoke.

*Magic.* Hari's voice echoed in my head.

I shook it off and rejoined Tristan. He had climbed to his feet, chains hanging from his body. He pulled them, but their weight tugged him forward, anchoring him to the ground.

"Captain, let me break the chains, please," I said.

He shook his head.

"If you're so concerned about your magic, we can leave the cuffs on…but the chains won't let us move fast."

Tristan scowled, his freckled nose wrinkling at the thought.

"Please," I pressured.

"Fine."

I unhooked my hammer. Tristan lay the chains down on the ground. Rusted and stained with dry blood, I could tell they were weak. Although not as instinctive as with the wood, I'd worked with enough metal to recognize its flaws.

I flexed my shoulders, then, with all my strength, I jammed the hammer into the chains.

Whack.

Whack.

Whack.

After a few thwacks, the chains shattered with a loud echo.

Nearby birds took flight, cawing in fear.

Except for Cheddar, who remained undisturbed on my shoulder.

I glanced over my shoulder and readjusted my hammer. "We should get moving before someone finds us."

"Where? Not like we can go back into town," Tristan commented.

I scanned the marsh. "We follow the water downstream…we'll at least reach shore and be able to find our ship from there."

Tristan nodded and motioned for me to lead the way.

The mud sloshed at our feet as we trudged through the swamp. Water refilled our footsteps with each step, hiding our path from any potential guards. Neither Tristan nor I spoke, settling into the song of the swamp. Breaths. Croaks. Sloshing. Wind. Around us, the swamp lived. We were in its domain, and there would be no mercy if we made the wrong decisions.

After a time, Tristan finally spoke, "I underestimated you, Mr. Beaumont."

I glanced back at him. "How so?"

"Thought you were some rich merchant's son tagging along to see the world. You've proven multiple times that you're more talented than that."

I smirked.

"But don't let it get to your head," Tristan punctuated.

I continued smiling as I led us forward, deeper into the swamp. Salt infiltrated the water, with mangroves mixing in with the cypress trees. Nearby, a log-like alligator sank into the water.

It was almost beautiful.

My heart thudded as we caught a glimpse of the sea. It wasn't far now. We just needed to wade through the grass until we reached the beach.

Then we would be home.

Free.

We exited onto the beach. In the distance, the pier waited for us. Specks of uniformed guards paraded on its surface, no doubt searching for Tristan.

I cursed under my breath, then turned to Tristan, "We'll need to be careful…there are guards."

"Won't matter…" Tristan mumbled.

"What?"

Tristan's gaze hadn't focused on the pier. Rather, his attention remained locked on the horizon.

I followed his gaze.

The recognizable obsidian body of the *Cobalt Hare* sailed away from shore, into the distance, without its captain.

# CHAPTER THIRTEEN

# Chasing a Rabbit

**W**hat do we do?" I asked Tristan, unable to pull my gaze from the *Cobalt Hare*.

"They may come back in a few days…" Tristan said, although he didn't sound too confident in his answer.

"Do we have a few days?" I retorted.

He frowned, his brows pinching over his nose. Focused, he looked older…confident even. Like a true captain. As he spoke, his voice remained level. "We might be able to catch them. The *Hare* is a slow ship. We'll have to find a small cutter or something similar that can catch the wind. But…it would be helpful if we knew where they're going."

I reached into my tool belt. There, the maps I had pocketed remained. I sorted through them, removing the next map in the sequence and handing it to Tristan.

"We don't have their piece of the map, but we'll know where they are heading."

Tristan examined it. "Looks like we're continuing along the Rosadian border."

I nodded.

Tristan handed the map back to me, then turned to the pier. "We'll need to wait until sunset…but then we can find ourselves a boat."

"Do we have enough time for that?"

"If we grab the right boat, yes. We wait."

"As you wish, Captain," I replied.

Tristan smirked. A spark ignited in his eye.

We stayed along the edge of the tree line, keeping our attention focused on shrinking the *Cobalt Hare*. Surely, they only left because of the guards. Perhaps they had plans to turn around, to retrieve us once the commotion had ceased.

Hari, Rémy, and Veta would never leave us behind.

Sybyl, on the other hand…

I pushed away the thoughts as Tristan and I trudged back into the marsh. We did not speak, letting the lull of afternoon turn to evening, and the horizon nod off to sleep, going from blue to purple to a navy black.

We found a place beneath the boardwalk at the edge of the marsh. There, we waited until the stars rose and the moon gave us a wink. Cheddar napped on my shoulder with her head nestled behind my ear. It was late for this little bird, but soon we'd be home. I made a silent promise of that.

This time, I had to put faith in my captain.

He hadn't spoken since we left our spot on the beach. Now, he eyed the docks, mouthing to himself as he counted the boats bobbing along the surface. Above, the occasional footsteps of merchants and guards echoed against the wood. But the marsh had hidden us from any onlookers.

"There's a cutter on the far end of the dock there," Tristan motioned with his metal-clad hands to a narrow boat, bobbing against the gentle ocean waves.

"Yeah, but looks like someone's watching," I replied. There was a single guard in a sweaty uniform, positioned at the end of the dock with a pipe in hand.

Tristan cursed. "This can't ever be easy…"

"That's the pirate's life, isn't it?"

He grumbled.

The guard paced up the dock, scuffing his feet along the wooden planks, hands behind his back. Tristan and I could probably take him alone…but we'd already drawn enough attention. Though our faces were bound to be plastered across Grover's Marsh and perhaps the entire nation of Rosada in the coming weeks. What was one more crime?

I squinted toward the boardwalk and counted each of the guard's steps. Fifty steps, turn, fifty steps, turn; the guard marched in the same rhythm, not missing a beat.

After counting for a few minutes, I removed Cheddar from my shoulder and placed her on Tristan's head. "Stay here."

"What are you doing?" Tristan hissed.

"I have an idea. But better I get caught than you, Captain. Not like I have magic."

"Lyam, wait," Tristan approached me.

I froze. He stood merely inches from my face.

Tristan realized this as well and stepped back at once. "Um…just be careful. I don't want to lose my carpenter. You've been valuable on the *Hare*."

I grinned. "Aye, Captain."

Tristan turned away from me, hunching his shoulders to hide his reddening ears.

My thudding heart carried me from the trees to the boardwalk. I didn't dare look back at Tristan. Every time I tried to push the captain from my mind, he came back to me like the sun rose each day.

I recomposed myself as I neared the boardwalk. Where the water met the sand, I stopped to remove my boots, roll up my trousers, and unhook my hammer from my belt.

Rather than climbing on the boardwalk, I waded into the water. Low tide offered its friendship. While the water still climbed up to my chest, it gave way so I could walk beneath the wooden structures of the walkways. The salt painted my lips, the tepid water weighing my tunic against my chest. Each step proved heavier than the last, with the sea grasses tangling my feet.

*Please don't let me step on some creature.* I hadn't a clue what might lurk in these brackish waters at night. An alligator? A large crab? A snapping turtle? I shook away the fears. Now was not the time to catastrophize.

I stopped halfway down the boardwalk, my head barely skimming the top of the wood. With my palm, I felt along the wood, searching for a piece that had succumbed to the natural elements. Each piece had its own age, replaced over the years from weathering storms and facing the waves.

I found a piece that had strips of mold along its surface. With the help of my hammer, I loosened the board, catching the nails before they fell into the water.

All I had to do was wait.

With only the ocean waves to fill the silence, I listened for the guard's footsteps.

One…

Two…

Three…

Each step echoed in my heart.

Nine…

Ten…

Eleven…

What if he stepped over the board?

Seventeen…

Eighteen…

Nineteen…

Would it make more sense to run?

Twenty-Six…

Twenty-Seven…

Twenty-Eight!

On that twenty-eighth step, the board snapped. The guard's leg fell through the opening, and his body hit the boardwalk above with a loud thud.

The guard cursed.

But I knew I had little time to act.

With my hammer, I hit the next board.

And the next.

Not hard enough to break them, but enough to send vibrations through the pathway above, so that the guard hit his head onto their surface and slipped into unconsciousness.

Once he stopped fidgeting, his leg hanging lifelessly through the hole, I reequipped my hammer and then heaved myself onto the boardwalk. I took one passing glance at the guard, blood oozing from his bludgeoned face.

*That worked better than I thought.* I smirked, but did not take time to linger.

I raced to the end of the dock. The ship waiting there was a narrow thing, able to cut through the waves with its single sail. I knew little about ships, except the basics of sailing, so I put my faith in Tristan. If he said this thing was fast, then I could only believe it as such.

I acted fast, using my little knowledge to untether the boat from the dock. From there, I found the anchor and raised it, letting it clunk onto the surface of the narrow boat. The waves caught the boat at once, pulling it away from the dock and toward the horizon.

"Merde…how do I do this again?" I mumbled as I pulled on the first rope. Nothing changed. Rémy had gone through how the sails of the *Hare* worked with me once, but this was different. So, I followed my gut instincts, alternating through a few more ropes, before the sail finally opened. I breathed out. Which way was the wind heading? I needed to turn south, back to Tristan and Cheddar…then we could head east, away from Rosada, and back to our home.

I spun a few times before finding the wind. With another tug of the rope, I adjusted the sail, then found the small tiller to steer. The boat circled once, and with a single gust of wind, I was heading back toward Tristan.

I laughed aloud. As I passed the boardwalk again, I noticed the guard waking from his slumber. He raised his head as I sailed past him and mouthed something I could not hear.

And I saluted him with a smile.

Past the boardwalk, Tristan waited with Cheddar. I navigated the boat, as best as I could, to the shore.

Tristan raced through the water, clamoring on board as I slowed. Cheddar jumped from his head and onto my shoulder.

"Go! Get out of here!" Tristan hissed as he hit the deck.

"I thought you would help drive this thing?"

"How am I going to do that? I'm wearing metal mittens!" He waved his metal-coated hands in my face.

"I told you that I can break them."

"Not going to happen." Tristan motioned to a rope by the sail. "Pull this here, that will turn us and get us moving out to sea. Let's get out of here."

"Aye, Captain," I said, then turned my attention to the endless sea, where I could only hope the *Cobalt Hare* waited just over the horizon.

We did not sleep as we sailed through the night to the north.

How could we?

Even once Rosada disappeared from view, the reality of our situation hit us. We had no food. No fresh water. Nothing.

Except for an incomplete map.

As the first signs of light climbed over the horizon, the realization hit me like a tsunami. We still had not caught up with *Cobalt Hare*. If we didn't find them in the next two days…well… we had to make a choice: turn back to Rosada…or die.

To be frank, I wasn't fond of either option.

"We'll catch her," Tristan mumbled. "We're averaging six or seven knots. On her best day, the *Hare* only goes six knots…and you know her current physical state. She's probably hitting four…at most."

"So what does that mean?"

"We'll catch her today."

"Assuming we're on the same path?"

"That's the question, isn't it?"

I glowered at the sea. We were alone, except for the occasional bird soaring above the clouds.

Cheddar hopped onto my knee and glanced at me.

"You know what I'm thinking, right, Cheddar-bird?" I asked her.

She bounced her head.

I had her step onto my fingers, approached the side of the boat, and threw my hand up, sending Cheddar soaring into the sky.

"Come back when you find the *Hare*!" I shouted after her.

"Aye!" She called as she flapped her wings once. She rose above our sail, taking to the sky, and out of sight.

I'd be lying if I said I wasn't worried. Every time Cheddar took flight, adventuring into the unknown, I questioned if she would ever return.

But she was a smart little bird. She'd be safe.

"You think she'll recognize the ship?" Tristan asked, leaning against the sail with his arms crossed. His wrists hung with the weight of the metal guarding his hands.

"She'll recognize it," I reassured him. That much I could be certain.

Tristan nodded, then used the crux of his arm to tug the rope slightly. The sail turned, catching another gust of wind. He then motioned to the tiller, "Can you turn our heading a few degrees north? Wind is shifting."

I obeyed. Tristan had a natural understanding of the ship, one that was far above my basic abilities. While I knew of the wood that constructed the small cutter, I lacked the knowledge to navigate it across the sea. Even if I did, Tristan was my captain. By agreeing to board the *Cobalt Hare*, I had also agreed to him as captain.

We sat in silence for a time, adjusting our heading as needed. I couldn't help but watch Tristan in awe. He worked with beautiful dexterity. His guarded hands did not hinder his abilities. Each movement cast the light over a different appendage. As he walked around the ship, his face glowed from the sun, so I could count each of his freckles. His hair, usually groomed back, hung in a sweaty disarray—like how it looked back in the *Aquamarine*. With only a tunic and a pair of dirty trousers, his lean stature was apparent, making it easy for him to rule over this cutter.

In contrast, I worried one wrong move might cause the boat to tip over.

I didn't want to spend time staring at Tristan like a love-struck fool. Instead, I sorted through questions in my head. I had so much to ask Tristan, and now he had no way to avoid them. But would it be too invasive? Would Tristan even answer anything? It didn't feel right to pry open my captain's life.

But it was Tristan who broke down that wall.

"Why carpentry?" He asked, not looking in my direction as he tied off a knot with his mouth.

"Oh," I stammered, "well, my father is a carpenter. It sort of came naturally to me—loved to carve things and build things when I was a kid. So, as I got older, I started to work with him." I reached for the hammer on my hip. "I liked it far more than all the trade negotiations my mother forced me to attend. Not that I regret going… I learned a lot."

"Like speaking multiple languages?"

"I learned Rosadian from my mother, but I actually learned Vernnes from my father."

"Impressive," Tristan sat down on the floor across from me. "I didn't get a lot of chances to learn other languages…or much of anything, really."

"You know how to sail."

"Only because I spent my entire adolescence in the military. I didn't have much schooling before then. Just whatever my father taught me."

"There was no school?" I asked. Even L'Perle, despite its small size, had a schoolhouse where I learned the basics.

"On Janis? Not unless you were wealthy, a merchant's apprentice, or in the militia."

"And you chose the militia?"

"It's not like I had a choice," he said pointedly.

"No one would take you as an apprentice?"

Tristan's nostrils flared. For a moment, it seemed like he wouldn't answer. But he couldn't escape me this time. There was no door to slam or deck to climb. Just the two of us, sitting alone, as the sea carried us in its arms.

"It's not like anyone would take me if I had asked. I was a criminal."

Now this was news to me. No one onboard the *Cobalt Hare* had mentioned the captain's criminal record…well, prior to being a pirate.

"What happened?" I asked.

Tristan sighed. "I discovered my fire. On accident. Was arrested on the grounds of arson."

"Sounds familiar."

"It happens."

"But…surely arson wouldn't prevent you from being a merchant, right? They must have understood it was an accident?"

Tristan frowned. "I still had to pay for property damages. My family couldn't afford it."

"So, you joined the military to pay that debt?"

"As I said…I didn't really have a choice."

"Your family didn't help?"

"They tried. Or, well, my sister tried. She sold herself into servitude to pay my bail…but I didn't know that until much later. Honestly, I believed for a long time that my mother took my sister and fled Janis."

"And your father?"

"He died when I was a boy. I had no one left."

"So…you didn't have a choice…" I mumbled.

He shook his head. "After about three months, the governor of Janis gave me the option of joining the military or staying in jail. I chose the former."

The plaque on Tristan's wall came back to me: *You belong to us. You deserve only the loyalty you give. Your freedom was sacrificed for peace.*

Now it made sense.

"Did you enjoy being in the military?" I asked, hoping to keep the conversation going.

"It made me into who I am today," he said, eyes cast out at the sea.

"But did you enjoy it?"

He kept his gaze locked at the sea without replying. He clenched his jaw.

It was enough for me to change the subject. "So…what do you want me to work on first when we get back to the ship?"

"Huh?" Tristan stared at me.

"The carpentry work. The reason we stopped in Grover's Marsh."

"Oh, whatever you think is best. I don't care."

"Well, there is a rotting plank in the mess hall that might snap any day, or there's the beam to the crow's nest, or—"

"You can figure it out."

"But I—"

"Mr. Beaumont, you can figure it out," Tristan retorted.

That was the end of the conversation. Tristan had filled the small hole I had created in his wall. Perhaps I had gone too far with my questions. But my last question echoed more than the rest. *Did you enjoy it?* Tristan's silence was enough of an answer.

Who was I to ask that, though?

I leaned my head against the edge of the boat. My throat scratched from lack of water, and every now and

again, my stomach rumbled. Lack of sleep tugged at my eye-
lids.

I drifted in and out of a half-sleep, helping Tristan
where needed, and keeping track of how the sun fell to the
west.

A single word, cawed from above, brought me back to
life. "Yam!"

Cheddar swooped down from above, flapping with excitement as she landed on the top of the sail.

"Yam!" she called again.

"Yam?" Tristan laughed.

"It's what she calls me. She calls you Feu."

"Feu?"

"That's 'fire' in Volfi," I said as I rose to my feet. "Did
you find them, Cheddar-bird?"

She bobbed her head.

"Can you show us?"

"Yam! Feu!" She jumped into the air and fluttered toward the northeast.

Tristan and I shared a smile.

It was time to catch a hare.

# CHAPTER FOURTEEN

# Snaring a Hare

Tristan gave the orders, and I took the helm. With the sails cast out in full and the wind in our favor, we rode the currents after Cheddar. She climbed and dove over the water, her orange tail feathers as our beacon into dusk.

After a little more than an hour, we saw her. The *Cobalt Hare*'s obsidian coating reflected the sea, glowing with the last bit of daylight.

Cheddar landed on my head. In a matter-of-fact tone, she chirped, "*Hare.*"

"Good job, Cheddar." I lowered her onto my arm.

Tristan approached the stern of our boat and eyed the ship. He fidgeted with his metal-cuffed hands, then turned to me. "You said you can get these cuffs off, right?"

"Yes…why?"

"We need to give them a sign so they know it's us."

"They might have seen Cheddar already."

Tristan scoffed. "Sybyl hates birds. She can't tell a parrot from a seagull."

"Why does she hate birds?" I asked.

"Pretty sure they kept pooping on her back on Janis or something. I don't know…it's petty and dumb. Can you break my cuff or not?"

I restrained the urge to laugh, keeping my amusement in line as I responded. "Right, okay, yeah…I can break it. It's pretty brittle…would be easier with one of my other tools, but I can do it."

"I need access to one finger," Tristan replied.

"Alright." I grabbed my hammer and sat across from the captain. He held out his left hand and turned his face away from the scene.

I lined up the hammer with the metal cuff on his hand. After testing its weight, I slammed it into the metal.

The metal rang but did not shatter.

"Give it more force."

"I don't want to hurt you."

"Do it. That's an order," Tristan hissed.

"Aye, Captain." I gulped, then raised the hammer again. With all my strength, I slammed it into the metal.

Clank.

The metal split open, and with a crunch, the hammer landed on the side of Tristan's hand.

Tristan winced.

"Sorry." I removed the hammer.

"It's fine. Probably just a broken finger or two," he lifted his hand. If a bruise had formed, I couldn't see it, not with the layering burns that coated his skin. Dark brown scars and calluses covered his fingers. Old and new burns marred the front and back of his hand.

I tore my gaze away before he caught me staring.

Tristan turned to the *Cobalt Hare*. He flexed his fingers. Smoke gathered around his palm.

Then he held his hand to the sky and shot three small flames above us like a beacon.

It took a few minutes before the *Hare* acknowledged us.

We waited in silence, drifting closer to the ship. Tristan kept his free hand close to his chest. Using the crux of his elbow, he adjusted the sails and motioned me to take the helm. I obliged, ignoring my grumbling stomach and scratchy throat. As soon as we boarded, I planned to beeline for the mess hall. It didn't matter what slop they put on my plate, I would eat it.

The *Hare* shifted her position as we neared her. A few crewmates moved about on deck. I recognized Veta and Rémy at the helm. When they turned toward me, I waved.

Veta jumped on top of a crate and waved both her arms in my direction.

As we approached, I caught sight of Hari hurrying around the ship, giving orders like a real quartermaster. Sybyl, as usual, was nowhere to be seen.

She motioned to us to sail toward the bow of the ship. While the *Cobalt Hare* wasn't a large ship, it felt like a giant compared to our cutter. We were like the moon navigating the earth.

A set of ropes and a narrow ladder waited for us at the bow of the ship.

As I tied the cutter to the ropes, I asked Tristan, "Shall I break open the other cuff?"

"And risk damaging my other hand. No, thank you. I'll wait until we're on board."

"How do you intend to get back on board the ship?"

Tristan scowled and crossed his arms. "I suppose you'll have to carry me."

"Carry you?"

"What? Are you not the big, strong carpenter that I thought you were?"

I approached him, smirking. "Oh, I can carry you."

"Prove it then."

"Aye, Captain." I locked my eyes with Tristan. For a moment, it was just him and me, standing on this small boat, sharing a memory. It brought me back to the first time we met in the tavern.

And I swear, his lip curled up in a smile.

But we didn't linger on this fantasy. Before I had time to act irrationally, I hoisted him onto my back, and with Cheddar leading the way up, I ascended back onto the *Cobalt Hare*. It wasn't a long trek, with only twelve rungs to the ladder, but with a heightened awareness of my surroundings, it might as well have been one hundred. With every muscle, I felt Tristan. He didn't hold tight, keeping his arms draped over my shoulders, but his warm breath hit the back of my neck, a constant reminder of his presence, like a dragon readying his flame.

We entered the *Cobalt Hare* through the storage hull. Cheddar fluttered onto one of the beams, guiding me inside. There, I took a knee so Tristan could climb off my back.

"Thank you, Mr. Beaumont," he straightened his back, "for everything."

"It was no trouble."

"It was a little bit of trouble."

"Yes, but it was worth it to keep the *Hare* with her captain."

His eyes twinkled. I am sure he saw through my pathetic excuses. It's not like I wasn't forward with my feelings.

"Well, let's get this thing off my hand then, c'mon—" Tristan turned down the aisle, then froze.

A figure stood amid the barrels and crates. One that we both recognized before it even emerged from the shadows.

Sybyl raced forward, "Tristan! There you are!"

She pulled him into a tight hug, petting his hair, her fingers soft on his arm. Tristan stiffened and clenched his jaw.

"I was so worried about you!" Sybyl continued fawning over the captain. Her fingers trailed on his skin, less in comfort, but more as if to say: *You belong to me.*

She patted Tristan's hair as she continued talking. "I've told you not to run from me. Of course you would end up stranded. That is why you need to stay by my side. I can keep your magic at bay. You know this."

"Pah!" The word slipped from my mouth. Really, the entire scene was absurd. Tristan and I both knew Sybyl's involvement.

She glowered in my direction.

The words continued to slip from my mouth. "*You* abandoned Tristan in Grover's Marsh. He didn't run off!"

"What do you know?"

"You left us behind. No one else made that call."

Sybyl dropped Tristan and approached me. Her lips curled into a faux smile. "The Guard was threatening to claim our ship. I had no choice."

"There's always a choice. A ship doesn't just abandon its captain."

"What do you know? You're only a carpenter."

"I know about loyalty…" I whispered.

Sybyl's nostrils flared.

I met her stern gaze. "And I'm loyal to the Captain of the *Cobalt Hare*."

"Your loyalty will not earn you anything," Sybyl said as she turned back to Tristan.

Tristan stared at Sybyl. He didn't smile, nor did he frown. His attention remained locked in place with his free hand clenched at his side. Sybyl fussed over him, like a mother with a child, adjusting Tristan's hair so it remained combed back.

Sybyl returned to lecturing Tristan. "You shouldn't have run off, Tristan—I told you, we had to stay together. But no, you insisted. This is what happens when you don't listen to me—"

Tristan interjected, his voice low, "Were you planning to come back?"

Sybyl stopped. "What?"

"When you took the ship…did you plan to come back?"

"We hadn't gotten that far."

"What did you plan to do then, Sybyl? You didn't have the map. You left behind your captain. What was your plan?"

"We were working on it."

Tristan stepped back from Sybyl and crossed his arms. "You had over a day to come up with a plan. Surely you discussed it?"

"It was in the works—we had a plan to, well, return at some point." Sybyl's hands twitched.

Tristan did not falter, a glimmer of his command shining through his callous demeanor. I leaned against a nearby barrel to watch.

"At some point?" Tristan asked.

"Yes, once it was safe."

"Even if it meant I was dead?"

"It was to protect the ship."

"The ship? I expect loyalty to the crew, not the ship. We are not in the military anymore."

"Well, that too—"

"So, when two of your crewmates are missing, you should not flee without a plan to find them!" Tristan's voice cracked. "Especially when one of them is someone you claim to love."

Sybyl simpered, the shadows cast over her face, hiding any life in her eyes. A deep chuckle rumbled from her. "You sound like a child, Tristan. I thought better of you. You might as well still be that little boy that my mother locked up in prison."

I sat up from my spot. Sybyl's mother? This was news to me.

"It was stupid of your sister to put you in charge of this ship. You're just not ready to lead. That's why you need me by your side," Sybyl stroked Tristan's cheek. "It's why you'll always need me by your side." She lowered her hand to Tristan's shoulder. She brushed her thumb along the side of Tristan's neck, down his collarbone, where she rested her finger.

Tristan gulped. His fingers flexed.

It reminded me of the night with sirens. Sybyl had approached Tristan. She had *touched* him on the shoulder.

Then there was the flame.

My gut told me that I had to act.

I lunged forward and tugged Sybyl back by her hair. She stumbled, then spun around, smacking me in the face with the back of her hand. I bit my tongue at impact. The taste of blood filled my mouth. I spat once, then spun back around to face Sybyl.

She had already unsheathed her cutlass.

I removed my hammer.

Let it be known, I had never fought with my hammer before, but it was my first instinct. As Sybyl cut through the air with her cutlass, I positioned my hammer so each jab hit the head.

Metal and wood clanked. The vibrations rocked through my hands and arms. Cheddar, who had taken to nestling in the overhead beams, screeched as she flitted around Sybyl's head.

It was certainly not a battle for the ages. Rather, I felt like a child, playing with sticks and stones in the streets, pretending to be a great warrior. But with Cheddar as a distraction, at least it gave me a fighting chance.

But, Sybyl still had more skill than me. While I managed to hold my own against her attack for a couple minutes, she eventually struck me just right, and my hammer went flying behind me. It landed with a snap of wood.

"Well, that was fun…wasn't it?" I half-laughed as I backed away from her. "We should do it again sometime."

Sybyl responded by lunging at me with full force. I toppled backwards and hit a nearby barrel.

"You should know that attacking a captain is punishable by death," Sybyl hissed as she leaned over me. She pressed the tip of her sword into my shoulder.

"You're not the Captain," I hissed.

"I might as well be." She raised her sword.

And hit the barrel behind me.

I glanced behind me. A single crack formed in the upper half of the barrel. Silver liquid oozed from it.

"What're you doing?" I gasped.

Sybyl hit the barrel again. More liquid seeped out, dripping onto my head and shoulders.

"Stop!" I shouted.

"If we get rid of this treasure, then there's no reason for you to be on board, isn't that right? We can drop you off at the next port, and we can be on our way. In fact, you can take Tristan with you." She slammed her sword down again. More liquid hit my head and crawled down my body.

As she raised his sword again, an object flew from behind and hit her in the head. She cried out, fumbled back, and dropped her weapon to the ground.

I scurried over to the sword and snatched it. A few paces away, the head of my hammer lay on the ground, glowing orange.

Sybyl sneered, gripping the ground, blood dripping down her face. She spun around as Tristan approached her from behind. Fire blazed in his palm.

"Enough," Tristan said, his voice low.

"Tristan, you saw—he attacked me!" Sybyl pleaded, holding the side of her head where the hammer hit her.

"He had every right to attack you," Tristan hoisted Sybyl up by the collar of her shirt. Flames lapped around his fingers, stroking the edges of Sybyl's face. I joined his side with Cheddar on my shoulder, holding the cutlass tight, my body shaking from adrenaline.

"Tristan, please, you know how much I care for you. Please love. I was doing everything for our ship." Sybyl tried to reach for his arm.

I snatched her elbow before she could touch him.

Tristan flinched but relaxed as I restrained her. His voice remained level. "It's over, Sybyl. As captain of this vessel, you are under arrest on the count of treason."

"So you'll have me walk the plank then?" Sybyl hissed.

"No…when we arrive in port, you will be extradited from the *Cobalt Hare*. I don't care where you go…but you will not be permitted to board this ship. again."

"But Tristan, come now—you know this is preposterous!"

"No. We're done." Tristan glanced at me. "I can take her to the brig. Can you deal with that barrel?"

"Aye, Captain," I replied.

"Good. Get some food and drink. It's been a long two days."

"Aye!" Cheddar squawked from my head.

I swear, Tristan laughed.

But it may have been the ship creaking.

# CHAPTER FIFTEEN

# Repairs

Rather than fixing the barrel, I syphoned the strange, magical liquid into a new one using a clumsy funnel. Well, what remained of it anyway. A slew of it formed a puddle on the floor, and the rest had stuck to me like tree sap. The old barrel sat there, broken and judgmental. But I wasn't about to reconstruct something with splinters sticking out of its skin.

With most of our treasure secure, I sought the broken hammer. Its glow had fizzled, and the handle had disappeared into the darkness of the storage room, no better than any other piece of dismembered wood. The head rolled off somewhere out of view. Gone. Abandoned. *Sorry* Père.

I called for Cheddar to follow, then climbed to the mess hall, where an overly excited Veta waited for me.

"I was so worried!" She flung herself at me, hugging me tight. "Why did you just disappear? I could have helped you find Tristan! Or you should have at least told us!"

"My plan was just to find where he was and come back, but I guess…my creativity got the best of me," I pushed Veta back a few steps. Cheddar fluttered around her, chirping.

"Are you sure you didn't want to be the captain's *hero?*" she chided.

"No! I just—I overheard Sybyl saying that the captain ran off…and a merchant told me there was an issue with magic. So I investigated."

"A'ight, if you insist…but you nearly died by the looks of it!"

"Eh, I'll be fine."

"Yes, but as the ship's doctor, I need to examine you!" She tugged at my arm.

"Can I at least get something to eat first? Or drink?"

"Here's some water…I'll grab food for you soon. C'mon!" she shoved a canteen of water into my hands, then dragged me by the arm out of the mess hall.

My stomach groaned.

"I know…" I grumbled back at it.

If Veta heard me, she didn't respond as she led Cheddar and me down a narrow passage to her and Rémy's room.

Veta and Rémy shared a room on the floor above mine. It was larger, with their two bunks pushed together, and a third cot against the wall. Beside it, shelves with salves, bandages, and medications dominated.

I chugged some water as I sniffed the air. It smelt of lilacs.

Veta ran over to the trunk at the foot of her bed and sorted through the clothes. She removed a tunic and a pair of trousers. "Here, let's get you out of those gross clothes and clean off that silver goo. This used to be Rémy's, but it should fit you. Might be a little short at the ankles."

I caught the outfit with my free hand. "I honestly think I'm fine."

"You've been dehydrated, attacked, and covered in goo. It's my job as the ship's doctor to examine you. Now go change. I'll go get you food."

She bounded from the room, leaving the door open a crack as she disappeared down the hallway.

I sighed and glanced at Cheddar, sitting on the bunk.

"What? I'm fine!" I said to her.

She bobbed her head.

I shook my head and peeled off my damp clothes from my skin. They came off like snakeskin. Replacing them with new clothes was worse. While the shirt went on with ease, the trousers were slightly too tight, sticking to my shins as I tried to tug them up to my waist.

"This must be what it feels like to be a frog," I grumbled as I buttoned the trousers.

As I pulled on my new tunic, the door behind me opened with a creak.

I turned, still fussing with the tunic. Tristan stood in the doorway.

"Oh, uh, sorry. I was looking for Veta…was hoping she could mend my hand," he muttered, tearing his gaze away from me.

I adjusted the tunic. "She'll be back soon."

"I'll come back then."

"Wait!" I stepped toward him. "Are you okay?"

"Why wouldn't I be?"

"Well, after everything—"

"It's just another day at sea."

But it wasn't. When the currents shift, we adjust. We do not ride them away from our destination.

Yet I only responded with a nod. "If you ever want to talk…you know where to find me. Besides, I have to knock off that other cuff at some point."

Tristan held up his cuffed hand. "Don't break my hand this time."

"I'll use a hack saw, don't worry."

"And you won't cut off my finger with that?"

"No promises."

Tristan smirked, then, without saying another word, left me alone in Veta and Rémy's room. I stared after him, a hollowness filling my chest as his footsteps echoed. Part of me hoped he might stay, continue to banter, and perhaps even share a laugh. On the cutter, we had shared in a quiet comfort.

But the currents changed. It would just take time to chart a new course.

Veta brought me three bowls of gruel. That was all I could call it—it wasn't flavored, it wasn't distinct. It was merely a lump of oats and dried fruits, mashed together in a bowl.

But my stomach cheered as I took a bite.

Frankly, it tasted like the best thing in the world, my hunger finally satiated.

As Veta examined me, using a wooden tube to listen to my heart and lungs, she started on another tirade. "You know, I heard you used a hammer to fight Sybyl."

"How'd you hear that?"

"It's a small ship. Word gets around. And I know things."

"Didn't think Tristan would say anything…"

"Who said it was Tristan? I told you…I just know things."

"Sybyl then?"

"Maybe. She was making quite a racket when Tristan locked him up in the brig. I'm proud of our little captain. He finally stood up to that bitch."

"Little? You're like half her height."

"You know what I mean." Veta removed the wooden tube, then pulled a rag from the shelf. She dipped it in a basin of water and wiped away the calcified silver liquid on my arm. It peeled from my skin, leaving behind a gray stain, tracing along my veins.

Veta frowned as she wiped another bit away from my skin.

"What is it?" I asked.

"Not sure. Never seen anything like this before."

"And that means?"

"It means that it might be a good idea for you to apply an antiseptic to the wounds until they clear up. Here, I have some here…I think." She rummaged through her shelf again, finding a burgundy bottle. She popped the cork. It smelled of whiskey.

"You sure that's right?" I asked.

"Alcohol, antiseptic, same thing," She poured a small amount into her cloth, then rubbed it on my arm.

A burning sensation shot up my tendons.

I gritted my teeth.

"Yeah, that'll happen. But it will heal any potential infection." Veta handed me the vial. "Dab it here and there where you can. Should do the trick."

"Great…thanks." I pocketed it. "Am I free to go? I haven't slept in almost two days."

"Yes, get some shut-eye. I know Rémy wanted to talk to you, but she can wait 'til the morning."

I thanked Veta again, then held out my arm for Cheddar. The bird leapt from a nearby shelf and landed on my arm. She pressed her beak to my cheek.

"Good bird," I stroked her feathers back, then left the room.

Outside, Tristan still waited, holding his bruised hand close to his chest. He glanced at me.

"Captain," I nodded toward him.

"Mr. Beaumont," he replied.

"Veta is free now."

"Good," he approached the door, then glanced at me. "I have a job for you, Lyam."

"Oh?"

"Once you're rested, go speak with Hari and Zo. They'll teach you how to use a sword."

"What? Was my hammer not good enough?"

"It was…untrained. If you're going to be part of this crew, you must learn to fight. Work with them for one hour a day. That's an order."

"Aye, Captain." I saluted.

Tristan smirked. It was always that same smirk, with the twinkle in his eye, as though acknowledging his rank gave him more confidence.

And it was that same smirk that always made my heart stammer.

*Merde.*

"Good night, Captain," I said as we turned away from each other.

"Sleep well," he replied, then entered Veta's quarters for his own treatment.

It was as though nothing had changed aboard the *Cobalt Hare.*

The next morning, I met with Rémy and Veta in the mess hall as usual. Over breakfast, I caught them up on my ordeal in Grover's Marsh, filling in the details of Tristan's torture. He hadn't spoken of the "cleansing ritual" to Veta, which didn't surprise any of us.

"I'll force him into another examination. That sort of torture doesn't sit right with anyone," Veta said. "I knew he went through something heinous, but it was not clear to me."

"If he's not physically harmed, what are you going to do? You might be a talented physician, but you can't go healing his mind," Rémy said as she pored over the newest map she requested from me. With Sybyl locked away, I was tempted to hand her the full map, but my mother's guidance remained with me.

Besides, while I was close with Rémy and Veta, and trusted Hari and even Tristan, I could not be sure about the other members of the crew. Were there others who thought Sybyl would be the better captain? The *Cobalt Hare* had only belonged to Tristan for a few months. When the *Tortuga* liberated the *Hare*, had sympathizers remained?

"I can heal heads! Talking can fix all of that, can't it?" Veta exclaimed, her mouth full of oatmeal.

"Whatever you want to believe, love," Rémy laughed.

I had missed the two women's bantering. There was something about tiny over-excitable Veta and tall stoic Rémy that complemented each other. A conversation with them was its own form of entertainment, and I found myself smiling every time I left, whether it was about Veta's healing capabilities or Rémy's excitement over the new cutter boat that had replaced one of our lifeboats.

It was that small glimmer of joy that carried me to the storage room. There, the piles of timber I'd acquired, which felt like a lifetime ago, sat in the back of the room. I grabbed a few boards, nails, and a set of old tools, then headed back toward the ladder.

Yet, as I passed the rows of barrels, the gray smudges on my arm began to sting, as though someone had pinched my skin and tugged on it. It pulled in the direction of the barrel of magic silver liquid.

"Shut up," I hissed at it. While it didn't stop, I pushed on ahead, repositioning the lumber in my arm to head up the ladder.

Once I left storage, the stinging stopped. I glanced briefly at the silver smudge. It hadn't changed.

Perhaps it was all in my imagination.

I returned to the main deck. Cheddar had already spent her morning flittering about, and upon seeing me, she produced a loud screech and landed on my shoulder.

"Let's get to work, Cheddar-bird," I smiled at her.

"Bang!" She replied.

"Right…bang."

My first order of business: fixing the beam on the main sail. Cracks had formed along the beam. We'd been lucky no storm had derailed us. That beam would certainly crack first.

I ran my hand over the wood, tracing where a few of the cracks formed. Like ripped seams, if I had a thread, I'd be able to weave them together.

I placed one board against the beam, measuring out the wood, then removed a rusted hacksaw and an old hammer from the toolbox. Upon weighing the hammer in my hand, I frowned. It didn't feel like the one my father gave me. It lacked the…love, for lack of a better description.

I held the hammer for a moment longer, then turned to the board leaning against the beam. Wouldn't it be nice if I could use wood like a sewing needle and thread it all together? Although when my mother tried teaching me to sew, I somehow made a second hole in a tunic.

I repositioned the board in line with the cracks, tapped it once with the hammer, patted it, then marked where to cut with my chalk.

When I pulled the board away, though, I froze.

The cracks had merged back together.

Had I put it in the wrong spot? I circled the beam, but to my amazement, they were no longer there.

"Mon oeil!" I exclaimed and squinted at the beam. As I looked closer, I noticed thread-like, fresh wood woven along the old cracks.

I flipped over the board lying beside me. From its smooth surface, markings identical to the old cracks cut into its skin.

"This doesn't make any sense," I whispered as I stared at the board. The only reasonable explanation was that this was in my head. Or perhaps there were no cracks in the beam. and I'd been wrong.

But then Hari's words came back to me. *Not everyone's magic is as flashy as fire.*

But if I had magic, why would it wait this long to show itself? At least like this?

"Cheddar, what's going on with me?" I asked my bird.

She hopped onto the board and hit her beak against it. With her chest puffed out, she exclaimed, "Wood!"

"Yes, wood…" I ran a finger along the beam. "It's just wood."

# CHAPTER SIXTEEN

# Melting

Magic became a constant thought as the days blended together. I tried my best to brush it off, but as I worked on rebuilding parts of the ship, reminders popped up at every corner. That beam, with its surprise repair, haunted me, occupying any space that once contained longing for my captain.

It was a fluke. Nothing more.

With each day, those thoughts weighed on me, but I forced myself out of bed and to the mess hall without coffee, then after my morning meal, got straight to work. No other anomalies occurred while repairing other sections of the ship. A board hammered, a rope cut, a chain sawed— each repair took my attention.

I only saw the captain once over the course of my first week back, to remove the metal cuff from his hand. He didn't speak, looking out at sea as I hacked off the last bit of his hand's prison. With a thank you, he left, disappearing into his quarters.

Where he stayed, for the most part, every day.

I caught glimpses of him now and again. He would bring food to the brig for Sybyl but never share in the humor and good spirits of the crew. It was as though everything we went through in Grover's Marsh meant nothing.

But he was the captain. If he wanted to forget everything, it was his prerogative.

Even if I wanted to seek him out, my evenings were filled with my newly assigned combat training. Zo and Hari wrangled me every day, and for that one hour before sunset, they forced me to train.

They had equipped me with a wooden stick as a weapon. Zo showed me the proper stances and motions, while Hari translated between us using clumsy hand motions. Training with Zo was interesting to say the least. They demonstrated with command, readjusted my position, and instructed me to practice the most basic stances.

Or, well, what they told me was basic.

While I consider myself fit and strong, my body was not used to moving like a warrior. Most of my work was done in stationary positions, lifting materials and aligning different equipment. This dodging, jumping, and flailing was far beyond my instinctual capabilities.

"Let's cut it short tonight, Zo," Hari said as I tripped over my feet one night. We'd been practicing for almost a fortnight, and the only progress I made, really, was being able to keep a grip on the weapon for longer than three strikes.

Zo crossed their arms and frowned.

"I think Lyam is tired."

Zo sighed.

"You can't expect him to become a master overnight. Come now…let us get dinner."

I thanked Hari as she led Zo away, her hand on their arm. Zo brushed the long side of their hair back, stealing another frown in my direction and shaking their head.

I didn't need Hari to understand Zo's disappointment.

Honestly, I was disappointed too. I could wield a hammer to build, but when it came to fighting…I struggled to make the connection.

Cheddar landed on my shoulder and pecked at my ear.

"I'm alright, Cheddar-bird," I said to her.

"Bang! Bang!" she cheered.

"Yes, I'm good at building…but you can't win a fight by building a boat."

"Bang!"

I smiled, then with my practice stick in one hand, I climbed from the stern and onto the main deck. There, I took a seat on one of the crates to stare out at the purpling edge of the horizon. The air had grown chillier as we headed north. While a tepid summer air remained, I still shivered. On L'Perle, we rarely saw a cold day, the air often humid and heavy. Now, the further north we sailed, the thinner it had become. How much farther would it be? While I could check the remaining pages of the map, wasn't the unexpected all part of the adventure?

I continued to turn the stick over in my hand. Would it be easier to learn how to fight with something shaped like a weapon? Zo and Hari wanted me to use my knowledge from woodworking, but this stick was nothing like a hammer.

But then again, using a proper weapon would probably result in the loss of an eye.

Cheddar pecked at my head, "Feu!"

I took a glance away from my stick and across the deck. Tristan stood there, staring out at sea, his palms open. A single glowing orb of fire hung in the air.

Composed.

Calm.

He closed his hand, and the fire sizzled.

He turned from the water. The skin beneath his eyes was puffy.

Upon seeing me, he wiped his face with the back of his sleeve and straightened his stance. "Mr. Beaumont…I did not see you there."

"Is everything alright, Captain?" I asked.

"Ay."

I rose from my spot and approached him. He kept his gaze past me, staring at the water on the far side of the ship.

There were so many things I wanted to ask him, but I couldn't quite find the words, silence chewing the air between us.

But Tristan broke that silence. Calm. Composed. "You were practicing with Zo and Hari?"

"Aye, Captain."

"How is that progressing?"

"Erm…not well. I can build things, but I can't fight."

Tristan nodded, "You create instead of destroy."

"I suppose so."

"We need more people like that."

I restrained the urge to smile, picking at the wooden railing with my nail.

"I am glad you have stayed busy since our little adventure," Tristan continued.

"Have you stayed busy?" I asked him.

"Managing the prisoner, studying maps…all the usual…" he trailed off as he spoke, his gaze still locked on the other side of the ship.

"Oh…you've been with Sybyl then?"

"I do not trust her around any other crewmate. She has her way of being persuasive." He glanced at me.

"Oh. I see." Another pang filled my chest.

"Trust me, I want her gone as much as anyone. I could send her overboard, but…the idea of *that* doesn't sit right with me. Once we reach land, I shall find another ship to bring her back to Janis," his voice cracked. "That's where she wants to go anyway."

"I am…sorry."

"Don't be. I was naïve to trust her." He shook his head.

"You said that you'd known each other for a long time, right? I imagine it is difficult to shake that connection."

"Yes, but the moment the *Sanguine Tortuga* liberated us and gave me this ship, I should have gotten rid of her. Why should I trust the governor's own flesh and blood?"

"The governor?" I recalled Sybyl mentioning her mother. "You mean of Janis?"

"Yes. That is right."

"She's the governor's daughter? And you knew?"

"Of course I did."

I didn't expect Tristan to say much else as he kept his gaze set on the endless horizon. He licked his bottom lip and continued, "The governor assigned Sybyl to me when I joined the militia to keep an eye on me. She had a…vested interest in keeping me in line."

"Because of your magic?"

"Ay…" he stared at his hands. "My father was the last pyromancer they had. Once he was gone, they started looking abroad for another…but no foreigner wanted to fight for a poor island. The governor saw me as an asset."

"So she asked Sybyl to watch you?"

"Yes, and I always knew that was her duty. She was older than me, and as a boy, I looked up to her. Say what you will about Sybyl, but she is a talented sailor. I thought if I impressed her, I might earn my freedom. Even if it meant…" He trailed off, unable to finish the sentence.

I didn't need him to say anything, though. It was easy to picture a young Tristan, trying his best to impress the governor's daughter. As a boy, could he really say no?

Tristan closed his eyes. "I fooled myself into believing that Sybyl cared for me. For years, I crawled back to her…because there was comfort there. But really, it was always about pleasing her mother. I was just a…treasure to her."

"But she didn't win," I whispered. "You escaped."

"Only because of your buffoonery."

"Excuse me?" I half-laughed.

"If she didn't attack you, I probably would have crawled right back to her once again."

I looked away to hide my burning cheeks.

He leaned back on his heels and peered at the sky. "The one thing that does not make sense, and she has not answered my questions either, is why she left me behind. Her duty was always to monitor me for her mother…but then she took the ship and ran. It just doesn't make sense."

My attention locked on the floorboards as my memory returned to the cellar where Tristan had been held hostage. While I didn't know Sybyl as well as Tristan, I could guess what the plan was with this new information.

"My hunch, and it is just that, is that she saw an opportunity when we arrived in Rosada. I don't think she was lying about retrieving you…but only after the Rosadian Guard tortured you for weeks." I whispered and glanced at Tristan. "She wanted you defeated, so when she rescued you, you wouldn't fight. You'd accept her as the captain and let her take you back to Janis."

Tristan's head dropped. "That sounds plausible."

"She didn't count on me making bad decisions, though."

Tristan said nothing.

I fidgeted. "You can let her go now, Tristan."

"Not until we get to our destination. Unless you'd have me send her to the plank…like Veta keeps requesting."

"No—not like that. I mean…you can let her go from your thoughts and just…be. You know? She's locked away now."

"It's not so easy."

"One piece at a time."

"I wouldn't even know where to begin."

Why was I the one making these suggestions? Better yet, why was Tristan even listening to me? I had no right to speak on this sort of experience.

But memories brought me back to childhood. It was a small moment, one that was a mere passing glance. My mother had been denied a seat on the Trade Bureau Council in Volfium. I'd woken to her cursing them out and tearing the letter to pieces. From my spot in the stairwell, I watched as she discarded each piece of paper into the fireplace…while laughing.

"I have an idea. Can I go into the captain's cabin?" I asked.

"Go for it. I haven't been in there in weeks."

I didn't need to ask why.

With Cheddar still on my shoulder, I rushed across the deck to the captain's cabin. The door opened without any resistance. I turned the nozzle on one of the gas lamps, illuminating the musky, stale room. Clothes lay scattered across the floor, while piles of disoriented maps and notes occupied the desk. The large cot sat beneath the window.

"This is its own sort of treasure trove," I mumbled to Cheddar.

She leapt from my shoulder and landed on a wardrobe, relieving herself on Sybyl's robe.

I paced the room and stopped at the nightstand beside the bed. On it sat the silver badge with an hourglass. I almost picked it up, then stopped myself when a glimmer of gold caught my eye. Sybyl's gold necklace stuck out from the drawer. I had never gotten a good glimpse at it. Now, I saw that inscribed on the rectangular pendant were those familiar words: *You deserve only the loyalty you give.*

I yanked it from the drawer and raced from the captain's cabin. Cheddar raced after me and landed on my head as I reached the captain.

"Here!" I thrust the necklace into his hands.

He gawked. "And what should I do with this?"

"Destroy it! Throw it into the sea…whatever you want! That's the first piece to letting go."

He furrowed his brow.

"Use these things to take out your frustrations. I know it will not fix everything…but at least…it's your way of facing Sybyl. If you want, that is. It's an idea, that's all." I took a step back from him. "You deserve to be free of this burden."

Tristan traced the words of the pendant, mouthing them to himself. His blue eyes grew distant, like the sea on a calm day. He turned it over once, then handed it back to me.

I frowned.

Yet, to my surprise, he didn't walk away. Instead, he removed one of his gloves and placed it in his pocket. He

184

turned his hand over, where an orange glow emanated from his skin.

I placed the pendant into the heart of his palm.

Silently, he held his hand over the railing of the ship, letting his palm face the sky. Heat gathered there, a yellow flame rising from his skin, pulsing with each breath. As it hit the pendant, the object began to melt…

Dripping from his skin…

Into the ocean, like blood.

# CHAPTER SEVENTEEN

# Talking to the Elements

Almost every night, after my daily duties and my hour of training, I waited on deck for Tristan. Together, we ventured into the captain's cabin, selecting different artifacts from the room for Tristan to destroy. Some nights, he hardly spoke, selecting an object and destroying it before leaving me alone on deck. But others, he spoke to me, in short quips and anecdotes.

"Have you ever seen an octopus?" He asked one night as he burned one of Sybyl's shirts. His red hair blew in the wind, unkempt, while his coat lay on the floor by his feet.

"Only dead in the market," I replied as I leaned against a nearby crate. My training stick sat beside me, still mocking me for a poor performance with Zo and Hari.

"They creep me out. Those tentacles. Their eyes. They're also smart. It's not right," he dropped the ashes from the shirt into the sea.

"You're probably angering them with all these ashes then."

"Well, if we get eaten by a giant octopus, then it's your fault for coming up with this idea."

"I didn't tell you to burn it. I just said destroy it."

"I'm the captain, and I say it's your fault. Understood, Mr. Beaumont?"

"Aye, Captain," I laughed. These conversations helped me peel open Tristan's layers. However complicated. Behind everything, he was but a boy…scared of octopi.

But not every night had these anecdotes. It didn't take me long to figure out when Tristan didn't want to talk. On the nights when he arrived on deck, still in his navy-blue coat, his hair combed back, I learned those were the nights he wanted silence, his memories strong, and his emotions locked in tow.

But I didn't want to abandon him even on those nights. Something told me he needed someone at his side to walk him to freedom.

On those nights, I brought out my flute, playing a quiet tune with the wind. Cheddar hummed along on my shoulder. The song of the ocean is eager to please, difficult to quell.

One of those nights, Tristan approached me after burning a few old letters. He took the flute from me mid-note and examined it.

"I can stop if it is bothering you, Captain," I said.

"No…I'm just admiring your instrument. Did you make it yourself?"

"Aye."

"It's well done." He handed it back to me.

"It comes naturally to me."

"Unlike combat?"

"I suppose Hari and Zo told you about my lack of progress…" I grumbled.

"I think you just need a weapon you're familiar with; you weren't all that terrible with your hammer."

"Just a little terrible?"

"There is always room to grow." Tristan eyed my practice stick at my feet. "Perhaps you could change that stick of yours into something more familiar. You may find improvements with it."

"You mean turn it into a mallet?"

"Or something that you know how to control."

"Oh, maybe."

"Consider it. That's all." The captain smirked. That was all he said that evening.

When I retired to my cabin that night, I didn't sleep, weighing the stick in my hand, imagining it as a wooden mallet. I ran my finger along its grooves. What would need to be done? It'd be easy enough to carve a handle and mimic the shape of a hammer. Even though I hadn't carved anything in quite some time, it was easy enough to visualize the movements.

But, as those thoughts washed over me, beneath my thumb, the wood shifted, bending like the handle of a hammer.

"What the—"

It sat in my hand, formed anew.

I threw it across the room and shouted at it, "Stop it!"

Cheddar woke and squawked from her perch.

"Sorry, Cheddar." I lowered my voice, still glowering at the stick. On my arms, the silver marks from the magical liquid pricked my skin. They hadn't bothered me in weeks, and in all truth, I had stopped applying the salve that Veta had provided to me. But now, the pain returned with a malicious sting, and I fumbled around the room until I found the salve beneath a pair of my pants.

My arms continued to burn as I lay in bed, forcing myself into a half-sleep until morning arrived.

I woke with a groan and toppled from my cot. Using my elbows, I crawled over to a pile of clothes, only to stop by my stick.

My stomach churned.

The top of the stick had reshaped itself into a knob that mimicked a mallet.

It wasn't perfect, but the idea filled the object.

"I'm so confused…" I whispered to myself. Part of me wanted to believe I carved this in my sleep. But I knew, deep down, that something had awoke within me.

For now, it'd be my secret. No one needed to know until I had answers.

No one noticed the change in my training stick. It did help a tad with training, though. I managed to strike Zo a few times each session and provide a solid defense against their attacks. I didn't show it to Tristan, though, instead returning to my flute on the nights he chose not to speak.

So, life continued. Tristan burned his past. I played my song and ignored my own problems.

It took nearly a month for Tristan to remove all Sybyl's belongings from the captain's cabin. Under a new moon, with a deep chill in the air, we stood in the cabin, examining the small pile of objects remaining. I shivered as I stepped inside, tugging my cotton sweater around my body.

Tristan stood beside me, silent, his hair combed back and navy-blue jacket buttoned tight.

I lifted a black coat from the pile. "Want to burn this tonight?"

Tristan took it from me. He held it up, the golden buttons shimmering in the dim candlelight.

"Just the buttons."

"The buttons?"

"The coat used to be mine. Sybyl took it from me and changed the buttons."

"I see."

Tristan snapped the buttons from the garment. He held the coat out with one hand. "I used to love this coat—was the one I got arrested in. Was always too big for me."

"And Sybyl took it?"

"As I said…it was too big for me." He held it out to me. "It should fit you fine."

"You want me to have it?"

"It's only going to get colder."

I took the coat from him, running my hands over the woolen fabric. A smile crawled onto my lips. "Thank you, Captain."

He shrugged, falling back in line with his silence as he carried the buttons from the room.

I pulled the coat on and stole a glance in the nearby mirror. My brown hair had grown long, falling to my chin, while a thin mustache and beard hid my chin. Cheddar landed on my shoulder.

"Do I look like a pirate, Cheddar-bird?" I asked her.

She bobbed her head.

I spun around one last time. Once I had a weapon to wear on my hip, the ensemble would be complete.

After straightening out the wrinkles on my coat, I joined Tristan on deck. He held his hand over the water, melting the buttons, sending their molten metal into the sea. I took a seat on a nearby crate and removed my flute. The song that escaped me emanated with pep and joy, bouncing like the waves in the distance.

Some days, it was easy to forget the freedom brought by the sea.

Tristan smiled as the last metal oozed from his fingers. He then turned his hand over and released a small fireball. It floated into the air, an orange orb taking on a life of its own. As it ascended, he released another, this time with a twinge of yellow. Each one danced to the tune I played.

Tristan released a third orb of fire, this time with a white flame.

"Do you think fire has thoughts?" He asked as the third orb danced.

I lowered my flute. The fire stopped midair, waiting for me to continue my song.

Tristan held his hand out to one of the orbs. It tickled his fingers. "Like, these little fellows here…I just made them, but now, they've taken on a life of their own. But do they have thoughts?"

"I'd say they have as much thought as any other element," I replied. "Some days, I feel like the wood talks to me, and I'm just a carpenter. So surely fire speaks to you."

"Yes, but fire is destructive…it does not get to live with its thoughts like wood or the water…unless it finds itself in the stars," Tristan bounced the orb upwards, letting it rise above our heads.

"What's stopping these little orbs from being stars right now?" I asked him.

"They'll destroy anything they touch."

"I don't think so. I think, if given the chance to be more, they can become as great as the stars." My eyes locked onto him. "They deserve freedom, just like the water and the air."

Tristan grimaced and closed his hand, eyeing the orbs rising above the ship. They shot about in the air like miniature comets, offering wishes to the entire crew. They did have thoughts of their own…but in a different sense from how Tristan or I perceived the world. Like how wood spoke to me; it wasn't a cohesive thought, but it was there, remembering its past and understanding its future.

"They're having fun," I said to Tristan.

Tristan did not reply, opening his palm again. Five more orbs shot into the sky, each dancing with a different color of flame.

A deep-throated chortle escaped Tristan's lips.

He was laughing. Out of practice and half-broken, but it was still a laugh.

I shared his enthusiasm, once again bringing the flute to my lips to play a jubilant tune.

# CHAPTER EIGHTEEN

# What Fire Sees

The little fire orbs followed the *Cobalt Hare* further north, unfazed by the growing chill in the air. As the nights wore on, the rest of the crew took notice, telling stories about the little orbs and their voyages ahead. Even Tristan stayed on deck to watch them, standing in the corner to listen. I kept my flute close, adding music to the tales of fairies, ghosts, and lost souls. And of course, there was Veta's tale that they were gumdrops sent to the sky.

I stopped playing my flute. "What is a gumdrop?"

"You've never had a gumdrop?"

"It sounds made up!"

"It is this sugar treat they sold back home. They take gelatin, sugar, and spices and form them into these little round chewable delicacies!"

"Interesting…" I wasn't convinced.

"Oh, they're delicious! Next time we're in port, I'll see if I can find them."

"Eh, you can keep them. They sound too sweet for me." I remarked and raised my flute back to my lips.

"I forgot. You prefer things on fire."

I sputtered.

Veta smirked.

Rémy placed an arm around Veta. "Leave him be, hun."

"What? We all know he spends his evenings with the captain! It's not really a secret!"

"Nothing happens between us. It's…cordial," I said as I wiped my mouth.

"Okay, if you insist. But—"

Rémy covered her mouth. "Ignore her."

How I would have loved to ignore Veta, but my insides churned at the mere mention of Tristan. I stole a glance in his direction. He wore his coat, but his hair had not been combed, the wind catching it, sending strands in uncoordinated directions. The chilled air painted his cheeks pink, and his eyes sparkled like the sea.

He met my gaze.

"Go!" Veta nudged me.

"Veta!" Rémy snapped at her.

I waved them off, then climbed to my feet. Even though I'd spent nights with Tristan, this time felt different. My entire body ached with each step. Was everyone watching? I stole a glance toward Hari and Zo. They stood by the captain's cabin, where Zo and Hari spoke in silence. They shared an intimate smile.

Tristan turned back to the sea as I approached him.

"Are you alright?" I asked.

"Yes…I believe so. I never thought that my fire could bring…this," he waved his hand in front of him. A few of the orbs danced around his fingers, then shot up into the sky.

"You mean happiness?"

"I suppose so."

We stood there in silence. I placed a hand on the railing, a few inches away from Tristan's hand. This wasn't like the *Aquamarine*. There, everyone was out seeking a reprieve. Here, if something went wrong…where else would I end up but the brig?

"Tristan…" I whispered.

"Yes?" He didn't turn.

"I…um, well…I wanted to say that—"

"Hold on." He removed his hand from the railing and reached for one of the orbs. It landed in his palm and crackled. Tristan listened to it, tilting his head to the side the same way Cheddar did when listening to me.

"What is it?" I asked.

"It's talking."

"The fire?"

"Yes."

"What's it saying?"

Tristan turned to me, "Land."

"You mean we're almost to port?"

"A day or so away, if I'm understanding it right. We're almost there," he sent the orb back into the sky.

"Oh…" A feeling of dread washed over me. If we were almost to our destination, would my role be complete? Had I proved myself loyal enough to the crew? To Tristan?

Once this was all over, would they still accept me?

The crew had welcomed me, but there was still that truth: I was a trader's son, only there to conduct business.

But…it was ridiculous to think they'd cast me aside. After all, we had come this far.

"Were you going to say something, Lyam?" Tristan asked.

I shook my head. "Oh, it's nothing…just that I'm happy to see that you've found joy in your magic."

"Is that all?"

"Aye, Captain."

"Very well." He turned back to the sea and placed his hand on the railing. His finger grazed mine.

But only for a moment.

With daylight, the sea turned red. The Blood Sea, as the crewmates whispered, was a tale like that of the Burgundy Sea in the south. This was its counterpart, thrashing beneath the weight of the cold air. The waves wavered around us, pooling like blood or wine, only made darker by the graying clouds mounting in the distance.

Tristan's fiery orbs did not follow us, staying back in the clear sea, twinkling as stars in the distance.

Upon waking and feeding Cheddar, I climbed straight to deck. Rémy stood at the helm. She did not acknowledge me.

"Here," I removed the last map from my pocket and unfolded it.

She snatched it from me and examined the page. "I knew it,"

"What?"

"Once we got out of Rosadian territory, I had a suspicion we'd be heading to Merton."

"Merton?"

"You haven't heard of it before?"

I shook my head. If any traders came from this Merton, my mother never mentioned them.

"Our old captain used to talk about going there—it's a city where magic is at its strongest. She believed we would become the strongest ship at sea if we could harness it. We should probably let Captain Davies know." Rémy grabbed an edge of the map with her mouth and used both hands to turn the ship slightly.

"Is he in the Captain's Cabin?" I asked her.

"Ay," she mumbled.

"I'll let him know."

She maintained her gaze set on the sea. I waved to her, then climbed back onto the main deck, ambling to the Captain's Cabin.

I knocked on the door. "Captain?"

"Enter..." he mumbled.

I opened the door a crack and peeked into the room. Tristan sat on the floor in an old tunic and trousers. He held his hands open, staring at them.

"Is everything alright, Captain?" I asked.

"Didn't sleep well...so I came in here to...investigate." He picked up a piece of paper. "Sybyl was documenting everything."

I sat beside him, "What do you mean?"

"She was keeping a record of everything I did for his mother. Every reaction I had. Like some sort of caged animal."

I picked up the papers and sorted through a few of them. Pages were missing, but those that remained told enough of a story.

*698-Spring-12*

*Joined the Cobalt Hare and made peace with Davies. No reason for him to lack trust. Will work with Ms. Platt to maintain order.*

*699-Summer-74*

*Davies has been growing in strength. Ms. Platt has expressed excitement. Will work on neutralizing the flame without disappointing the order.*

*699-Winter-59*

*Flame has been neutralized in San Joya. Will take time for incision to heal.*

*700-Summer-34*

*Ms. Platt has met her demise at the hands of Captain June Lok. Davies has been assigned as captain. Will continue to neutralize potential affects.*

*701-Spring-51*

*Davies showed a hint of resistance. Appropriate communications have been sent.*

*701-Summer-62*

*Davies threatened to take charge today and cast light to ward off an invisible foe that the crew called a "siren". Attempt to mitigate with words failed. Stabilized with the incision. He continued his defiance, but his magic is subdued. Worried if external pressures continue, he may act beyond typical control.*

"This last one was recent…" I murmured.

He nodded.

"What does he mean by 'stabilized with the incision'?"

Tristan sighed. At first, I thought he wouldn't elaborate, but then he lowered the shoulders of his shirt. On his shoulders, two different scars, shaped like the letter 'X' marked him.

"When I joined the military, they needed to find ways to subdue my magic. I was…erratic and untrained. The governor had a local doctor, one who practiced magic, create these incisions. The right side stops my magic and the left side ignites it." He adjusted his shirt. "Sybyl took me to San Joya a couple years ago to deepen the incisions."

"So when Sybyl made your magic react—"

"She was pressing on my shoulder to set it loose."

"And you couldn't control it?"

"That's right," he heaved and turned to face me. "As I said…I was an experiment."

"But you're free now."

"Yeah, for now," Tristan crossed his arms, walling himself off again. "Why did you come here, Lyam?"

"Oh, right, um…" I licked my lips and turned away from him. "I just gave Rémy the last piece of the map. We have our destination."

"And that is?"

"Merton."

"Merton…" he repeated. "That's a name I haven't heard in many moons."

"Rémy said your old captain spoke of it plenty."

"She did. Our missions never sent us this far north, though. She wanted to acquire more crewmates with magic."

"That sounds like chaos waiting to happen."

"Oh, I am sure. Our sister ship, the *Sanguine Tortuga*, proved that to me."

"A lot of magic on board then?"

"Untrained magic, mostly," Tristan shook his head. "It makes them quite dangerous."

"I guess we better get this trade done for them, huh?"

Tristan nodded and walked across the room to the small window overlooking the bloody water. He laced his gloved hands behind his back.

"Captain?" I called.

"Hm?"

"Um …just…let me know how I can be of service these next few days, alright? I want this to go well."

"I will, Lyam."

That was enough for me.

# CHAPTER NINETEEN

# Talking to the Elements

The coastline of Merton was nothing like I'd ever seen. In the distance, hills of black and white checkered flowers filled the landscape. It was like stepping into a painting leeched of all colors. The entire crew stood on deck, gawking at the approaching land. With the blood sea beside it, the transition to the black and white fields was even more dramatic.

Cheddar did not speak, sitting on my shoulder, taking in the unusual sight like the rest of the crew.

The city appeared with a splash of colors. Multicolored boathouses lined the dock, with a collection of ships bobbing in the harbor. Like the homes, their sails bore a prismatic array of colors. The *Hare* was a stain beside them.

The silver marks on my arms itched as the city's skyline came into view, soaring over the colorful homes, with its towers climbing to the sky. Honestly, I'd never seen buildings so tall. The hill I grew up on was the highest point on L'Perle, and these—in comparison—surpassed even that.

When I thought I had picked out the tallest point, another tower caught my attention.

Tristan emerged from the captain's cabin as we arrived in port, his coat buttoned and hair combed back. His eyes darkened at the sound of the first anchor falling, and he turned to face our small crew.

No one spoke. This was it; we had made it.

Now, what would the captain have us do?

Finally, he spoke, his voice low but commanding. "I know it's been a long voyage, but from what our sister ship told me…we have something onboard worth more than a chest of gold. That barrel of silver liquid, as unusual as it is, will grant us the freedom that we never imagined. And I thank each one of you for staying by my side."

"Woo!" Cheddar chirped from my shoulder.

"Shush!" I hissed at her.

Tristan smirked, then continued. "I have a job for each of you once we're docked. Here, let me see," he removed a small note from his pocket and pointed at members of the crew, ordering pairs to conduct repairs and restocks, deal with merchants, and swab the decks. When he came to me, he paused, "Mr. Beaumont, I need you to seek out details about this trader your mother knows."

"Aye, Captain."

"Good." He resumed his orders, "Hari, Zo, you're with me. We need to find transport for our prisoner."

"Aye, Captain!" the crew recited.

At once, everyone dispersed, preparing for their assignments.

I headed down to my room to deposit Cheddar, wracking my brain. My mother had given me one name, and I had committed it to memory, deep in the confines of my mind. I hadn't spoken it…but did I remember?

It was odd, at least to me. What was it? Aric Peck? No…that wasn't it. Taric Beck? No…that was closer, but no.

I closed my eyes, rolling names over my tongue, however obscure, before it returned to me.

"Tarek Kek," I recited the name to myself. "Tarek Kek. I need to find Tarek Kek." Hopefully, it was an uncommon name in Merton…otherwise, we would have a whole slew of issues.

But my mother would have been wise enough to consider that.

"Kek! Kek!" Cheddar said as I opened the door to my quarters.

"Keep that to yourself, Cheddar-bird," I said as I put her on her perch.

She banged her beak against the wood.

"Good bird. I offered Cheddar a few seeds, grabbed my tool belt, and then left my quarters and headed to the gangway. Other members of the crew had already climbed ashore. My feet wobbled as I hit the pier, but then I smiled.

Land.

Last time came with its own challenges, but without the Rosadian Guard threatening us, we might enjoy the next few days ashore.

The port bustled, alive with trades and civilians even in the early hours of the morning. With countless traders waiting for us to disembark, it reminded me of L'Perle. They called out to us as we climbed off the ship, offering wares and goods, thrusting objects in our faces.

*Keep walking. They'll thin out.* My mother always mocked these types of merchants, calling them predatory scum that had no other skills. But every trader had to start somewhere; I knew my mother once did the same, even if she hated to admit it.

As I expected, once we exited the pier, the obnoxious merchants spread out, replaced with a line of organized stalls.

*Where should I begin?* I glanced amongst the array of merchants. There had to be someone, like my mother, who knew everyone and could point me in the right direction. I scanned each booth as I walked by; the merchants with their heads down wouldn't know. I had to find the one who not only ran a successful booth, but also the market itself.

Their products wouldn't tell me. It was all about the person.

Until I happened upon a stall toward the end of the market. There, a woman with bushy red hair sat, her arms crossed, with unique pieces of ore on her table. A presence of command exuded from her. Subtle, but it was there.

She was not a simple merchant, but someone gathering information. Even in silence.

She leaned back in her chair as I approached, her eyes narrowing.

"Vernnes, Rosadian, or Volfi?" I asked.

She responded in Rosadian, "What is a Volfi? I've never heard that language before."

"It's the language spoken in Volfium between Gon-vernnes and Rosada—oh, no matter." I waved it off and rubbed the back of my neck.

She rolled her eyes. "What do you want, pirate?"

"Is it that obvious?"

"No formal uniform, a stench that I can smell from here. Oh yes, it's obvious."

I flushed.

"Well?" She pressured.

"Right, um, sorry. You have a look about you—"

"I ain't interested in an affair, if that's what you're after. Don't know where you've been—if you want someone like that, try the brothel by the pier."

"No! Not that!" I raised my hands, the blood thickening in my cheeks.

"Then spit it out!"

"Do you know a trader by the name of Tarek Kek?"

She leaned forward, "Who's asking?"

"Me—well, the *Cobalt Hare* as a whole…but me."

"And who are you?"

I rubbed my hands together. "My name is Lyam Beaumont, son of Madame Claudine Beaumont of L'Perle."

"And that should mean something to me?" The woman asked.

"Well, maybe not…but, a few months ago, the *Cobalt Hare* approached my mother regarding a magical artifact. While she could not provide proper compensation for it, she did have the name of someone who could. Tarek Kek."

"And what sort of artifact is this?"

I leaned forward, pressing my hands on her table, "We have a single barrel of an odd, silver liquid."

The woman's eyes twinkled. "And where did you find this barrel?"

"I won't disclose that until I speak with Tarek Kek."

The woman crossed her arms. She eyed me, a piercing stare that sent prickles down my spine, then said, "This evening, follow the main road there to the central plaza. In the wall, between two slate-colored buildings, there is the

*Crossbar Inn*. Tarek will be there. I'd recommend bringing proof of this…artifact."

I lifted my hands from the table. The wood absorbed my handprints, leaving a weak outline.

If the woman noticed, she said nothing.

"I look forward to meeting them," I said.

The woman did not reply, leaning back in her chair, eyes watching me like a hawk as I backed away, into the market, and toward my ship.

I was the first one back on board the ship. Rather than retiring to my room, I mulled about in storage. After finding a small jar on the back shelf, I loitered about the barrel of silver liquid. As I approached it, the gray marks on my arms pricked. Wounds remember their culprits. This was no different.

While Tristan hadn't given me permission to harvest a sample of the magical liquid, I took it upon myself to fill the jar. I opened the barrel only a crack and stuck the jar halfway into the liquid. Without letting my fingers touch it, I filled the jar halfway, then removed it.

Outside of the barrel, I finally had a good look at the liquid. While I'd seen it in other lights, this was the first time

I could observe it, sitting there in a glass jar. As the light flickered from a nearby lantern, the silver liquid seemed to change colors, capturing different images on its surface like a mirror. But unlike a mirror, the liquid remembered. In other glances, I swore I saw the shadows of miniature figures moving. Of whom or what…I did not know.

I placed the jar in my satchel and continued my meandering amongst the boxes. Only when I heard someone climbing down the ladder did I stop.

"You're making this quite difficult," Hari hissed.

I peered around a box. Hari led Sybyl down the ladder, her hands tied together. I hadn't visited her in the brig. No one had—except for Tristan. In a short couple of weeks, she'd transformed into a monster. Her hair fell past her shoulders in matted clumps, while dirt smudged her face. A blue bruise painted her forehead. She stared forward, her dark eyes like those of a wild beast.

Zo followed in the rear behind Sybyl. Whenever she protested or issued a slew of curses, Zo took the hilt of their sword and nudged her.

I kept to the shadows as they led her to the gangway. Tristan waited on the pier. As they approached, he held up his hand and approached Sybyl.

They exchanged a few words, ones that I could not hear. Tristan's face went pale before Sybyl spat in his face.

Yet Tristan did not flinch.

With a single wave of his hand, he motioned for Hari and Zo to take Sybyl down the pier, toward a ship at the other end of the dock. She twisted against the ropes, glowering back at Tristan, only for Zo to once again knock her in the back.

Once Sybyl disappeared down the pier, I climbed down the gangway. I approached Tristan. "Captain, I—"

"Did you find the trader?" he asked without looking at me.

"Yes, they'll be at the *Crossbar Inn* tonight in the main square. I already got a sample of the treasure." I handed him the jar.

He snatched it from me. "Who said you could take this?"

"I was trying to help."

"Whatever. Thank you. I'll handle it from here."

"Captain—"

"I said I'll handle it, Mr. Beaumont!" He jammed the jar into his pocket. "Go back onboard and await further instructions."

"Tristan, I can help—"

"You've done enough!" he shouted. Tears filled his eyes.

I gaped at him.

Without another word, he marched off, disappearing into the droves of merchants and civilians mingling on the pier.

"But you don't even know where that is!" I yelled after him.

He showed no sign of hearing me.

I cursed under my breath. We didn't need a repeat of Grover's Marsh. While we didn't need to worry about the legalities of magic here, I felt obligated to ensure that our captain returned to us. Safe.

"Merde," I whispered, then bolted after Tristan.

With the late afternoon upon us, crowds had thickened on the pier. One step forward, and another person emerged. Where did everyone come from? Had they crawled up from the floorboards, creating an organic blockade against me?

It took a few minutes before I escaped the sea of people. A cobblestone road granted me silence, and there I took a breath to gather myself. No sign of Tristan. I cursed under my breath. Didn't he trust me? I thought over the last few weeks, we had built that repertoire.

But now—

No. It made little sense. This morning, there was a new light in his eyes. Excitement even.

What did Sybyl say to him on the dock?

The only way to find out was by finding Tristan.

So I would start at the one place I knew of in this unfamiliar city: the *Crossbar Inn*.

# CHAPTER TWENTY

# The Crossbar Inn

The instructions were simple: follow the road to the main square where the *Crossbar Inn* waited.

But getting there was anything but simple.

The streets of Merton did not follow an orderly pattern. Named after trees, it was hard to know which one was north and which one was south. The buildings all merged after a time, their towering structures blocking any guidance from the falling sun and rising moon.

Although even with the misleading street names, the central square did not hide. Lined with marble buildings, the square itself exuded regalness. Hints of magic flourished in the streets. Two children ran past, mystical sparks appearing and vanishing on their fingers, while a man strode up the walk with flowers blooming from his fingers. As I entered the plaza, I bumped into a woman who gasped out a cloud of multicolored smoke.

As I spent longer in the square, I noticed more of the little pieces of magic. Fountains flowed with iridescent water. Carvings and statues watched with humanized eyes. Even windows blinked.

Or perhaps I imagined everything.

I stayed close to the perimeter, checking the signs and crevasses of each building. Two slate-colored buildings. I recited to myself. That would have been a great distinguishing factor if all the buildings were different colors, not just black and white. The dim lights along the path failed to differentiate the shades.

Even with night upon the square, the crowds did not thin, nightlife emerging from the corners and allies. Windows, peaking out of basements, glowed with excitement. Any of them might have been the *Crossbar Inn*.

I sighed, slowing my pace as a few people walked past me. A giant fellow, with orange hair slicked back like Tristan's, passed me a smile.

"Excuse me!" I called out in Rosadian, taking advantage of the friendly face.

"Yes?" The fellow turned, his voice soft. His red eyes glowed in the lantern light.

"Do you know where the *Crossbar Inn* is?"

"Ah, yes. It's right there," he pointed between two narrow, slate buildings, bordering a quiet alleyway. "Be careful. There was some commotion going on around there."

"Thank you!" I called, then burst into a run, pushing past another slew of people toward the slate buildings.

*Tristan, you best be there.*

Sybyl had to have said something to Tristan. It was the only thing that made sense.

Between the two buildings, a door with two metal bars, shaped like an "X", hid. No sign. No text. Only the two metal bars.

I pushed the door open.

My heart dropped.

Smoke waited on the other side.

Followed by flame.

And my uncontrolled shout.

"Tristan!"

The fire dissipated at my shout, leaving behind a trail of smoke. A gathering of individuals stood by the bar, arms crossed, watching Tristan as he spasmed on the floor. The frizzy-haired trader from port stood over him, the jar of silver liquid in one hand, and a sword pressed to Tristan's left shoulder. Char marks covered the ground. Embers gathered around Tristan's hands, his breaths heavy.

"Now tell me again," the frizzy-haired trader hissed in broken Vernnes, "where did you find this?"

He grunted, "I told you…our sister ship."

"That's not an answer," she pressed the blade deeper into his shoulder.

Tristan cried out. Another flare escaped his hands, shooting across the floor and toward my feet.

"It's all I…it's all I know…please…" Tristan begged.

"You stole this from us!"

"No…gah!"

The blade dug deeper. As Tristan cried out, smoke bubbled from his mouth, sparks shooting from between his teeth.

"Ay!" I ran over to them. "Stop this!"

The trader turned to face me, lifting her blade ever so slightly from Tristan's back.

"I thought Tarek Kek would be here?" I asked.

Her lip twitched. "Who's to say they're not?"

I eyed her. "Because I am sure my mother would have given me the name of a respectable trader. This seems more like an ambush."

"They'll be here."

I crossed my arms. "Well, this behavior doesn't make me eager to trade with anyone here in Merton. Maybe we'll take our business elsewhere."

The woman smirked. While keeping her saber blade pressed to Tristan's shoulder, she reached into her pocket with her free hand. She removed something small and glistening. Before I even registered it, the item expanded, transforming into a long, sharp blade. She pressed its tip to my chest.

I froze.

"You're in my domain now. You boys don't understand the true prowess of magic like mine…so I recommend
you listen to me."

I exchanged a glance with Tristan. Sweat gathered on
his brow.

The woman did not remove the blades. "Now, both of
you come with me. I have a lovely place for you to wait for
Kek to show their face."

With the help of two large individuals, the trader
dragged Tristan and me to an empty room, but for a bunk
and a grotesque chamber pot in the corner. They stripped
us of our coats, emptied our pockets, stole Tristan's gloves,
and took my tool belt, leaving us with nothing but our un-
dershirts.

Once the door slammed behind our captors, I helped
Tristan to the lower bunk. He sat down and brought his face
to his hands.

"Tristan?" I sat beside him.

He shook his head.

"What happened? Why did you run off?" I pressured
him.

"Why do you care?"

"Because you're my friend."

He wiped his nose with the back of his hand, then stole a quick glance at me. Tears stained his cheeks. It made him look younger, boyish even; the poise and determination stolen from him by a mere altercation.

"Sybyl said something, didn't she?" I asked.

Tristan's shoulders fell.

"You can tell me."

He sighed. "It had nothing to do with you, if that's what you're wondering."

"Then what was it?"

"It was nothing."

"Really? It doesn't seem like nothing."

Tristan picked at a scar on his hand before whispering, "She said, 'Without someone to light your flame, you're nothing more than a candle that won't burn.'"

"That's rather…elegant."

"It's what Governor Pierce said to me to convince me to join the military…" Tristan closed his eyes. "I had nothing then. And now…I guess…I wanted to prove I could be a captain without anyone's help."

"So that's why you didn't want me to come?"

"Yes."

I went to take his hand but stopped myself short. Instead, I inched closer to him and continued to pry. "What happened when you got here?"

"Took a seat at the bar, got myself a drink. I didn't even notice that woman sitting at the bar beside me." He scanned the room, recalling the events. "It was like she already knew I had the treasure with me. She started interrogating me almost at once."

"She might have seen you in port after I spoke with her."

"So she was the one who told you about the trader here?"

"Yes."

"I'm guessing it was just a ploy."

I shook my head. "Not sure. She was civil when I told her about it…and she knew the name Tarek Kek."

"Could *she* be Tarek Kek?"

"I don't think so."

Tristan leaned his head back against the wall. "Well, I only hope you are right, Mr. Beaumont. If not, we have lost this trade for good."

He'd already returned to that stoicism—the same I had seen after his imprisonment in Rosada. A momentary lapse of emotions, followed by a staid countenance. But I couldn't forget the fear in his eyes as the woman pressed her sword into his shoulder. The uncontrollable fire. The sweat and tears.

But bodies remember trauma, even if our minds suppress it.

"Are you okay?" I asked him.

"I'm fine," he closed his eyes, hugging himself around the waist.

"But she was stabbing you."

"Am I bleeding? No? Then I'm fine."

"Well, I haven't checked——"

Tristan groaned and turned so I could examine his shoulder.

Blood stained the top of his shirt.

I lifted the edge of his shirt. He stiffened but did not argue. A small cut etched its way across the X-shaped scar on his left shoulder, leaving a crossbar through its center. It did not ooze but spotted his skin with red.

"It's bleeding a little. I don't want you to react if I clean it, though," I said.

"Just dab it gently with a cloth. I'll be alright."

I used the thin blanket on the bed to clean the wound, dabbing it with care to not put pressure on his scar. He remained stiff, his breathing slow, in and out. Despite how he reeked of sweat, I yearned to lean in and press my lips to his spine, drag them up his back, to his neck, and then——

I let the desires fall into the crevices of my heart. It was ridiculous to consider.

Especially right now.

I stepped away once I finished cleaning the wound and paced the length of the room to quell my building excitement. Why would a daydream like that come now, of all times? No—not now. We were prisoners!

Tristan raised his brow as I paced back in front of him. "Now I need to ask if you're alright?"

"Yes, I'm fine," I gulped and turned to him. "Sorry, just thinking is all."

"About?"

I flubbed my way through a statement. "Just…that we don't know when Tarek Kek will come. We could be here all night with only that chamber pot as company."

"Well, you better not stink it up then, huh?"

I scoffed, "Same goes for you."

"I'm the captain, so I have more of a right than you."

"Aye, Captain," I laughed and gripped onto the bunk's ladder.

He nearly laughed, a smile peeking through his callous emotions. "Well, if we're going to be here for a while, I suppose we should rest."

"Good idea. Top or bottom?"

"Wha—what?" he sputtered.

"Bunk. Top or bottom bunk?"

"Oh, right. Bottom then."

"Very good. 'Night Captain."

"Good night, Lyam."

# CHAPTER TWENTY-ONE

# Tarek Kek

I did not sleep. As far as I could tell, neither did Tristan. We lay there in silence, waiting, unsure of how much time had passed. Every now and again, I opened my mouth to speak, but bit my tongue, letting the darkness remind us of our prison sentence.

The door finally opened to a blinding light, ripping open the darkness. I shot up from my spot, nearly hitting my head on the ceiling. A lean figure, with short-cropped curly hair, and a long white gown, stood in the doorway. Their dark eyes darted around the room. Behind them, the red-headed trader smirked.

The figure waved their hand at the trader, "Edith, leave us. I can take it from here."

"Oh, but I would love to watch," she replied.

"Go."

Edith grumbled, but left, leaving us with the newcomer.

They entered the room with their hands laced behind their back. With beady black eyes, they shot a glance over both Tristan and me.

"I understand you have been looking for me?" They asked.

I swung my legs over the side of the bunk. "Are you Tarek Kek?"

"Yes. You can call me Tarek. Or Kek. Whatever you please," they smiled, their voice calm. "I apologize for Edith's behavior. She is impulsive and reacted irrationally to discovering you have a piece of our Divitiae."

"Divitiae?" Tristan asked from the bottom bunk.

"The silver liquid you so graciously brought us." Tarek Kek removed a vial from around their neck and held it up to the dim light. It sparkled just like the liquid back on board the ship.

I rubbed my prickling arms as I stared at it.

"I know Edith asked, although not so nicely, but I must inquire…where did you find it?"

Tristan shifted on the bunk beneath me, then answered with leveled authority. "Our sister ship found it. They asked us to find a buyer…which led us here."

"And how did you find *me*?"

I interjected, "My mother knew your name through her trade network."

"I see." Tarek Kek nodded, placing the vial back around their neck before continuing. "Do you know what my Divitiae is?"

"It's magic," Tristan remarked.

"Yes, but do you know what it does?"

"I have seen it react to my magic, but otherwise…no."

Tarek motioned for us to follow. "Come—let me show you."

I hopped off the top bunk and glanced at Tristan. He grimaced.

We had no other choice but to follow Tarek Kek out of our prison and down the stairs. They strode through the inn and into the kitchen, where Edith sat on the counter, picking at her nails with a dagger. She glowered in our direction but said nothing.

Tarek took a bowl from the cabinet. They half-filled it with water, then removed the vial from around their neck. Once again, they held it to the light.

"This liquid, In Domumus Divitiae, was created a millennium ago by a powerful alchemist. Their initial task: to create an elixir of life. But in their quest, they developed something far more powerful than immortality. An elixir that has served as a base for thousands of different concoctions. At its core, it's unpurified magic. But with the right element, its properties could be changed into anything." Tarek's eyes lit up as they spoke. "You're correct that Divitiae is magic—but I would say it is the most powerful magic in the world."

I exchanged a glance with Tristan. He raised his brow.

"I understand if you're skeptical. Here, let me offer a demonstration. Come, gather around." Tarek Kek took the vial and poured it into the bowl. The silver liquid slipped beneath the water, swirling as it filled the translucent space. Tarek took their finger and stuck it into the bowl. The silver liquid of Divitiae gathered around their finger, and with ease, they raised it above the water like a string.

Tarek smiled as they spoke, "The unaltered Divitiae reacts differently depending on the person. I am an alchemist just like its creator, so it obeys my every whim. It connects with me, transforms with me, and obeys me." They dropped the silver strand back into the water and called into the other room. "Edith, could you spare me a moment, please?"

"What is it!?" She shouted from her spot.

"I need you for a demonstration."

"Fine." Edith sauntered in, stealing a glower in Tristan's and my direction.

"Place your hand over Divitiae, please," Tarek instructed.

Edith obliged, holding her hand over the bowl. This time, the silver liquid attacked her hand like a magnet, forming marble-like balls on her fingertips. She gathered them, reshaping them into a knife.

Tarek answered our questions before they exited our mouths. "Edith can manipulate metals, and as such, Divitiae behaves like the very thing she transforms." Tarek nodded at Edith to release her hand. The knife fell into the water and re-liquefied. They then turned to Tristan, "Now you…captain-boy—"

"Davies. Captain Davies," Tristan muttered.

"Yes, well, I know you have magic yourself, yes? Give it a gander. Let's see what the Divitiae does for you."

Tristan tensed up, but with rigid steps, approached the bowl. Like Edith had, he placed his hand over the liquid.

The surface boiled, then shot upwards, producing a white flame.

He jumped back from it, nearly landing against my chest.

"Fire magic brings out Divitiae's strength," Tarek said with a smile, and then glanced at me. "And you—what is your specialty?"

I shook my head. "I don't have any magic."

"Are you positive?"

"I am a carpenter…nothing more."

"Well, if that is the case, this will allow us a control element to all of this. In a case of no magic, Divitiae should not react."

I approached the bowl. The silver liquid spun around the water. The grayish scars on my arms prickled. What if

Divitiae did respond? With all the anomalies occurring with my woodworking, would this finally give me an answer to the burning question? Did I have magic?

My fingers trembled as I placed my hand above the bowl.

It happened in a blink. Divitiae shot out of the bowl in sharp stakes. They flew in my direction, cutting into my arms, legs, and chest, and slamming me into the far wall.

I screamed out as the stakes dug into me. Spots filled my vision. I couldn't even process what had happened. My chest burned, my arms screamed, and my legs trembled. Each silver stake carved away at my skin. Did I bleed? I couldn't even look down at my body.

"Lyam!" Tristan raced over to me.

Edith blocked his path.

Tarek approached me, their head cocked to the side, beady black eyes piercing into my entire body. "Well, this is rather convenient."

"Help…" I sputtered.

"Fix him!" Tristan shouted. He sounded a league away from me.

"Only when you bring the rest of Divitiae. Until then, your carpenter will stay here," Tarek's face darkened as he spoke, eyes locked onto me.

"Tristan…" I mumbled. I wanted to tell him to leave, sail off without me, and find another way to offload Divitiae.

But my head drooped, my body caved in, and everything disappeared into a film of silver sleep.

# CHAPTER TWENTY-TWO

# Splinters of Magic

In my half-baked sleep, I was aware that someone carried me. Who? I couldn't say. One moment, I was on the ground. Next, I was in someone's arms, my head lolling to the side as they carried me down a flight of stairs.

When I finally climbed out of that strange sleep, I was back in the bunk from earlier. My skin ached as if a thousand splinters embedded themselves.

I raised my head slightly as my vision stabilized.

"Easy now," a figure offered me a glass of water. "Take it slow."

I inhaled the water, then turned to the person beside me. It was the same man I saw in the plaza—the tall one, with red hair and red eyes.

"What happened?" I croaked.

"Kek will be here soon to explain. After we removed the Divitiae stakes, they asked I bring you down here to rest."

"Everything hurts," I groaned.

"I am sure. Rest. Kek will be here soon."

I gripped the cot beneath me, wincing as I rested my head against the firm pillow.

"My name is Varden, by the way. I do not think we had a chance to properly meet," the man said.

"Lyam Beaumont…" I whispered.

"Beaumont…that name is familiar."

"My family has a strong trade network in the south."

"That must be it…I was down there several years ago."

"I see." I closed my eyes. Any other time, I might have inquired further, but I just wanted to rest.

But sleep was not welcome as the door opened. I kept my eyes shut, but I recognized Tarek Kek's voice the moment they spoke.

"Thank you, Varden. I'll take it from here."

"I understand." Varden's footsteps filled the room, heavy as he left.

Tarek approached me. Without opening my eyes, I knew they were there, hovering over me, observing my every breath.

They rolled up my sleeve. I shut my eyes tighter as they trailed a finger up my arm and pressed a sharp, needle-like instrument into my skin.

I cursed and shot upwards at the pain.

"What did you…" I trailed off. The splinter-like pain in my arms had subsided.

"The reaction is over. Your pain should be gone," Tarek sat down in the chair beside my cot.

"What…what happened?" I asked them. My heart pounded in my ears.

"Divitiae reacted to your magic."

"I don't have magic," I protested.

"But you do. It has been suppressed for many years…so when Divitiae detected it, your body fought back against the magic. A sort of…self-imposed disease, if you will." Tarek laced their hands together. "I have seen it a few times with unaware Magii."

*So the wood has been reacting to my magic. Hari was right.* I swallowed. As much as I had tried to ignore it since Grover's Marsh, it hadn't gone away. Now, in Merton, there was no denying its presence.

"So…what does this mean for me?" I asked Tarek.

"Your body will forever be locked in this battle; your magic may grow, but as it has been suppressed in the crucial years of childhood, it will never be strong enough to fight off the effects of Divitiae." Tarek motioned to the graying scars on my skin. "Essentially, you are rotting."

I held open my hands, observing the recent scars forming on my skin. They had etched into me, like permanent splinters of wood. On my wrist, a wider mark than the rest lay visible, like bark stripped away from a tree. "Is there anything you can do?"

"I have never been able to solve it…even after a millennium."

"A millennium?" I recited, staring hard at Tarek. They did not look that old, perhaps ten years older than me. But their dark eyes had seen wars across millions of rising suns. It was the sort of heaviness that only experience carried. "You created Divitiae, didn't you?"

Tarek smiled. "Ah, so you figured it out."

"You kind of gave it away."

"Ah, so I did."

"The elixir of life was a success then?"

"It would seem so then."

"So, you solved death, but you haven't figured out this?" My voice squeaked at the proclamation. "How many people have died from this?"

"You can live a fulfilling life with this rot, I promise. Perhaps now that I'll have my Divitiae back, I can solve it."

"What are you talking about? You didn't have it before?"

Tarek stood up and strolled across the room. "Years ago, there was a war. The events do not concern you, but it resulted in Divitiae being taken from me. I was left with one singular basin, one where I could continue my alchemy work. A neutral emissary was responsible for guarding

234

Divitiae's new location, and they did for a thousand years. But then, only a few years ago, I received a report of their death…and since then, the location of Divitiae has been lost."

"So they were immortal too? And they died?" The questions kept flowing. All of this seemed implausible, but here it was, being spoken to me like some common fact of life.

"My elixir halts the aging process, but it does not protect against drowning or stabbing. The emissary made a name for themselves, and many wanted to see them dead. You may even know what they called themselves in your region."

"And that is?"

"Venom Mouth."

*Venom Mouth.* Their legend had reached all the way to L'Perle. Everyone across the sea knew their name. "The pirate?"

"That's right. They certainly made a name for themselves down in Malva Strait."

I scoffed to myself. This was all ridiculous. I could accept magic, but immortality? Legends coming to life? It was preposterous! This was supposed to be a simple trade, not some ridiculous tale filled with twists and turns.

Tarek placed a hand on my shoulder. "I understand this is quite a lot of information, Mr. Beaumont. Rest—I will let you know when your captain returns."

"Wait, where's Tristan? What happened?"

"All in due time," Tarek released me. With a smile, they left the room, leaving me to wallow in my confusion.

I drifted. Even with the medication, I didn't have the strength to get out of bed. I rubbed the peeled skin on my arm. The larger silver mark itched, but I kept myself from scratching, using my constant barrage of thoughts to distract me. Immortals, magic, a powerful substance; it was preposterous! For Tristan's sake, I hoped he didn't return. He could find a different trader and forget about me. It wasn't worth bargaining with threats and obscurities.

But, if he didn't return, what would happen to me? Would Tarek let me rot beneath the weight of my magic? Would I splinter away into nothing more than sawdust?

But then the door opened after what felt like hours.

"Lyam!"

Veta rushed into the room, carrying a bag nearly as big as her.

I sat up, using my better arm for support. "Veta? What're you doing here?"

"Came with Tristan and Zo. Wanted to make sure you were okay. How are you feeling?" She removed a few of her instruments and began her examination, placing a metal tube to my chest, then proceeding to pick at the splintering wounds on my arms.

"I'm okay. It doesn't hurt anymore," I said.

"Your chest sounds odd…like there is water in it. Are you breathing a'ight?"

"Yes…I feel okay."

"Are you sure? You look like shite if you ask me."

"I've been worse, trust me."

"Fine. I'll give you a better examination on the ship."

"So I can leave?"

"Yes. That Tarek person said you can come out if you're able."

I forced myself to sit up, then swung my legs over the bed. My body wobbled as I stood.

Veta caught my arm.

"I'll be okay…" I muttered.

"We brought a cart with us if you can't make it back to the ship."

"Oh, that will be a sight to behold," I took a few shaking steps forward, clutching the wall for support.

Veta helped me to the stairs. Taking each step, one at a time, I managed to climb back into the heart of the inn, where Tristan and Zo stood beside the barrel of Divitiae.

Upon entering the room, the splinters on my arms seared.

I bit my lip to hide the pain.

"This is it then?" Tarek asked Tristan.

"It is what our sister ship gave us."

"They only took one barrel?"

"It's all they gave us."

"What about the rest?" Tarek's nostrils flared.

"They traded the rest to someone else."

"To who!?" Tarek stepped closer to Tristan. Their voice cracked.

"I don't know! They didn't tell me!"

Tarek's face went pale. They shared a glance with Edith and Varden sitting across the room.

"Well," Tarek regained their composure, "this certainly changes the nature of our trade."

"What do you mean?" Tristan asked.

"The fact your sister ship is selling Divitiae to an un-known party is concerning. In the wrong hands, it could alter the world."

"I cannot control what the *Tortuga* does with their treas-ure."

Tarek wrung their hands together, their composure breaking, nerves etched into their voice. "No, you cannot control what has *already* happened. But you can control what the future may hold."

"I don't understand."

"Think of it this way: I will give you a partial payment today, as a thank you for bringing me this much…but it will come with a caveat."

"And that is?"

"Stop your sister ship from continuing the trade."

"And if we don't?"

"Well…you won't have a choice." Tarek removed a vial from their pocket and turned toward me. Edith stepped in front of Zo before they could unsheathe their saber.

I stiffened.

"Wait…what're you doing?" Tristan called.

Tarek did not reply. They shook the vial and popped open the cork.

Veta tried to block Tarek, but they pushed her to the side. In a swift motion, they grabbed me by the arm, then pried open my mouth, holding my face back. I was too weak to fight as they poured the liquid down my throat.

At first, nothing happened.

Before the searing pain from earlier returned. One hundred times over. Ripping through my body.

I fell to the floor, holding my head, unable to even scream. The room spun around me. The peeling skin on my arm howled, like a tree being chopped through its trunk.

"Lyam!" Veta knelt beside me.

"What are you doing!?" Tristan shouted, his voice quivering.

"Finishing an experiment," Tarek replied.

"He's in pain!" Veta exclaimed.

"And it will stop once your captain agrees to my terms."

"Tristan…" I begged. *You don't need to do this.*

My captain stared at me, his hands shaking. Embers flickered on his bare fingers as he turned to Tarek. "What will you have me do?"

"As I said, stop your sister ship from continuing their trade…and then find where my Divitiae is hiding. If you succeed, you will be granted riches far beyond your imagination."

Tristan chewed on his lower lip, pondering the offer. "And how will you know we're obeying your instructions?"

Tarek motioned to me. I blinked away a few tears, the carving pain continuing to press me into the floorboards. "I'll know."

"And why do you think I'll keep Mr. Beaumont on board? Wouldn't it make more sense to taint me with whatever concoction you put together?"

"You do not have the same rot as Mr. Beaumont does. Besides, something tells me that you will not be letting your carpenter go." Tarek approached Tristan. "I think you understand the power of Divitiae now. Imagine what it will do in the wrong hands. Cultures will be altered. People will be killed. And it will be on your hands if you do not stop it."

"And what if it's too late?"

"We will determine the best course of action if so."

Tristan remained silent, pondering. Tarek made sense to a degree. If this Divitiae could torture me like this…then what would stop it from harming others?

But as another wave of stabbing rippled through me, the thought dissipated, leaving me further to wither.

When Tristan finally spoke, he sounded muffled and distant, as though suffocated by a cloud.

"I'll agree to your terms."

"Very good," Tarek waved a finger in my direction. The pain simmered to a faint whistle. My veins thumped with my racing heart.

I closed my eyes. Only now could I feel the tears staining my cheeks.

"Breathe slow," Veta said beside me. "We'll get you back on board soon, and you can rest."

I swallowed back a sob.

Tristan had saved me.

But at what cost?

# CHAPTER TWENTY-THREE

# Fire Hundred Doubloons

Veta and Zo carted me back through Merton. I had tried to walk, but my body gave out after two steps, so like a parcel of goods, I lay on the cart, flittering in and out of consciousness. Tristan stayed behind to finalize the trade—alone, per Tarek's request.

The buildings passed in blurred colors as I lay on the cart. Veta rambled to either Zo or me, but none of the words stayed with me. Despite Tarek ending the torture, a twang etched its way through my skin, a splintering reminder that Divitiae had not left me.

Hari and Rémy waited for us outside the *Cobalt Hare*. They raced toward me and, with the help of Zo and Veta, carried me onto the ship. I mumbled a hello to each of them, but otherwise, teetered into a half-conscious state as they carried me up the ladder and into my quarters.

I must have fallen asleep as soon as I hit the cot. A dreamless sleep washed over me, where I stayed.

Drifting…

Until Cheddar produced an obnoxious squawk. "Yam!"

I opened one eye. The bird sat on my forehead, staring down at me with wide gray eyes.

"Yam!" She berated me.

"Cheddar-bird…I'm resting."

"Yam!"

I grunted and waved her from my head. My joints ached. Splinters pulled from my skin.

"Yam! Yam! Yam!"

I squinted around my quarters. A set of clean clothes sat folded on my end table. Beside it, a glass of water waited, the liquid sloshing back and forth in the vessel. We were moving.

I hoisted myself up to glance around the room.

Then froze.

Tristan slept in a chair by the open door, his arms crossed over his chest, and his hair disheveled.

"Captain?" I whispered.

He shifted, then opened his eyes, "Oh, Mr. Beaumont. Good. You're awake."

"How long have I been out?"

"A couple of days."

"Merde…"

"We've set sail again."

"I see. Um, what…what are you doing here?" I asked.

"Wanted to make sure my carpenter got better, that's all."

"I see…"

He stood and approached me. Trembling, he pressed the back of his arm to my forehead. "How are you feeling?"

"I've been better."

"But you're alert? Not in pain?"

I shook my head. The silver markings on my arms twinged but otherwise remained quiet. Even the deeper mark on my wrist, the one that ran from the base of my hand and halfway up my forearm, did little more than ache.

"Good," Tristan took a step back. "I was…worried. You did not deserve to be tortured like that."

"All part of the fun," I forced a smile.

He did not smile back at me, his frown a permanent fixture on his face.

I rubbed my hands together, words once again escaping me. There was so much running through my head. But every thought added weight to the strings of exhaustion tugging on my eyes.

"Thank you, by the way," I finally said.

"For what?" Tristan asked.

"Saving me."

"Why wouldn't I?"

"Because now I'm a burden. You could have just left me to rot and found another trader."

"You're a vital part of my crew. I'm not in the business of sacrificing people loyal to me." Tristan crossed his arms. "And frankly, it is clear now that this Divitiae is bigger than us. I just wish you didn't have to pay the price."

"I'll be alright. It's just a splinter."

He eyed a few of the marks on my arms.

"It's more than a splinter," Tristan mumbled. "It gave me quite a scare, Lyam."

I stared hard at him. With his gorgeous blue eyes, his narrow countenance, and unkempt hair, it was hard to shake my feelings after all these months. Gently, I placed my hand on his arm.

"I'm here now," I whispered.

Our eyes remained locked. I eyed his lips. But I couldn't act. Instead, we sat there, gazes unable to be torn.

Any instinct to act ceased as the door opened. Veta stood in the doorway. "Oh, am I interrupting something?"

Our gaze broke. Whatever bonding Tristan and I shared had vanished, and he turned his attention to the far wall.

"Oh…oh, this is exciting!" Veta clapped her hands. "You two were going to kiss!"

"Ms. Nunez, I would appreciate it if you left now," Tristan croaked.

"Oh, but—"

"Now!"

"Fine…but I'll be back later. I need to check on my patient." Veta rushed down the hallway, giggling like a schoolgirl.

My face warmed. I sputtered, then leaned back in bed, trying to ignore the slew of frustration and embarrassment locking me in place.

Eventually, Tristan spoke again, his voice low, "I have your payment by the way. From Tarek. It's less than your mother expected…but it's something."

"Oh, thank—merde!" I cursed to myself.

Tristan raised his brow.

"I forgot to send my mother a letter! She's going to be livid!"

Tristan chuckled.

"Well, she is!"

"Aren't you old enough to set sail by yourself?"

"Yes, but she asked that I keep in touch."

"It'll be fine. Once she has her payment, she'll forget your minor indiscretion," Tristan rose. "One second."

He strode from the room. With a moment alone, I glanced at Cheddar sitting on her perch. She bobbed her head up and down, and I swear if birds could smile, she would be beaming.

*Damn bird is in cahoots with Veta.* I adjusted my pillows so I could sit up easier as Tristan reentered the room. He handed me a small pouch. I peeked inside at a handful of gold coins.

"This is my share, then?" I asked.

Tristan replied, "Tarek did not give us a lot. Five hundred gold doubloons total. You get one hundred as your cut."

"My mother won't be happy."

"I wasn't going to argue for more. You are worth more than five hundred doubloons. I think your mother would agree."

I could feel my face warming again, but I hid it by sorting through the coins.

Tristan backtracked, speaking fast, "I mean my entire crew is worth more than five hundred, but, well…" He didn't finish his sentence, his own face reddening.

I placed the pouch of coins on my end table. "You're a good captain, Tristan. Not every captain would feel the same way."

"Every member of my crew has helped me. I couldn't abandon them," he replied.

I rubbed the silver mark on my wrist. Tristan grabbed my hand to examine the scar.

"Do you feel anything there?" he asked.

"Some slight pain."

"You don't feel like someone is watching you?"

"What do you mean?"

"Tarek said that, through this scar, they'll be able to track our progress. I don't know what that means, but that's what they told me when we finalized everything."

I poked at the scar. The silver surface shimmered. "Well, I hope they can't see everything I do. They don't want to know where this hand has been."

Tristan's lip twitched. "They deserve to be scarred for life after what they did. I was close to roasting them alive, in all honesty."

"Why didn't you?"

"Because I have restraint, for better or for worse." Tristan stared at his hands. "In the back of my head, I kept saying to myself…Leena wouldn't have restraint. She would have destroyed Tarek right there. But…I'm not Leena."

"Leena?" I had never heard the name before.

Tristan blinked, pulled from his reverie. "Sorry…my sister. Leena."

"You haven't spoken about your sister before…"

"There isn't much to say…" Tristan picked at the wall.

"That usually means there is much to say."

Tristan shrugged. "She has fire magic like me."

"And she wasn't recruited into the military?"

"No…she only discovered it a few years ago, when she was already aboard the *Sanguine Tortuga*. It's…untamed. Powerful, but she has no restraint. I'm almost envious."

"Wait…wait…you told me that your sister and mother left Janis. You found her again?"

"You didn't know?"

"Know what?"

"Leena is the first mate on the *Sanguine Tortuga*. It's why I was given command of this ship. Because she didn't want it." Tristan sat on the desk. "Nepotism at its finest, I suppose. They put me, an unqualified pyromancer, in charge. One of many reasons for Sybyl's…distaste."

I hoisted myself up a little more. "I think you've earned your place aboard this ship."

"People are just scared of my flame."

"No. The crew respects you. Over the last few weeks, you've been spending more time with everyone, too. I honestly believe they would follow you into battle without question."

"Then why did they listen to Sybyl?"

"Because they were scared of her, not you."

Tristan frowned.

I placed a hand on his shoulder. "Listen to me. You are fantastic. Not just because of your magic, but because of the thought you put into every action. You trust your crew to make decisions, and you take time to listen. Back when we sailed through Siren's Bay, you could have easily ignored what we were saying and taken Sybyl's word over ours. But you didn't. Sure, you make mistakes—we all do. But, considering the weight you carry on your shoulders, I can look past them." My words exploded from my mouth, uncontrolled, emotions acting as a guide. "Merde, we're not much older than kids. You're what? Eighteen? Nineteen? That's nothing. I'm barely twenty and I don't have a clue what I'm doing. So the fact that you can keep this ship running is amazing. Don't let anyone tell you otherwise. You've proven yourself to be a confident leader. A kind leader. And someone who I am happy to call my friend.

"Sure, when we first met in the *Aquamarine* all those months ago, my mind was in one place. But as I've gotten to know you, I haven't been able to get your blue eyes or calm smile out of my head, Tristan. I am—" I stopped myself. My throat tightened. What did I just do? Was this a confession? I had kept my thoughts quiet all this time. Sure, I thought Tristan might know…but now it was in the open.

And he stared at me, wide-eyed, silent.

Instead of taking back my words, I set them free. "I was once enamored by you for only your physical appearance. That much I admit. But now, Tristan…you have kindled my heart, and it burns with such desire…adoration…love. If anything, for you as my captain and as my friend."

Tristan still didn't respond, his eyes locked onto me.

I curled in on myself and closed my eyes, "I don't expect you to return the sentiment…but I wanted you to know."

My body shook with the confession. It wasn't like my feelings were a secret, but the words had been building up for months. Now, they were free.

And I might have destroyed anything that was possible.

Tristan placed a kind hand on my arm. "Lyam."

I opened one eye.

"Thank you," he whispered, "for being patient with me."

I waited.

"I do share…similar feelings. But…after Sybyl…you must understand."

"I do."

"But…I am scared that I might lose you…if I give in to my reservations."

"You don't have to worry about that."

"But I do."

I lifted my head. "I will wait until you are ready."

His bottom lip quivered as he continued, "I don't want to wait, though. When we were at the *Crossbar Inn*, all I could think about was how I had to save you. It didn't matter to me how; I didn't want to lose you. I tried to convince myself that I would do it for anyone on the crew, but that's a lie. If it were Zo or Veta or anyone else, I don't think I would have conceded the same way. But…I can't imagine a life without you on this ship. You've helped me find myself after years…and…I want to be ready."

"What do you propose?" I asked him, my voice shaking.

"That we try."

"Is that an order?"

"Ay…" He reached for my cheek. Through his gloves, the warmth of his palm radiated. He dug his fingers into the hair behind my ear.

And he kissed me.

It wasn't a soft kiss either. He pulled me forward, his lips encapsulating mine, breath heavy and desperate. Warmth washed over me, and I pulled him closer, our bodies so close that our heartbeats matched like a drum. It wasn't like the kisses I shared with one-day flings; this one wore a cloak of desperation, locking us in place.

Until Tristan finally pulled away from me. Shaking.

"Captain?" I asked.

He opened his mouth to respond.

Only to cry.

# CHAPTER TWENTY-FOUR

# Freedom

I sat with Tristan all night as his emotions poured from him. The kiss had broken open a wall, and everything that Tristan had locked away came out like a flood. At first, it was in mere sobs, rocking through his body. I offered him privacy, but he shook his head, begging that I stay at his side.

So, we sat together on my cot. Tristan sobbed into my shirt. While I wanted to provide comforting thoughts, this time, I offered only a comforting arm around him. Promising that I would not leave his side.

"I'm sorry," Tristan mumbled as he wiped the snot from his nose.

"Don't be," I soothed.

"This has been building up for a while. It is not exactly how I wanted to confess to you," Tristan half-laughed.

"If I can't accept you now, then who's to say I deserve you at your best?"

Tristan snorted.

We sat there, embraced. Tristan's breathing slowed, his sobs dissipating.

Thoughts raced through my head. Was I still asleep? Was this real? I'd been lusting after Tristan for months, but now…here he was, opening up to me. I was holding our captain in my arms…and he was holding me.

*He* kissed *me*. I touched my own lips and smiled. It had been a powerful kiss, too. One that I didn't expect, as he had pulled me into his embrace.

"You know," Tristan whispered, "I honestly thought, for a long time, that Sybyl was who I deserved. I had other partners before, but then Sybyl sauntered in and made me feel like I didn't deserve them."

"*You deserve the loyalty you give…*" I whispered.

"How do you know that saying?"

"I…saw it on the plaque in your room."

"Right…the plaque." He didn't seem shocked that I had seen it. Quietly, he recited, "*You belong to us. You deserve only the loyalty you give. Your freedom was sacrificed for peace.*"

"But now you're free."

Tristan didn't reply.

"I'll prove it to you. Here, help me up…I want to show you something," I swung my legs out of bed. Tristan caught my arm and hoisted me up, helping me walk across the room. My legs ached, out of practice, but slowly I led him from my quarters and across the hall to Tristan's room.

"What're we doing here?" Tristan asked.

"Proving your freedom." I opened the door and stepped inside his quarters. There were more charred than I remembered, a permanent film of ash marking the room. I lit the lantern on the wall. Beside it, the plaque with the Janis Militia's mantra glistened.

Tristan eyed it.

"Hold on a second," I muttered and stumbled across to my room again. Without disturbing Cheddar, who had fallen asleep on her perch, I rummaged through my toolbox on the floor and pulled out that hideous hammer I'd been using around the ship. Even after repairing half the ship, I hated how it felt in my hand.

But it would do the job.

I returned to Tristan's quarters. He had taken a seat on his bed, staring hard at the plaque.

I tapped the plaque with my hammer. "Do I have your permission to remove this, Captain?"

Tristan stared at it, then in a single breath said, "No."

I pulled the hammer back from the plaque. "Oh, um, right. Never mind then. I got ahead of myself."

"No, it's not that. Hold on," Tristan hopped off his bunk and opened the chest on the floor. He rummaged inside and threw a few pieces of clothes onto the floor until he found a small parcel. He held it close to his chest as he approached me.

"Use this instead," he removed the old mallet from my hand and gave me the parcel.

I took it from him and unwrapped the paper.

"Tristan…" I gasped as I opened it. Inside was a hammer, forged with iron and hints of gold. Its head, undoubtedly, belonged to my old hammer, the one I had long down in the storage room, while its handle glistened with an artistry unlike any other.

"I've been trying to repair your hammer for weeks, but didn't have the means to do so until we arrived in Merton. The day before we left, after everything with Tarek, I found a blacksmith…and they helped me forge this for you," Tristan kicked the ground.

"You made this for me?"

"I provided the flame."

In that moment, I wanted to kiss Tristan again, but I restrained myself, holding the hammer tight. "This means…so much to me. Thank you."

"You can repay me by removing that plaque," Tristan said.

"Aye, Captain." I weighed my new tool in my hand, then took the claw of the hammer to the wall. Despite the twinging pangs in my arm, I was strong enough to yank the plaque from the wall.

It fell with a clatter to the floor.

Tristan melted the plaque over the sea. He helped me onto deck, where all sat quiet, and held the plaque out just as he had with Sybyl's belongings. The golden material oozed from his fingers, sliding down the side of the ship and into the water. We stood there as the last of it disappeared, then retired to our separate quarters for the night. I hesitated to kiss Tristan as I stood outside our rooms, but just as I opened the door, he took my hand and kissed it.

My skin tingled all the way into my bed.

But the next morning, all was normal aboard the *Cobalt Hare*. Tristan had already left his quarters for the day, and I climbed up the ladder to the mess hall.

Where Veta cornered me with a bowl of mushy oatmeal.

"Well!?" she asked, forcing me to sit on the bench beside her. "What happened!?"

"What happened where?" I feigned innocence.

"With the Captain!"

"Nothing happened! We were talking, that's all."

"As if I believe that. I saw the way you two were looking at each other."

"It was nothing, really," I muttered as I stuck a spoonful of oatmeal into my mouth.

"You can't hide this from me, Lyam Beaumont. I always know!"

"Veta, leave it be," Rémy said as she took a seat beside me. "How would you feel if Lyam asked you about our love life?"

"I'm an open book."

"Maybe too open…" Rémy grumbled, then turned back to me. "Happy to see you back on your feet."

"It was a tad difficult this morning. Felt kind of sore," I said, mouth full.

"I need to give you a full check again. I don't trust that Tarek Kek person and what they did to you," Veta said.

"I feel okay, I promise."

"Well, I don't believe you."

I groaned.

Rémy interrupted our banter. "Well, the ocean looks clear for a bit. Take it easy while it's smooth sailing…no reason to put too much pressure on yourself."

"I take that you have a new map?"

"Aye. Acquired a series of new maps, detailing the Blood Sea, all the way through the Malva Strait and toward Jrin Ayl. Should help us avoid any unexpected obstacles as we head south."

"Do we have a course of heading?"

"The Captain said 'south' for now."

"I see." I placed my spoon onto the table.

Rémy continued, "It shouldn't take as long. The maps I gathered show an oceanic current that follows along the continent into the Malva Strait. We were sailing against it on our way north. I'd gander we'll cut our time back by a third."

"So, you know, if you want to return home to your mother, it shouldn't take too long," Veta added with her mouth full of oatmeal.

I had put little thought into what I'd do after this initial trade. At first, I might have considered returning home…but now?

"The *Cobalt Hare* is my home," I remarked. "Although I need to get word to my mother at some point."

"I'm sure we'll pass near L'Perle in the coming weeks. It won't take long now. Once you know the seas, the world becomes all the smaller," Rémy said.

I didn't know if I agreed. With the endless ocean cast out before us, and its currents guiding us into the unknown, some days I felt like the one growing smaller. The world was vast and full of mysteries—ones that a day in port did little to solve.

Unable to finish eating, I returned my bowl of porridge to the kitchen, then climbed onto the deck. Cheddar greeted me with an excited squawk.

I removed my new hammer from my belt and weighed it. A smile inched over my lips. Over the last few weeks, repairing the ship had been difficult. But now…with this new tool…it would be like molding clay.

I chose my job just outside the captain's cabin. While I could have rested, as Rémy said, I just wanted to return to my work. I knew there was a loose board beside the door that needed repairing. With my tools set up and a smatter of new wood and nails, I began working on replacing the board.

It was strange, though, working with the wood. I couldn't ignore the prickling sensation every time I touched the board. It spoke to me. Saying what? I couldn't be sure. But I knew the wood spoke, trying to help me complete the best repair.

Had it always spoken to me like this? A subconscious message, instructing me in how to best create, build, or repair?

Did it speak to my father all the same?

It took me far longer to repair the board than I cared to admit. My mind kept arguing with the strange sensation.

And my body kept searching for Tristan with every footstep.

As I finally nailed in the new board, someone approached me.

"You are looking much better, Lyam," Hari said from behind me.

I turned to face her. Zo stood beside her, a smirk on their face, arms crossed.

"Oh, hi Hari. Yes, I'm doing alright now," I replied.

"Good. We were all worried about you." She smiled at me. I wondered if Tristan might make her his first mate. She was more than qualified. Really, she already took on those duties without question.

It would make sense for the sake of the *Cobalt Hare*, at least. Why wouldn't we want a leader like Hari? She was kind, orderly, and insightful.

More insightful than most.

Just like in Rosada.

"By the way, Hari…you were right," I remarked.

"I'm right about a lot of things. You'll have to be more specific," she replied.

I stared down at my hands. "My magic. You saw it before I wanted to admit it…and now…I know it's there."

Her lip curled upwards into a half smile. "You're not the first one who denied their own capabilities. It's hard…when so many places have placed sanctions on magic. There are a few places that put efforts into promoting magic's growth."

"Like Merton?"

"Merton, São Caméliosa, even Janis…just to name a few."

"Kind of a shame."

"Just the world we live in," Hari exchanged a glance with Zo. "We wanted to stop by to say that whenever you're ready to continue your combat training, let us know. It is still a good idea for you to build your defenses…might even help with your magic."

"Give me a couple days," I grumbled as I hooked my hammer to my belt. My body still felt weak. The idea of spending an hour throwing around a fake wooden hammer did not sound like a good afternoon.

"As I said, whenever you're ready," Hari repeated, still smiling. "We're just glad you're okay."

After I thanked them, Hari and Zo left me alone. I leaned against the wall of the captain's cabin. Listening.

Not just to the bustle of the crew, but to the ship.

The way it creaked.

The way it moaned.

The way it spoke.

And my heart sank. Would I ever know silence again now that I could hear?

Tristan emerged on deck in the evening, as he usually did. I greeted him with a smile. But he only nodded with a half-smirk.

We didn't touch each other as we approached the railing of the ship. Although we hadn't discussed it, we both shared the same sentiment; for now, even if the crew speculated, we would not show affection in a line of sight.

Instead, Tristan cast a small orb of fire into the sky. He poked it with his fingertip, sending it out toward the sea.

"How do you know what the fire is saying?" I asked him.

"Hm?"

"The fire. You said it told you things."

"Oh," Tristan pondered. "It's…not really a language. It's a feeling or understanding."

I ran my finger over the beam. Its smooth texture breathed serenity.

"Why?" Tristan asked.

"The wood is trying to talk to me…but…I don't know how to understand it."

"Haven't you already been understanding it?"

"No—"

"How else would you be such a talented carpenter? You know what it is saying." Tristan cast another flame on his palm. "When I think back, before I discovered my magic, I used to understand fire. I talked to it…knew when it needed more fuel…and learned stories from its flames. Magic starts with stories after all."

I stared at the railing. A memory came back to me of when my father helped me build my first simple crate. I pointed out to him that a beam looked like it had a pouting face. As a child, I didn't want to hurt the wood, so we put that beam aside.

A few days later, my father discovered rot forming on that very board.

Tristan interjected, "I think it's best not to overthink it. Your magic is part of you."

I traced the grain in the wooden beam. One straight, perfectly trimmed; another jagged. What did it tell me here? Someone had done a poor job with a repair?

Or perhaps that this beam had seen a battle, leaving it cracked? Or had the weather left it struggling?

*Don't overthink it.* I reminded myself, trying to let the wood speak.

But the questions only continued.

Tristan cast the flame in his hand into the sky, then closed his palm. He eyed me, then placed a warm hand on my arm.

I relaxed, placing my free hand on top of his hand.

Where we stayed, watching the little fire orbs flutter in the sky, like shooting stars above the water.

# CHAPTER TWENTY-FIVE

# Quelled

And so, our days and nights resumed in this routine. I completed my repairs, then in the evening, stood on deck with Tristan, sharing stories and warmth. We took small steps with our intimacy. Some nights, we only held hands as we stared out at the water. Others, if we were sure no one was on deck, we kissed.

Soft.

Gentle.

Nothing with the abrupt passion of the first night.

As night waned into the early morning, we walked together back to our separate quarters, saying goodnight with a light kiss and a smile.

At daybreak, our duties resumed, keeping to ourselves so as not to create a distraction.

But night always brought us back together.

One night, as we approached the ladder into the belly of the ship, I paused to steal a glance at the captain's cabin.

"Why don't you move up here? You work in your cabin most days." I asked him.

Tristan frowned, staring at the cabin door. "It's…difficult. There are a lot of memories in that cabin."

"With Sybyl?"

"And others."

"I see," I approached the door and ran my hand down it. The wood did speak. But with tension, sadness, and fear. Those emotions shot through me and left me hollow.

Tristan sighed and opened the door to the cabin. The room was now empty, except for a desk, a dresser, a couple of chairs, and a bed. He approached the desk, eyes glazed over.

"I would love to stay up here. It's bigger, closer to the ocean…but the memories remain. I could replace the furniture, reshuffle the room…but it would still be the room where…" he swallowed, "my sense of self was stolen."

I joined him at the desk. "You also reclaimed it."

He shrugged.

I took my hand to his cheek. "Remember. This is your ship. It doesn't belong to a rogue first mate—this room should be yours."

He leaned into my touch, pressing his lips to the corner of my hand as he closed his eyes.

We stayed there for a moment, a quiet intimacy holding us in place. In times like this, I wished I could freeze time, locking us in place, sharing something impossible to replicate.

Understanding.

Tranquility.

Love.

We left the captain's cabin, hands locked. Tristan glanced one more time into the room before closing the door. One step at a time; one memory unraveled each moment.

It was his battle to face, but I would remain at his side.

As we reached the hallway outside of our quarters, Tristan stopped me before I entered my room.

"Lyam," he whispered.

"Ay?"

"I, um…" he shook his head. "Sleep well. I will see you tomorrow."

"You too, Captain."

I leaned forward and kissed him. This one lingered for a few seconds before we both stepped back toward our doors.

Screams woke me.

I toppled from my bed and raced into the hall.

"Tristan?" I called.

No response but for another scream.

Without thinking, I jammed open the door with my shoulder. The wood gave out without argument, letting me rush into the room.

Smoke poured from the doorway, steaming like a boiling kettle. Embers coated the floor. On the cot, Tristan flailed in his sleep, casting smoke and embers from his body.

"Tristan…" I approached him slowly.

He tossed in another direction.

"Tristan?" I spoke a little louder.

Nothing.

I knelt beside the bed, wincing as a puff of burning smoke hit my face. As gently as possible, I touched his arm.

"Tristan…it's Lyam. Wake up."

He exhaled again, rolling onto his back. Sweat covered his brow.

"It's okay. I'm here," I took his hand and kissed it. "I'm here."

As the smoke died, I remained there, staying by his side as his night terror dissipated.

And he finally awoke.

"Lyam?" He croaked.

"You were having a nightmare," I whispered, brushing back his hair.

"O-oh. Not again," he groaned. "Did I hurt you?"

"Not this time," I said.

"This time." He frowned, and his eyes darkened.

"And I don't think you ever will."

"I already did, remember?"

Of course I remembered, but it was my own foolishness that led to that injury. I was unaware of his magic then, though.

"That wasn't your fault."

"But who's to say that it won't be my fault one day?"

"Captain, if you're trying to get me to leave, it won't work. I do not fear your fire." I motioned to the bed. "Now move over—I'm not leaving your side."

Tristan's lip quivered as if to protest, but he obliged, scooting over on the bed and letting me climb beside him. It was a tight squeeze, the cot barely big enough for just one of us, but we made it work.

We lay there in silence for a moment, our breathing uniform, hesitant in touch.

Tristan broke the silence, "I've had these nightmares ever since I boarded the *Cobalt Hare*. Had them occasionally when I was younger, but they've grown more consistent. Sometimes…I wonder if it was punishment for abandoning Janis."

"I thought the governor put you on this ship?" I asked.

"Not at first. Initially, I joined to find my sister. Or, well, I joined to find her killers."

"You thought she was dead?"

"I had learned that pirates took the *Sanguine Tortuga*…so my assumption was they slaughtered everyone. So I left with a vendetta."

"You don't seem like one for vendettas."

"I honestly did not have a plan. Just knew I had to find them. Sybyl joined a few months later, claiming she missed me…but I know she just wanted to watch over me for her mother. It was in those months that the nightmares began. I…haven't been able to shake them."

"If I can ask…what are the nightmares about?"

Tristan hugged himself and inhaled. "Remember the scars on my shoulder?"

"The ones that can control your magic?"

"Yes. Those were a…proud experiment of the governor. But she wanted to ensure that every captain in her military knew how to use them. As a part of their training, they would put me in different demonstrations, where they spent time…manipulating my flame. It drained me…and some nights…those memories come back to me." Tristan choked.

"Tristan…" I stroked the side of his face.

He continued, staring at his hands. "My magic was supposed to be mine. But they took it from me. Any joy I had with the fire, any artistry I conducted with it, was lost. I can still make some images with it, but it does not grant me any sort of joy. Not like my sister. She's free and powerful. I don't think I'll ever reach that sort of raw talent." He opened and closed his hands. "She doesn't fear her magic."

I waited a moment, then responded, "You know, when I was building houses with my dad, I used to get frustrated that I couldn't keep up with him."

"What're you talking about?" Tristan asked.

"Stay with me, I promise I have a point."

"Okay…"

"Right, so my father would finish a roof in half the time it took me. While I knew he had more experience, it still angered me that I couldn't do better. But one day he told me, he said he wished to be precise as me. He told me that every roof I made had this artistic quality to it. So, what I'm saying is, while I don't know your sister…perhaps your restraint complements her freedom."

"Perhaps…" Tristan mumbled.

We settled into silence. I placed my arms around Tristan. He did not push me away, settling into his thoughts. The embers on the floor had disintegrated. All that remained was a memory.

And a moment to dream.

"Try to sleep, Captain," I whispered. "I'll be here."

Tristan and I continued to spend our nights together. It was innocent in all matters, really. We kissed. We talked. Even Cheddar joined us in the evening, perching on the top of the bunk.

"Feu! Yam!" She chanted one morning after we slept past sunrise.

"Cheddar-bird…please…" I groaned as I rubbed my eyes.

"Feu! Yam!"

"Okay, okay, hold on," I sat up slowly.

Tristan grumbled beside me. "What does she want?"

"Food, probably. Can you reach into my coat pocket? Should have some seeds in there?"

Tristan grunted and reached for my coat. He removed a handful of seeds from the pocket and offered a hand up to Cheddar. The bird took them with a happy little dance.

I caught a glimpse of a smile on Tristan's lips.

"She's usually not so demanding. I rarely sleep past sunrise," I said as I swung my legs out of the cot.

"Sorry," Tristan muttered. The night before, we'd spent too long talking, and much longer kissing, before falling into a restful sleep.

"Don't," I grinned.

Cheddar flew around us in a circle, whistling.

"Well, she's a smart bird," Tristan remarked.

"She is." I raised my hand up to Cheddar. She hopped onto my fingers and bobbed her head.

"Did you train her?"

"In a way. She's been with me for a long time. In some ways…she's my best friend." I stroked back her feathers.

"Not many friends back home?"

"I mean…living on L'Perle, it was hard to build long-term connections. A lot of people were transient…and at a young age, I was always working for my parents. So, when Cheddar came into my life…it was nice to have someone always by my side."

"You've always been social and charming on board here, though."

"I never said I didn't make friends, just that they were short-term. Until now at least."

Tristan smirked.

In our morning daze, we slowly dressed. I paused at the mirror near the door, adjusting my tunic and trousers. After brushing back my shaggy hair, I ran my fingers through my thickening beard.

"Do you think I should shave?" I asked Tristan.

He shook his head. "Nah, it makes you look like a pirate."

"Is that a good thing?"

"I think so."

These morning flirtations had become more common with each passing day. But as soon as we passed the threshold of his room, we put on our masks, releasing our hands and returning to our positions on board.

Usually, when we reached the mess hall, we went our separate ways. But this time, Rémy waited outside, tapping her fingers on her crossed arms.

"Captain! There you are!" Rémy called as we emerged from the ladder.

"Rémy, good morning," Tristan approached her. "What's wrong?"

"I was looking over the maps this morning. We're on track to arrive in the Malva Strait in two days."

"That's wonderful news."

"Yes, but…only if we go through the Siren's Bay again tomorrow…" Rémy glanced between Tristan and me.

Tristan laced his gloved hands together. "Well, we survived last time."

"Yes…but we could just add a week or so to our voyage if we bypass it. Would it not be safer?"

"It would be"—Tristan glanced at me—"but Mr. Beaumont's idea worked so well last time. I don't think we have a reason to fear them. And this time we do not have someone trying to stop us."

"Are you sure?" I asked Tristan.

"Positive. I'm confident in our little crew. But I'll discuss with Hari before we make a final decision. For now, keep a steady course, understood?" He said to Rémy.

"Yes, Captain," she replied.

Rémy returned to the mess hall. Tristan and I shared one last look, the same one that we shared every day.

We would discuss more later when the ship was quiet. For now…we had work to do.

An uneasy silence fell over the ship as word spread of returning to Siren's Bay. Everyone remembered last time. But this time, we had a chance to prepare, without Sybyl barking orders or holding us hostage to her anger. Instead, we were Tristan's crew, working as a unit to prepare.

I secured the weaker sections of the ship's hull, applying new layers of wood to the sections that begged for support. It was a subtle feeling, like how I imagined a parent might feel when their child cried. Once I bandaged the wounds with a fresh layer of wood, the crying stopped, and I moved on to the next imperfection.

Yet so much of how I reacted was based on guesswork. Maybe this wasn't what the ship wanted, and I was only making assumptions.

I never doubted my knowledge of carpentry before, though. Why should I start now?

Once evening came, I met Zo on deck to practice my defense training. Hari remained preoccupied with preparing the ship for Siren's Bay, so Zo and I practiced in silence. My skills had improved enough to block an attack, but if I were caught amid a sword-fight, I doubted I'd last more than a minute.

But, like every night, I put my best effort into practicing.

If anything, for Tristan.

I hopped back as Zo threw a parry in my direction. They hit my fake weapon, sending it flying into the air. I stumbled, trying to catch it, but it landed a good distance away from me. Zo approached, a smirk on their face as they raised their sword to pin me.

My mind raced. If this were an actual fight, what would I do? I scanned the ground, looking for something. My eyes locked on a floorboard with a missing nail.

*That floorboard is weak. What if it snapped?* I tapped my foot.

Zo stepped onto that board.

And to my surprise, it snapped. Zo tripped, losing their stance long enough for me to dart over to my disarmed weapon. As I snatched it from the ground, Zo dislodged their foot, then lunged in my direction.

They pinned me to the ground with their weapon before I had a chance to react.

"Merde," I muttered.

Zo helped me up and patted me on the back to tell me, "Good job."

Elation bubbled in my core. It was the first time I'd use my magic in one of these practice sessions. While it might have been luck, and it had been a minor fluke, it worked.

Once Zo dismissed me, I raced to where Tristan stood, staring out at the water. With the crew still on deck, I did not sweep him into my arms, but stood beside him, the edge of my hand brushing up against his hand.

"So we're continuing to Siren's Bay?" I asked him.

"Yes. We know their weakness. It doesn't make sense to delay."

"We're not in a rush, are we?"

Tristan ran his fingers over my silver-coated wrist. "That's the thing. I do not know what Tarek is expecting…or when they are expecting it, for that matter. I'm worried that if we delay too long, that… Well, you understand."

"What instructions *did* they give you?"

"Terminate the trade and locate the source of the Divitiae. No time horizon. No guidance. If I fail…they'll know." He pulled his hand from my wrist and turned back to the sea. "So it only makes sense to go through Siren's Bay."

"What does the crew think?"

"They know that Tarek gave me instructions—they're loyal and haven't questioned me. At least not to my face."

"I see…" I followed his gaze out to sea. "Are you comfortable with the preparations then?"

"I can control my flame enough for this," he removed a glove and held his hand out over the water. There, another orb of fire formed. Hundreds followed us in the sky. If someone saw them from afar, they might have called them fairies or spirits or something else fantastic. But they were just our little followers.

Seeing more than we could ever imagine.

Telling stories.

Speaking with crackles and pops.

Tristan sent the new flame into the sky, poking it once to set it in motion.

"I wonder if they could help," I said as the flame became a speck on the horizon.

"Huh?"

"The flames. Couldn't you ask them to shoot ahead to Siren's Bay and see that everything looks alright? They could even stay with us to add more light."

Tristan's eyes lit up at the prospect. "I didn't even think of that!"

"It's just a thought." I etched my nail into the wooden railing. The wood responded with stiffness, its intention to remain strong against my invasion.

Tristan formed another orb in his hand. This time, he spoke to it, "Go find the others. Seek out the sirens. Let me know by tomorrow their status."

The fire twinkled with understanding, then spiraled upwards and into the sky.

Tristan spun back to me with a grin. "You are amazing!"

My face warmed. "I have good thoughts sometimes."

"More than sometimes. I honestly don't know what I would do without you, Lyam Beaumont. You have saved this ship in more ways than I can count."

"It's nothing—"

Tristan pulled me forward and kissed me, right there on deck, surrounded by the crew.

We didn't care.

Sharing that moment, undisturbed.

Not by the thrashing waves.

Not by the whistling wind.

And not by Veta cheering from across the ship.

# CHAPTER TWENTY-SIX

# Return to Siren's Bay

Our celebration did not last long, as time was of the essence. Tristan and I turned in early, although nerves kept us both awake. We lay in that narrow cot, laced together, not speaking as we tried to find a path to sleep. Sure, we survived Siren's Bay before, but if one thing was certain, the sea was unpredictable.

The morning greeted us with calm currents. A few clouds dotted the distance, but otherwise all seemed right as we made our preparations. Hari led the cause, ordering the crew to erect torches along the sides. We obeyed without question. While there still had not been a formal declaration, we all knew that Hari was the first mate.

Tristan waited on the bow of the ship, conversing with his fiery orbs as they returned with news. Every now and again, he would pass a few words over to Hari or Rémy, to change course or assemble another few torches.

While we had entered Siren's Bay sometime midafternoon, we pocketed our fear until sundown.

Where Tristan lit the first torch.

The silence that followed permeated the ship. A distant shriek carried across the water.

Tristan lit the next torch.

I gripped the railing. The wood clung to my hands.

One by one, the torches caught light, igniting every side of the ship. The orange glow cast over us. While Tristan remained a commanding flame, moving from torch to torch, the fire bowed to his whim. Controlled. Calm.

Loved.

The howling remained in the distance. It poked at my head, trying its best to pull me into its clutches. Why did sailors fall for it? The noise itself wasn't beautiful. Nor was it enchanting.

Nevertheless, I could not stop listening.

That was it, though. Other than the desire to listen, the fire kept the sirens at bay.

Tristan's fiery orbs hovered about in the distance, navigating the siren's realm without fear. They were a constellation, each one holding a specific position.

All calm.

Until one turned.

I didn't notice at first. What I did see was Tristan's back straightening. He held out his hand, catching an orb in his palm.

It flickered rapidly, shouting almost.

I approached Tristan's side.

His eyes widened, then with a shaky finger, he pointed to the horizon. A thin strip of clouds moved in our direction.

*Rain.*

We didn't need to say it aloud. When we first entered Siren's Bay, it was too far from us.

But now it moved, like an army marching across the sea.

"Captain!" Rémy shouted from across the deck. She had seen it, too.

Tristan's fear dissipated. With his back strong and his head high, he took command of the *Cobalt Hare.*

"Ready the course, Rémy. We keep sailing. We're too deep into Siren's Bay to turn back now," he shouted. Then he waved over Hari.

She joined us on the bow.

"Get everyone below decks. Lock the doors. Close the windows. Stuff their ears with cotton. We won't lose anyone tonight. I'll take control of the helm."

"Yes, Captain," she darted off on his orders.

"You too, Lyam. Help Hari secure everyone. Afterwards, I ask you stay below deck, too."

I stared at him.

He continued, "I might be able to keep the fire going amidst rain…but there are no promises. If I fail, I won't have your blood on my hands."

"Tristan—"

"Please."

"Ay, Captain," I took his hand and squeezed it, then let him return to the sea.

While I didn't want to leave him, I honored his need to focus. So, I assisted Hari in rounding up the crew, including a reluctant Rémy, who insisted she continued to drive the ship, then headed below deck.

While Hari ensured everyone went to their quarters, I gathered wood and steel nails from storage. I didn't have a lot of time. At each door, I nailed two boards in the shape of an 'x' once each crewmate was secured. If anything, it would derail them from jumping overboard and into the siren's clutches.

I secured Hari last in her room.

"He's stronger with you at his side, Lyam," she said to me in the doorway.

"I know…but I should trust him."

"Yes, you should…but I think without you, he wouldn't have come this far."

I grimaced.

"Take that as you will."

With that, she closed the door, leaving me to board her door.

As I hammered in the last nail, I headed back to my quarters. Cheddar waited there, chirping furiously as I shut the door. I adjusted a plank against the door.

"Feu!" Cheddar shrieked.

"He's protecting the ship, Cheddar-bird."

"Feu! Feu!" She flew around the room, stopping at the porthole window. She banged her beak against its glass.

I dropped the board and joined her. The subtle glow of the ship pulsed outside, reflecting against the rough waters. A gentle rain had begun to fall.

In the distance, the fiery orbs rose high, clamoring above the clouds to avoid the rainy slaughter.

Cheddar and I stayed at the window. Enchanted. The howling in the distance grew louder, permeating through the walls of the ship.

But the light remained.

Yet, with each passing moment, the rain increased.

One drop.

Two.

One drop.

Three.

One drop.

Four.

It did not cease.

And the light dimmed.

First with a flicker.

Then with a gasp.

"Feu!" Cheddar shouted again.

"I have to help him." I glanced at Cheddar. She bobbed her head. "Stay here."

"Feu! Feu!" Cheddar chanted, remaining on her perch as I rushed from the room and back onto deck.

The rain hit me like a sheet of metal. I stumbled backwards, nearly falling down the ladder. Through it all, the howling had grown louder, a detrimental song that could not be shaken. I squinted. The song demanded I come toward it. To its warmth. To its embrace.

*Tristan. Where are you?*

It took everything I had to push through the water and towards the bow of the ship. The helm stood empty.

While Tristan stood by the back railing, staring out, a single pulsing flame in his hands. Water drenched his body, while he swayed back and forth to the shrieking song.

"TRISTAN!" I shouted.

He didn't hear me.

I ran toward him.

In his hands, the flame had fizzled to an ember. He leaned over the railing, staring toward the water. He reached his hand out, sending his body curving over the side of the ship.

"NO!" I held out my hand, but I was still too far away from him. "STOP!"

I still don't know how I did it, but it was almost as though the wooden railing grabbed Tristan. It splintered upwards in thin strands, and like string, they wove together around his ankle to catch him before falling.

His body hit the side of the ship. I raced over and yanked him back on board, holding him close as he sputtered.

"Ow…" he mumbled.

"You're safe now, Captain," I lowered him on deck. With the wood still obeying me, I had it lock his hands and feet in place. He didn't fight it.

Once I was sure I had secured him, I climbed to my feet. I glowered into the water.

There, a siren stared back at me.

It was as though a thousand distinct faces stared at me. Its translucent body thrashed with the waves.

When it opened its mouth, a hideous song filled the area. The noise choked on the air, gargling and hacking. As it moved in the air like a leech, it spoke to me with deceptive whispers. It promised me adventure, romance, freedom, a home, and good health. Was this the song it sang to everyone? Attempting to latch onto one thing we so desired?

But I shook it away; the siren offered nothing to me.

So, I turned my back on it and took control of the helm, keeping the boat steady as we sailed through Siren's Bay.

The rain stopped in the early morning. I maintained the helm, keeping the boat afloat as the rain continued its hammering throughout the evening. Once the rain ceased, but before the sun rose, the little orbs of fire descended from the sky, serving as a final layer of protection against the creatures lurking in the deep.

With light again as my guide, I left the helm and joined Tristan. He sat there, awake and wide-eyed, his red hair matted to his head, clothes drenched as though thrown into the water.

"How long have you been awake?" I asked as I knelt beside him. With a single tap, the wood rescinded its restraints.

"I'm not sure. It was hazy for a while..." he mumbled. "You...the sirens...they didn't affect you?"

I shook my head. "They didn't have anything I wanted."

Tristan stared hard at me.

I pulled him to his feet and brushed back his wet hair. Around us, the fiery orbs hovered above, casting their glow of protection over the ship. Tristan caught one in his hand and listened.

He smiled, then sent it on its way.

"We're almost out of Siren's Bay. Another hour and we'll be free."

"Good." I brushed back another strand of his hair. "We're safe then."

"Because of you."

"I didn't want to survive in a world without you."

He placed a warm hand on my cheek. "As I with you, Lyam Beaumont."

Nothing held me back, and I pulled him into a kiss. This one was different. We pulled close to each other in desperation, our breaths heated, our mouths unhindered. Our skin squeaked as we touched, the residue of rain and sweat interjecting the peaceful thrashing of the waves. But what did it matter?

Tristan's mouth traveled down my neck, while his hands found their way lower. My groin warmed. My body yearned.

It was everything I'd held back for months.

We landed against the side of the captain's cabin. Tristan laced his fingers around my belt. My heartbeat rose in my ears. Already, my knees shook as a tremble of excitement rocked my body.

But before we went further, a loud gurgle interrupted.

Tristan paused. I glanced around the corner.

"Do you see anything?" Tristan breathed, straightening his back.

"No."

Tristan raised his voice. "Who's there!? Show yourself!"

Nothing.

Trembling, my body suspended in an untapped release, I followed Tristan's gaze around the corner and onto the main deck.

What looked like a pile of seaweed lay against the wooden boards.

But as we approached, I placed a hand in front of Tristan.

The seaweed had moved. Etching closer to us.

*A siren.*

The siren lay there, a pool of water around it. With the early morning light and the dancing orbs above us, it failed to produce its ugly song.

Tristan and I approached it. Now, lying before us, we could see it in full.

Its face was nothing more than a mask, shifting between countenances every few seconds. One second, it was a man with blond hair, the next it was a woman with a bird-like face, and the next it was me. But other than its face, everything else about it was inhuman. Its body mimicked both a human and a cephalopod, with multiple tentacles and limbs protruding from its torso. Seaweed was attached to its limbs. Smoke rose from its body.

While stories spoke of a gorgeous creature, luring sailors to their demise, this was not that.

No. It was just a façade to lure us into its home, deep beneath the surface.

Tristan shuddered beside me, "It's an octopus…"

"To think, you almost went overboard for something you hate."

"I don't hate octopus…they just…scare me."

"Well then, it makes a perfect siren."

Tristan scoffed.

The siren's face continued its odd shifts. It gurgled again, flailing another tentacle-like arm in our direction.

"You know, when I tried to jump… I swear, it had your face. I guess that's part of its act…" Tristan said.

"Yeah, but was it as good-looking as me?" I winked at him.

"There was something incorrect about it."

I chuckled.

"So…what do we do with it?" Tristan asked.

"You're the captain. That's your decision."

Tristan took a step toward it. The creature locked eyes with him. Even as its face shifted, there remained a sadness in its permanently black irises.

"It's not its fault that it's a siren…" Tristan whispered. "We should help it back into the ocean. Show some good-will to it."

"Aye, Captain." I restrained a smile. This was the reason why I adored Tristan; it was this kindness, hidden beneath his otherwise serious exterior. While he was a pirate in name, he was not a ruthless dictator of the sea. In his core, he just wanted peace.

Even as the siren thrashed its tentacles as we approached.

Tristan jumped.

"We're not going to hurt you," I said to the siren.

It gargled, its beady eyes narrow. When it opened its mouth, a collection of pointed teeth threatened us.

Carefully, I swooped my arms under the siren's lower body, hoisting it over my shoulder. The creature flailed, slamming its tentacles into my body.

To lull it, Tristan ignited a flame in his palm. It produced a half-made shriek at the light, but when it hit me again, it did not have the same force. This time, like a wet fish, its tentacles slumped against my body.

We carried the siren to the edge of the ship. I turned around, allowing the siren to see the water from over my back. It kicked, trying to escape my clutches.

"Be free, creature," Tristan said beside me.

I loosened my arms.

The siren wiggled from my grip and dove into the water.

Tristan and I watched the waves for a moment to see if the siren reemerged. But all was quiet.

No song exited the waves.

Perhaps that was the way it expressed gratitude.

# CHAPTER TWENTY-SEVEN

# Toward the Horizon

Within an hour, we exited Siren's Bay.

An hour after that, we removed the boards from the crew's doors.

No one suspected that the Captain or I had taken a fervent detour.

The crew crawled onto deck to assess the damage. Cheddar shot out behind them, cawing with excitement. Despite the bombardment of the storm and the clawing of the sirens, the ship sustained minimal damage. The worst of it came from where I'd locked Tristan in place, with the splintering planks.

Veta ran over to Tristan and me as we examined the damage. "Captain! Are you okay? Do you need anything?"

"I'm perfect, Veta," Tristan smiled at her. "Really."

"Are you sure?"

"Lyam made sure of it."

"Lyam!" she spun to me, "Why were you out in the storm!?"

"Why do you think?"

"I swear by the Gods…" she muttered. "I need to examine both of you later. Understood? The two of you are bound to run a cold being out in that rain."

Tristan and I shared a smirk.

Veta continued to mull about us as I worked on repairs. Others came over to check on the captain as well, but for the most part, everyone fell in step to ensure that the *Cobalt Hare* continued to sail.

I kept stealing glances at Tristan, admiring how he leaned against the wall, talking to Hari. He held an aura of nonchalance, relaxation, and pride. Something had shifted within him.

Was this the start of a new Tristan Davies? One for the better?

It might take time, but I could see the sparks forming. The beginning of a fire ready to burn.

I finished mending the broken planks on the bow of the ship and joined Rémy by the helm. She scanned the horizon.

"You alright there, Rem?" I asked her.

"Tired, but here. Spent the night trying to stop Veta from jumping out the window."

"Did the sirens not affect you?"

"Oh, they did. They offered me something impossible, though…so it helped me stay grounded. I'm guessing you weren't affected by their song either?"

I shook my head. "I have everything I want…so their song was pointless."

"Wasn't aware you were that shallow."

I blushed. "What!? I don't just mean Tristan."

"Oh?"

"It's this ship—the *Cobalt Hare* is my home. I feel like I belong here, not just as a passenger. You and Veta welcomed me without any questions. Hari, Zo, and all of them have taught me so much about this ship. And then of course there's Tristan. The sirens couldn't offer me any of this."

"You wanted to belong somewhere without the shadow of your past," Rémy stated.

"Isn't that all we ever want?"

Rémy pointed her chin toward Tristan, talking with Hari. "You know, you've helped the captain with that. I think he's smiled more in the last few months than he had in the last few years. We've all seen it. The moment you came on board, there was a shift."

As if on cue, Tristan smiled in our direction. I waved.

Rémy chuckled and adjusted the helm again. But halfway through turning, she frowned.

"What is it?" I asked.

She removed a spyglass from her belt and pulled it to her eye. After a moment, she replied, "There's a ship out there."

The seas had been calm throughout our entire trip. Ships rarely took a voyage down the entire strait. What was one doing all the way out here?

"Can you see the flag?" I asked.

"No. It's still in the distance. I'll tell the captain." She dropped her spyglass, then hopped over the barrier and onto the main deck. I followed her over to Tristan.

His shoulders fell as she approached. "What is it?"

Rémy held up her hands. "I know, I know, I always come here with inconvenient news. But…there's a ship on the horizon."

"What does it look like?"

"It's too far to tell."

Tristan wrinkled his nose and squinted out at the horizon. Rémy pointed to the small blotch bobbing in the distance.

"Keep our heading to the southwest. We may avoid it if they don't notice us. I'll send a scout ahead."

"Aye, Captain," Rémy replied and hurried back to the helm.

Tristan removed his glove and gathered a new orb of fire in his palm. He cast it into the air, where it crackled once, then raced across the sky.

Tristan and I waited in the crow's nest for the little orb to return, drinking a pint of water-downed ale. Cheddar sat on the mast of the sail, watching us as the sun fell in the distance.

"We probably should stop calling them fiery orbs," I said to Tristan as I finished my drink and kicked the mug to the other side of the crow's nest.

"What do you propose then?"

"I don't know. Something more…magical?"

"Throw me a name. Let's see if it sticks," Tristan placed his empty mug on the ground beside him.

"Feuból?"

"Doesn't that just mean 'fireball' in Volfi?"

I laughed, "You speak Volfi now?"

"Cheddar calls me 'feu', I was going to at least remember that. And ból? I might not speak Volfi, but even I know that means 'ball'."

"Do you have something better?"

He eyed the orbs in the distance. "They're just my fellas, that's all. My little orb fellas."

"Very poetic."

"Well, they give themselves names, but I cannot speak fire. It would be a grumbling of pops and snaps, which honestly sounds profuse coming from my mouth." Tristan leaned against the rail of the crow's nest. "I think they're my little fellas. That's all."

I chuckled to myself.

"But if you need something more formal, we can call them feubóls, I suppose," Tristan chided.

"I think I will."

Tristan smiled.

We stood there in silence, watching Tristan's little fellas—or as I chose to call them, feubóls—bob in the distance, analyzing the blurry image of the ship. Tristan placed his hand over mine, letting his fingers trace the silver scar on my right wrist. Unlike the other splinters across my body, this one still shimmered with the same life as Tarek's Divitiae. All the other splinters had turned gray.

"It doesn't bother you, does it?" Tristan asked.

I shook my head. "No. It's been quiet."

Tristan ran his thumb over it. The silver reflected his shadow. "It's like a mirror."

"Yeah, I use it to trim my beard," I joked.

"I'm sure Tarek enjoys that sight." Tristan smiled.

"You think they're watching me through the scar?"

Tristan shrugged. "It is possible. The magic of the Divitiae always perplexed me. I knew it was powerful, but now…what Tarek said to me…it makes me wonder what the *Tortuga* has unleashed."

"Well, I hope your sister is reasonable when we find her."

"Yes, that is the hope…" he leaned forward against the railing. "I'm thinking, we head toward L'Perle. We'll hopefully gather some news about the *Tortuga*, and if anything, we can send out a message for a rendezvous. Plus, you can visit your parents and bring their share of this trade."

"And tell them I'm not coming home," I added.

"Do you think they will be disappointed?"

"They will be…but they'll also understand."

"Good…because I'm not losing my carpenter," Tristan squeezed my hand.

We sank into silence as daylight drifted into dusk. The feubóls danced like comets in the distance, growing closer with each passing moment. On the deck below, other crewmates watched our messengers as they approached. It was just like the voyage to Merton. If only I had brought my flute out before joining Tristan on the crow's nest.

The first of the feubóls arrived back just before the sun dipped below the horizon. It landed in Tristan's outstretched palm, where it crackled. Tristan tilted his head to the side as he listened.

He furrowed his brow.

"What is it?" I asked.

"It says that the ship is…dead."

"What?"

"Burnt, with no one alive."

"So what does that mean?"

Tristan let the feuból shoot in the air. "Not sure. But we'll proceed with caution. There is no reason to get caught in the crossfire."

# CHAPTER TWENTY-EIGHT

# The Graveyard

Within an hour, we exited Siren's Bay.

An By the next morning, we could see the bobbing carcass of the burnt ship in full. Tattered sails, a cracked mast, and a cavernous body sat in the water, with no signs of life. Even the wood did not creak with the wind, suffocating beneath the remnants of smoke, whatever story it had lost to the wind.

Like any graveyard, all was silent. Cheddar did not squawk, and the crew did not speak. Tristan watched from the crow's nest with Rémy's spyglass in hand.

We moved closer, but still far enough that no weapon could reach us. The last thing we wanted was to get caught in the same crossfire. We weren't out in the sea to take blood. Tristan wasn't that kind of captain.

And we weren't that kind of crew.

Did that make us bad pirates?

Tristan crawled down the crow's nest and handed Rémy back her spyglass. "It's the *Crimson Fox*."

"That is part of the Obsidian Fleet, right?" Rémy asked.

"Obsidian Fleet?" I asked.

"Other ships like the *Hare* and the *Tortuga*. The Commeant commissioned them," Tristan stated.

"You mean there are others like you?"

"I think we're the smallest. The *Tortuga* is a bit bigger—and faster, for that matter. The *Crimson Fox* was one of the largest."

I glanced back toward the ship in the distance. The charred exterior of the ship hid the obsidian coating.

"What happened to it?" I wonder aloud.

"A battle, probably," Rémy said.

We'd been fortunate not to engage in a battle at sea. Those, like sirens and sea snakes, were legends to me. The rest of the crew had taken part in them, but part of me couldn't shake the devastation of the ship. It wasn't just attacked; it was used as kindling for a flame.

Tristan rubbed his gloved hands together as he continued to stare out at the ship. In the distance, the feubóls hovered over the tattered sail.

"Do you want to go in for a closer look, Captain?" Rémy asked.

He shook his head. "No. Keep this distance. It's not worth the risk to get closer."

"Aye, Captain."

Rémy returned to the helm. I stood beside Tristan, paying more attention to him than to the sea. His eyes darted back and forth as he took in the scene. He flexed his gloved fingers again and frowned.

"What is it?" I asked.

"This was…more than just a battle," he whispered.

"What do you mean?"

"This was the result of magic," he bit his bottom lip.

"How can you tell?"

"Because I've seen it before. The governor used to take me into the shipyard and burn the old boats. They looked just like that," his voice shook.

"But this wasn't your fault." I placed my hand on top of his hand. "You're not in the shipyard again."

"I know. But…if it wasn't me… I only know of one other pyromancer who *could* do this."

I pondered, then whispered, "Your sister?"

He nodded.

"Would she, though? There must be other pyromancers out there."

"Another pyromancer on a vendetta against the Commeant? I think not."

"But *would* she do this?" I asked again.

His eyes trembled as he stared out at the shipwreck. "I don't know. That's the problem. I saw what she could do on the *Sanguine Tortuga*, but I still thought that she was the girl I knew growing up. A bit scatterbrained, easily distracted, adventurous…but not destructive without cause.”

“There might have been a cause.”

“I hope so…” Tristan swallowed. “Because if not, then I don’t know my sister.”

We continued sailing to the southwest over the next few days. The *Crimson Fox* had rattled Tristan, and during the day, he withdrew to his cabin. I knew better than to bother him, so I continued my duties, securing parts of the ship and making necessary repairs.

But three days later, another ship emerged on the horizon.

Like the *Crimson Fox*, it too was only ashes.

I first noticed it while helping Hari mind one of the sails. We both paused, taking in the sight, where the feubóls hovered about to gather information.

“Another one…” Hari mumbled.

“We must be a couple days behind whoever is responsible,” I added.

“You mean the *Tortuga*?”

“How did you know?” I asked.

Hari tied off one of the ropes. "I lived on that ship for years. I know her work."

"Tristan thinks it is his sister's responsibility."

"Most likely," Hari sighed.

"You really think she did this?"

"With the way things were going, yes…I do think Leena is capable of this."

Curiosity piqued, I inquired. "Tristan seemed distraught by the idea. I'm guessing she has changed since they were children?"

"Oh, definitely. I knew her when she first joined the *Sanguine Tortuga*. She was innocent, easily embarrassed, overwhelmed…but, as time went on, the sea hardened her."

"As it often does."

"Yes, but…it was more than that," Hari said. "She grew close with Captain Lok, the young woman who freed the *Sanguine Tortuga* from the Commeant. Captain Lok is…ruthless, for lack of a better word. She will spill blood, for better or for worse."

"So you think that this…Captain Lok…ignited Leena?"

"I know she did. Leena Davies is not a diplomat by any means; she does not fear her fire or what it can do." Hari smiled sadly. "I was sad to see her lose some of that innocence…but she makes a fine pirate."

I could imagine the cognitive dissonance that surrounded Tristan's view of his sister. He had an image of his sister from childhood, but in reality, the girl had changed into something unrecognizable. Did she feel the same about her brother?

Hari took a step back from our work. "I shall tell the captain that we found another ship."

"Something tells me that he already knows," I said, noting the feubóls approaching us. That didn't stop Hari from heading toward the captain's cabin, leaving me alone to take in the sight of the new member of the ship graveyard.

What had happened here? If the *Sanguine Tortuga* was responsible, where were they now?

And would we run into them sooner rather than later?

Burnt ships continued to layer the path to L'Perle, but with no sign of the *Sanguine Tortuga*. Every day, we found another ship. Some days, we found multiple, dotting the horizon with ash.

With repairs few and far between, I resorted to sitting with Tristan in the captain's cabin during the day. The cabin was empty now, except for his desk and chair. On the far wall, he hung a map, where he marked the location of each burnt ship. We weren't far from L'Perle, from what I could tell.

And with each day forward, only more ships appeared.

Tristan sat in his chair, staring at the far wall, another mug of watery ale on his desk. He hadn't touched it since I came into the cabin, his own thoughts taking him far away from the present. Cheddar hopped on the desk and hit her beak against the mug.

"Tristan…what's on your mind?" I asked as I took a seat across from him.

"Just…pondering."

I frowned. "And what are you pondering?"

"It's…all of this," he waved at the map. "I'm trying to decipher *why* Leena would do this."

"She's a pirate."

"So are we," Tristan laced his hands together and leaned his forehead against them. "Or maybe we're not…I don't know anymore."

"A pirate is but a name," I stated.

"But it has a meaning."

"It means we are free."

Tristan raised his head so our eyes locked. Freedom; that's what the *Cobalt Hare* signified. We were not dripping in blood or ruling the seas. Here, we sailed for a calm current. Not bloody tides or a crimson sea.

"We won't be free until we're completely untethered." Tristan glanced at my wrist. "We're still being…held hostage, in a way."

"I told you it doesn't bother me."

"That doesn't change anything. One wrong decision and… Well, I don't want to think about it."

I gripped his hands. "Right now, I am unharmed. We are going to ensure this Divitiae does not get into the wrong hands, but until we speak with your sister…we cannot do a thing."

"Yes…my sister…" Tristan mumbled, then pressed his lip to my wrist. He held it there, with a silent promise passed into my skin. I wish I could have quelled his fears, but I didn't know his sister. Part of me shared in his fear: if she could burn countless ships, who was to say the *Hare* was safe?

The shared blood of family did not surpass the bond of a crew.

Not when the seas became home.

I ran my fingers against Tristan's cheek. We sat there, silent for a time, watching the waves waltz outside the cabin window.

In the distance, the feubóls continued their excavation of a charred boat.

Tristan sighed, "I wish they would find something more definitive. A reason or something for the destruction."

"But nothing?"

"None," Tristan shook his head. "You must understand, every one of those ships deserved to burn…but…there were many innocent lives onboard as well. The Commeant has a way of…convincing people to follow. For better or for worse."

"My mother never liked them. She said it was slavery."

"That is one way to describe it," Tristan replied.

"Could your sister have freed them then? Like she did with the *Hare*?"

"We can only speculate."

That was the truth.

For now, we could just sail toward L'Perle, no matter how thick the smoke.

# CHAPTER TWENTY-NINE

# Back to the Start

Eleven ships.

We saw eleven burned ships before the first signs of L'Perle.

By the last one, the marveling had turned to a nonchalant observation, added to the tally and rumors. The entire crew whispered about the *Sanguine Tortuga.* If nations along the Malva Strait hadn't heard of the ship, without a doubt, they would soon.

There was a day-long reprieve before we finally caught a glimpse of L'Perle, creating a frontage of paradise against a wall of burning death. There, in the distance, I recognized the hills of my home, rolling across the island. Small boats clustered around the pier, white dots on the horizon.

Except for a much larger ship.

One that I knew—that we all knew—even from afar.

Its black sails cast a shadow over the island, the flag of a skeletal tortoise waving in the breeze. My chest tightened as we approached, my thoughts as rampant as a stormy sea.

But L'Perle was calm as we approached. Other than a few damaged roofs from the summer storms, the lush greenery and dripping humidity remained. Traders and merchants dotted the boardwalk, watching as we made our way through the harbor.

We docked opposite the *Tortuga*. Not only was it larger than us, but it had seen more. Even from where I stood, the wood of its hull told that story: this ship had entered battles, pillaged for treasure, and fought foes beyond our wildest imagination. Its crew, who watched from deck as we pulled in alongside us, more than quadrupled our crew. Part of me expected to see Tristan's sister standing at the bow of the ship like her brother, with an equally determined stare.

The silver splinters along my skin prickled for the first time in weeks.

I rubbed my arms but didn't show any sign of discomfort as Tristan joined my side. He didn't say a word.

Despite the shadow of the *Sanguine Tortuga*, a bubble of excitement filled my chest. I was back on L'Perle, the place I had called home for my whole life. My parents would be exuberant! I had so many things to tell them.

Well, after my mother lectured me for not writing.

I gripped the railing as I analyzed the bustling boardwalk. To my disappointment, my mother was not among the traders. I frowned. Part of me expected my mother to be waiting for me, right on shore, hopping between her feet with excitement as I disembarked.

"Lyam, what's troubling you?" Tristan asked from beside me.

I turned to him. "Honestly? I thought my mother would be waiting for me."

"Well, if she's a trader, it is possible she is talking with Captain Lok?"

"That's possible." It would align with my mother's behavior.

"I'll ask Hari to see if your mother has been on the *Tortuga* when she heads over there."

"You're not going aboard with her?" I asked.

"Not yet. Hari knows that crew better than me. I'll let her handle the reunion," he fidgeted with the tips of his fingers. "Once all that is out of the way, I'll talk with my sister about the…treasure."

I rubbed the scar on my arm. The silver encasing it seemed to shift beneath my fingers, reflecting the blue sky above us.

"Why don't you get off and stretch your legs? I'm sure you've missed home," Tristan said to me as he leaned against the railing.

"I told you that I'm not leaving the *Hare*. You've got a permanent resident."

"I know—but it doesn't mean you cannot visit your old home, right?"

"You should come with me then."

"What?" Tristan blinked.

"You're not doing much else, right? Let me show you my old stomping grounds." I smirked at him and crossed my arms.

He glanced toward the *Sanguine Tortuga* beside us, then back at port. The corner of his lip etched upwards, but he didn't allow himself to fully smile. "Fine. Show me L'Perle, Mr. Beaumont." He turned back to me. "That's an order."

I led Tristan off the *Cobalt Hare* and onto the dock. The salty air of L'Perle greeted me, followed by the whiff of lime, garlic, and peppers. *Home*, I sighed, letting the scents wash over me for a moment. I hadn't realized how much I missed L'Perle until then. While I wouldn't trade anything for life aboard the *Cobalt Hare*, there was still a part of me that loved my home.

Cheddar leapt from my shoulder and took flight, circling the market before vanishing over the trees. I wasn't worried about her. This was her home too; she would find her way back to me after sharing her adventures with the other birds.

We followed the boardwalk along to the main road, where the Postal Bureau looked out over the sea. Beside it, the narrow blue entrance to the *Aquamarine* sat, dull and insignificant in the daylight.

Tristan slowed outside of it.

"This is where we first met," he whispered.

"You remember?"

"Of course I do. It's hard to forget the first time a burly fellow flirts with you."

"Was I that forward?"

"You are the opposite of subtle."

"What can I say? I know what my heart desires."

We stared at each other for a moment. If we had continued our flirtation, if things had progressed to a one-night rendezvous, where would we be now?

"What was the plan? Were you going to sweep me off my feet and take me to your childhood bedroom?" Tristan asked, closing the gap between us.

"It's worked before."

"And I suppose it's working again."

"It never failed before," I brushed a finger over Tristan's chapped lips. He took hold of it and kissed the top of my hand. Warmth escaped his lips.

We abandoned the *Aquamarine*, side-by-side, our fingers brushing. I pointed out different homes I had repaired with my father, places I frequented in my youth, and even the path where I first found Cheddar. Tristan hung onto my every word, quiet as always, taking in my stories. His home had been tainted; was there anything left that brought joy? But when he spoke of his childhood, it sounded more like a dream, lingering with only small gasps upon waking.

We took the long way up the hill to my parents' house. Out of practice, my glutes and calves ached as we ascended the steep stairwell. I fought through the pain, blathering about different moments throughout my childhood. Sweat gathered on my palms. I wasn't just bringing another boy home; I was introducing him to my family, opening myself up to him in ways I'd never considered.

What would my parents think of Tristan? Would they be appalled that I fell in love with a pirate? My mother had urged me to hold guard to my trust. I could almost hear her saying I sacrificed the integrity of the trade.

On the other hand, I knew my father would welcome Tristan with open arms.

Cheddar waited for us at the top of the stairs, sitting on a familiar perch. She didn't speak as we approached. Instead, she stared toward the house, alert, with her wings tucked back and head cocked to the side.

"What's wrong, Cheddar-bird?" I asked her.

She clicked her beak but said nothing.

"Maybe she's just tired?" Tristan asked.

I bit the inside of my lip. Cheddar was a smart bird, but she could only say so much. Tristan was probably right, though; she was excited upon arriving in port. Now, she needed rest.

A few additional birds fluttered around the house as I approached the door. As usual, it was unlocked. The door creaked as I entered the cluttered sitting room.

"Mère? Père?" I called.

No response.

"They might not be home," I said to Tristan.

He stepped into the sitting room and brushed his hand along the sofa. He didn't blink as he analyzed the room, taking in the piles of books and artifacts.

"It's a treasure trove in here," he commented.

"My mother struggles to get rid of, well, anything."

"Means she always has something to trade." He removed a cracked coffee mug from the end table, "Although, she probably could get rid of some things."

"It's quite a bit, I know."

"My mother would have been envious…" Tristan placed the mug back on the table.

That caught my attention. Tristan never spoke of his mother. And for a good reason.

He glanced at me, noticing my interest. "She always wanted the finest things."

"Would you call my mother's collection 'fine'?"

"It's 'fine' to those who have little."

I glanced at the mug. It was one of many mugs that we had in the house. I'd never given it a passing glance. Growing up, how many mugs did Tristan have? Did they all have to share one? It was hard for me to fathom.

"Do you think your mother has found the finest things in life?" I asked Tristan.

"I…do not know…" Tristan hesitated before continuing, "and I do not know if I care."

"You don't want to find your mother someday?"

He frowned and kicked the ground. "Perhaps someday…just to show her that I'm thriving without her help."

"You're more than thriving."

His frown disappeared, and that twinkle reappeared in his eyes.

I placed a hand on his arm and guided him from the sitting room to the kitchen. Didn't I have a dream, months ago, where he sat at the kitchen table awaiting a cup of coffee from my mother? Now, it had become a reality.

Now—

I froze at the entrance to the kitchen.

My throat tightened.

My stomach dropped.

My knees buckled.

Smatterings of dried red blood coated the kitchen table and floor.

In the chairs at the table, both my mother and father sat tied to chairs.

Their throats slit open.

And no breath to be had from their lips.

# CHAPTER THIRTY

# The Quartermaster

I couldn't feel my body. Around me, any sounds disappeared into a vacuum of silence. All I saw were their bodies, lifeless at the table, stripped of their dignity and wealth.

I didn't even send them a letter. They didn't even know if I was alive. I gripped the wall, my ankles quaking beneath my weight. What kind of son was I? The one promise I made was that I'd send a letter, but I hadn't even done that because I was too enthralled with my own feelings.

No, they couldn't be gone. Not like this.

I took a trembling step forward, but Tristan caught my arm. "Lyam, wait."

"No…" I mumbled.

Tristan grabbed my arm tighter. "Lyam."

I shook my head and blinked away the tears.

"You need to breathe. Come outside. You don't need to see this."

"No—"

"Please."

My shoulders sank, and I obliged, letting him guide me away from the scene and out onto the front step. My knees gave out once the fresh air hit my face. Tristan caught me, helping me take a seat.

The world continued to spin. My heart thudded. Everything moved fast and slow at the same time.

But Tristan stayed, his arm tight around me, his warmth a promise.

There, in his arms, I finally succumbed to tears. Every blink brought back images of their bodies. My mother and father tied to the kitchen chairs, blood pooling from their necks. Their blood was dry, but the deaths were fresh. It had to have happened in the last two days. If we hadn't been caught with the sirens, they might still be alive.

"Lyam," Tristan took me by the shoulders. "Breathe. One at a time. Breathe. In and out." He inhaled and exhaled to demonstrate. I followed, my quivering breaths choking on each beat. The air was heavy, and my lungs struggled, as though a rock sat in their base, taking up space.

Who was I without my mother to guide me? Or without my father to lecture me? Even at sea, I turned to them. I had so much to tell them about my adventure.

All of it was gone.

Lost.

"What do I do?" I sobbed.

"For now, you need to breathe," Tristan whispered.

"But…I don't understand. I can't imagine who did this. They didn't have any enemies or…or anything like that!"

"Perhaps something happened while you were gone?"

"I can't think of anything," I choked.

"Hm," he brushed my hair back. "I'll go investigate. Stay here."

"Be careful," I gripped his hand.

"I will." He brought my silver wrist to his lips, held it there for a moment, then climbed to his feet and headed back into the house.

With Tristan gone, I brought my hands to my face and succumbed to another bout of tears. *It's a dream. They're fine. They have to be fine.*

But I'd seen their bodies.

Their blood.

No. It couldn't be true.

And why did I feel like it was my fault?

"Yam?" Cheddar chewed at my finger to get my attention.

"It's okay, Cheddar-bird," I mumbled.

"Yam!" She bit my finger harder.

"Cheddar, I swear." I groaned and raised my head.

The bird fluttered into the air and squawked.

"What—" I stopped. Footsteps approached from the brush.

I wiped my eyes and sat up ever so slightly. A figure emerged from the bushes.

"Merde!" I jumped backwards from my spot. "Sybyl!"

She grinned widely. Her hair fell to her face in matted clumps, while a permanent scar sat etched into the side of her forehead. Her dark eyes, bloodshot, stared at me without blinking.

"Well, well, well, if it isn't Mr. Beaumont," she said as she leaned against a nearby tree.

"What're you doing here?! You're supposed to be on the way to Janis!"

"Ah, I was…but you see, most ships stop in L'Perle on their way to Janis. Or did you not know?"

I blinked. Right. We were a trade hub. The gateway to the south. The pearl of the sea.

"And they just let you go when you got here?"

"Well, let's just say a savvy trader saw me locked away in their cargo hold and recognized me from a previous trade."

My throat tightened. "You mean my mother freed you?"

"She was quite worried about her little boy. How could you not write?" Sybyl pouted at me.

"I—well—um—"

"I told her you were caught in a mutiny aboard the *Hare* and that I could save you if she acquired a ship for me."

"And she refused?"

Sybyl laughed. "Oh, no, she wholeheartedly agreed."

"Then why did you kill her!?"

"Kill her?"

"She's dead!" I motioned at the house.

"Oh." Sybyl's face fell for a moment. "Well, that is quite unfortunate. I was on my way to ask if she had found a boat. Although now that you are here, I do not really need one," Sybyl's conniving light returned as she stepped toward me. "Thank you for making this all the easier. This is a pleasant surprise."

"You didn't know we were here?"

"I've been keeping a low profile," she took another step, "Your island here has plenty of places to stay out of sight."

I reached for my hammer. Cheddar leapt from a nearby branch, diving toward Sybyl. Before she landed, Sybyl threw out her arm, sending Cheddar flying into the air.

"Cheddar! Stay back!" I cried after her.

"This can be easy, Mr. Beaumont. Tell me where the captain is, then I'll leave you to mourn your dead parents," she unsheathed her sword.

"Why would I know where he is?"

"Oh, don't play a fool. It was always you creating disorder on the *Hare*. You do not know Tristan Davies as I do; he needs to be neutralized. His magic is uncontrolled and unsound. You'd be doing him a favor by sending him back to me."

Before I could respond, Tristan's voice came from behind me.

"No. He wouldn't."

I spun around. Tristan sat in the sitting room window, arms crossed.

"Tristan!" Sybyl's voice softened as she raced forward to him. "Oh, you must understand—I never wanted to harm you! It's important for me to protect you, as I promised I always would. Don't you remember?"

"Stop with this bull already, Sybyl," Tristan shook his head. "I'm no fool."

"Is this what Mr. Beaumont put in your head? Tristan, love—"

"Stop!" Tristan rose.

"I told you when he first climbed aboard—"

He removed his glove. Fire danced around his fingertips.

"—you'd become untamed," Sybyl finished.

Tristan did not further his fire, maintaining it on his fingertips, his attention unchanged.

324

His anger did little to hinder Sybyl. She took another step in his direction and placed a hand on his shoulder. "Come with me, Tristan. Let's go home."

Tristan's eyes widened. Fire built around his palm.

I acted fast, removing my hammer from the belt and lifting it in the air. I aimed at it with great care and then set it loose.

It flew through the air and hit the wooden wall of my familial home just to the right of Tristan and Sybyl.

The wood splintered, and despite my weak control of magic, it obeyed my command. The pieces shot forward, miniature stakes, and pierced Sybyl's side.

She cursed and released Tristan. It gave him enough time to rekindle the flame on his fingers, and with an artistic twirl, he whipped the fire through the air, lassoing around Sybyl. The wooden stakes in her side caught aflame, searing up the side of her body, and singeing her shirt. She fumbled backwards and into the brush. Cheddar lifted off from a nearby tree and screeched as the leaves caught aflame.

Sybyl gathered herself. With wild eyes and a snarl, she lunged in my direction, her sword unfurled. Some of Zo's training had stuck with me, and I jumped back, landing a few paces from my hammer on the ground. Tristan sent another plume of fire toward Sybyl. It caught the surrounding air, knocking her back off her feet again.

"Lyam! Get inside!" Tristan shouted.

"I'm here and I'm helping!" I yelled back at him.

"My magic—"

"—will only burn brighter with me here! I'm not going to lose you!"

Tristan huffed, but with Sybyl rising again, undeterred by the flame, he did not find another argument.

I snatched my hammer off the ground and readied my defenses. Sybyl was dynamic, moving through the brush, a warrior ready to strike at any second. I tracked her while Tristan's flames remained flickering on his fingers. Her shadow moved, like the other creatures lurking in the trees, waiting.

Embers flickered on the leaves. The bark of the trees flinched at each touch of flame.

Seconds later, Sybyl stormed from the trees at Tristan. She slammed into his right shoulder, causing him to fall to the ground with a grunt. The fire fizzled out on his fingers as Sybyl held him there.

"Not so strong now, are you?" Sybyl snarled.

I took a step forward with my hammer in hand.

"Don't you dare," Sybyl snapped in my direction. "I can turn his flame off permanently if you dare to take another step."

I froze. Tristan's eyes darted about, his breathing ragged. Magic, at its core, was more than just a talent. For someone like Tristan, his magic was his life.

Taken from him, what more would he be?

I knew he was more than his magic, of course, but if it kept him alive, if it gave him purpose…then what would he be without it?

But maybe Sybyl was lying. Tristan said the scar on his right shoulder neutralized his magic…but it was only when touched. Right?

Unless there was a more malicious reason behind the scar.

"Now, you're going to come with me. Understood, Davies?" Sybyl glowered down at him.

"And where do you intend to take me?" Tristan grunted.

"I have reinforcements coming from the Obsidian Fleet, don't you worry."

The next words exited my mouth without hindrance. "No, you don't!"

She glowered at me.

"They're all destroyed! Burnt to the ground! We saw them about a day outside of L'Perle!" The countless ships, burnt to a crisp, filled my mind.

Sybyl frowned. "That's a lie."

"No, it's not!"

"You want me to believe that Tristan Davies burnt the Obsidian Fleet to the ground? He doesn't have that sort of power!" She pressed harder into his shoulder. He groaned.

"But I do." A voice came from the brush.

A woman emerged from the trees. I didn't need to know her name. Her flaming red hair and deep blue eyes told me everything.

Tristan's sister, Leena Davies, stood amongst the trees. One of her eyes had been removed from her skull, leaving an etched scar as a memory of her socket. Fire rode up her arms, lacing around the saber in her hands. If Tristan was a flame, Leena was a bonfire, burning with fury and fueled by determination.

Sybyl released Tristan and spun to face Leena. I raced over to Tristan's side, hoisting him up and away from Sybyl.

She stared at Leena, her fingers twitching.

But Leena was not one for a performance. Leena knocked Sybyl over with a single wave of her saber. Sybyl fell to her knees.

Leena dropped her saber. She held out her hand and pressed it to Sybyl's face.

The fire in her hands exploded.

It pooled around Sybyl's mouth, eyes, nose, and ears.

Suffocating...

Melting...

Skinning...

She held her hand there for a few moments longer.

Then released.

Sybyl stumbled backwards from Leena and fell to the ground.

Breathless.

Eyeless.

And faceless.

# CHAPTER THIRTY-ONE

# Siblings

I held Tristan tight in my arms. He gripped my shirt, shaking still from the altercation. Across from us, Leena paced around Sybyl's body. She poked it once with her saber, then smirked in Tristan's and my direction.

"Leena…" Tristan breathed.

"Hello, brother. It's been a bit, hasn't it?" She smiled.

"What have you done?" he sputtered.

"I think I saved you." Leena crossed her arms. "I was watching for some time but waited until the time was right for a dramatic entrance."

"But you killed her!"

"Nothing changes unless there is blood."

Tristan stared at Sybyl's body. "This was my battle to fight."

"Well, you weren't doing too well."

"I swear…" Tristan cursed and shook his head. "What were you doing here in the first place?"

"Well, I was a little disappointed you didn't come visit me on the *Tortuga*." Leena pouted.

"So you stalked me here?"

"No! Well…yes. I was just curious."

"I was going to speak with you later," Tristan grumbled.

"Took out the latter part, we're speaking now."

Tristan sighed. "Fine. Can you give me a few minutes with Mr. Beaumont, though?"

"Mr. Beaumont?" She eyed me. Her good eye flickered with understanding. "Oh, I see. Fine. I'll be right around the corner."

Tristan observed his sister as she departed. Once she disappeared around the corner, he turned to face me. He gathered my face in his hands. "Are you okay, Lyam?"

"Yeah, yeah…I'll be okay. Are you?" I gripped his arms.

"Yes. I…am shaken…and annoyed…and saddened…but here."

"Good. It's good you're here."

Tristan kissed me in full, his hot breath hitting me and warming my face. I held him close. We just needed a second to ensure everything was okay. We were here. Still. Alive. Unharmed.

Cheddar landed on my head. "Yam?"

"Are you okay, Cheddar?" I asked the bird.

"Yam! Fire!" She exclaimed.

Tristan and I smiled at each other. That was a yes. We were all okay.

Well…at least physically.

I stole a glance back at my childhood home. My parents' bodies still lay inside, rotting away, their affairs as disorganized as their house.

"We can stay in L'Perle as long as you need," Tristan whispered.

"Thank you," I replied. Did they ever speak with an advocate about their estate? Was there a will? These were things I had never considered. Part of me always thought that at least my mother might live forever. I placed my hand against the wall of the house. "Did you find anything inside?"

"Oh, um, yes. I found this." He removed a piece of paper from his pocket and handed it to me.

I unfolded it. Inside was a flyer, written in Vernnes.

*WANTED*

*CAPTAIN TRISTAN DAVIES of THE COBALT HARE*

*ON GROUNDS of MUTINY, TREASON, ROB-BERY, and ABDUCTION*

*REWARD: 10000 DOUBLOONS*

*Please report any information to Madame Claudine Beaumont.*

332

I recited the flyer to myself, then glanced at Tristan. "Sybyl told my mother that the *Hare* abducted me. She must have put out a bounty."

"A bounty can cause violence."

"Perhaps someone gave false information…or something…" I frowned. Part of me still believed Sybyl was responsible.

"We will make this right, Lyam. Do not worry."

I nodded and put the flyer in my pocket. Tristan and I exchanged a single glance, then side-by-side, joined Leena around the bend. She waited there, her gaze falling down the mountain, to where both the *Sanguine Tortuga* and *Cobalt Hare* bobbed in port.

"Oh, good, you two are done necking," Leena smirked at us.

"Shut it," Tristan grunted.

She chuckled to herself, then glanced down the path. "One thing, then we can head back to port."

I raised my brow.

She marched down the path, back toward the house where Sybyl's body lay. Seconds later, a bright orange light exploded, coating the sky for a moment, then dissipating into smoke and ash. The ground shook with the explosion. Birds fluttered and cawed. The bark from the trees groaned.

I screamed, "No!"

Tristan grabbed hold of me to prevent me from running toward my home.

Leena walked back toward us with the fire as her backdrop. Her hair fluttered behind her, as bright as a flame, her eye twinkling.

"What did you do!?" I shouted.

"I had to get rid of the evidence. Now, it just looks like a fluke forest fire."

"That was my home!"

Leena's face softened, and her shoulders fell. "Oh. Well. I apologize. We can pay for any damages."

"No…you don't understand…my parents…you don't understand…" I whimpered.

Tristan placed his hand on my back.

"I'm sorry, I did not know," Leena said quietly. "I didn't want anyone investigating your attacker's death."

"It's because you don't think before you act. You never have," Tristan replied.

Leena did not argue with that statement. She bowed her head, seeming to accept the criticism.

My body shook as I held back a new round of tears. With Tristan's hand on my back, I swallowed them, focusing on my breathing as we turned away from the fire and from my home.

We didn't speak as we descended the hill. To avoid the commotion and curiosity brought by the fire, we took the long way, trudging to the far side of the island where only the empty beach waited. From here, we couldn't see the port or the ships; only the sea, tapping against the shore, unscathed by the slaughter in the hills.

I felt like a ghost as I walked. Nothing was left. My childhood home. My parents. It was all gone. It was a circumstance of puzzle pieces, meeting to form one storm. Only Cheddar remained, nesting on my head, as silent as the rest of us.

Tristan's sister was only one of those pieces. She left her mark, scarring L'Perle as she had the ocean with the corpses of the Obsidian Fleet.

"What's gotten into you, Leena?" Tristan finally asked after a long walk of silence.

"What're you talking about?" Leena retorted.

"I'm talking about the eleven burnt ships in the Malva Strait!"

Leena glanced at him, a similar smirk on her lips that I'd seen on Tristan's face. "Oh, right…you saw that."

"It was hard to ignore," Tristan replied.

"Every one of those was self-defense. The *Crimson Fox* had been chasing us for weeks. When they finally caught up, we had to defend ourselves."

"And the others?"

"They were reinforcements. They attacked, we countered. It's not my fault they can't defend themselves."

Tristan frowned.

"You'll get used to it. Your crew is young and inexperienced. You haven't been doing this for all that long," she waved her hand in the air. "Soon enough, you'll understand, nothing changes on the high seas unless there is blood."

That statement irked me. She said it with authority and determination, as though this was the law of the water.

The words came from my mouth without filter, "Things can change without blood. There are other options."

Leena scoffed, "Didn't seem to work with that loon you fought on the hill."

"Sybyl is different…" Tristan mumbled beside me.

"Is she? Honestly, I'm surprised you didn't roast her. What happened to that military boy who attacked the *Tortuga* over a year ago? Have you gone soft?" Leena leaned forward on her toes. "You almost burned the *Tortuga* alive right then and there."

Tristan rubbed his right shoulder. "I've changed, Leena."

"You won't survive like this, though." There was a hint of worry in her voice. Her snarky remarks came with familial care. The sea had sharpened her words, though, making them more pointed and direct.

"I'm still a pirate," Tristan replied.

"Are you?"

"I'm free…isn't that what it means to be a pirate?"

I held back a smile at Tristan's remark.

"Point taken," Leena beamed. She placed a hand on her brother's arm. "It's good to see you again, Tristan."

"You too, Leena."

She turned to face me and raised the eyebrow over her good eye. "I guess we haven't been formally introduced then. Leena Davies, first mate of the *Sanguine Tortuga*."

I nodded. "Lyam Beumont. Carpenter."

"He's more than a carpenter," Tristan said as he returned to my side. "He is my crewmate and my confidante."

"*Confidante*?" Leena's eyes twinkled.

Tristan's ears turned red. Cheddar hopped off my head and onto Tristan's shoulder.

"Feu! Yam!" she exclaimed with her chest puffed.

Leena's grin returned. "Well, my *confidante* is waiting for us back on the ship. And I am sure you have quite the tale to tell us both."

Leena detailed her misadventures to us as we returned to port. The *Sanguine Tortuga* had been spending its time sailing across the Malva Strait, making connections from Gonvernnes and to the nations in the west. They had found more treasures, encountered multitentacled monsters, and battled many ships that crossed their paths. Compared to the *Tortuga*, the *Hare*'s adventures were far more subdued.

The smoke from the hilltop had reached the docks by the time we arrived. It bubbled over the tops of the trees, dismantling any last sign of my childhood home. I froze just outside of the *Aquamarine* to watch. No one even knew I had returned to L'Perle. Honestly, they probably only spoke about the two ships in the harbor.

The pirate ships, with their skeletal flags.

"We can't stay here…" I whispered.

Tristan paused, following my gaze.

Leena joined us, "Oh, I'm sure my crew is already preparing to leave. You should as well. Once we're at sea, we can use a gangplank to connect the ships."

"Are you okay with that, Lyam?" Tristan asked me.

"What else is there for me here?" I replied.

"But do you need time to get your affairs in order?"

"The only thing left are my mother's trade contracts. I don't need to spend days negotiating with the merchants on them. Let them fight amongst themselves." I continued to watch the plumes of smoke. Only a year ago, I might have stayed behind to claim my mother's empire. But it didn't matter anymore. There were other traders and other carpenters on L'Perle. No one needed to remember my name.

"We can always come back if need be," Tristan remarked.

"Thank you." I turned to him.

He smiled softly, just so his dimples showed on his freckled face.

"Well, this is quite lovely, but we should get going," Leena interjected. "You two can climb in the crow's nest later."

Tristan and I exchanged a smirk. With our fingers brushing against each other, we followed Leena down toward the pier, where the *Sanguine Tortuga* and *Cobalt Hare* awaited our return.

# CHAPTER THIRTY-TWO

# Pirate Talk

Hari waited for us on the dock. Before she could inquire about our whereabouts, Tristan pulled her aside and told her to prepare the ship for departure. Hari did not question, eyeing the smoke in the distance with her lips pursed into a frown. Leena returned to her own ship, passing Hari a friendly wave before boarding the *Tortuga*.

As we boarded, Hari filled Tristan in on the details of her time visiting the *Tortuga*. She had informed Captain Lok of our adventure around the trade we had promised to complete. While Hari hadn't gone into the details, she did tell Captain Lok that it had not been as lucrative as hoped. It would be Tristan's job to elaborate on the details.

"How did she take that?" Tristan asked Hari as we reached the main deck.

"Captain Lok was…dissatisfied, to say the least," Hari replied.

"I see," Tristan glanced at me. His finger stroked the side of my wrist.

"But, I know from my time with her, she can be reasonable as well," Hari added.

"We'll see. For now, let's prepare for departure."

"Understood, Captain."

Hari left us to begin preparations. Tristan turned to face me, placing both his hands on my shoulders. After staring at me for a second, he pulled me into a tight hug.

I sank into his arms. Tears poked at the corners of my eyes.

"Get some rest," he whispered, stroking back my hair. "Use the captain's cabin. It has the better bed. Don't worry about any of this. Understood?"

I didn't argue, pressing my forehead against his head, letting his warmth cradle me for a moment.

He kissed me lightly before saying, "I'll join you once we're at sea. Please, Lyam, get some rest. You've been through plenty today."

"Okay," I murmured, our lips brushing again. All I wanted was to sink into the comfort of his arms and restart the day.

Tristan guided me to the captain's cabin. He planted one last kiss on my forehead, then closed the door to continue his work.

Cheddar fluttered about the room, landing on the empty desk staring out at the sea. I offered her a couple of seeds, then removed my tool belt, letting it fall to the floor beside the desk. On the far side of the room, a curtain divided the wide bed that oversaw the opposite window.

I took a seat on it and brought my face to my hands. It didn't feel real. None of it felt real.

The fire. The blood.

But here I was, with the memories etched into my skin.

Like the silver splinters that began to twinge.

The sound of the gangplank hitting the deck woke me. I didn't remember going to sleep, but when I woke, a blanket covered my body, and my boots had been removed. The haze of the rising sun against distant storm clouds cast its light through the bay windows.

Tristan stood by the mirror, buttoning his shirt. Upon seeing me sit up in the reflection, he smiled.

"Morning," he said.

"I didn't know I fell asleep, to be honest." I rubbed my head. The night had been dreamless, though my eyes still weighed with the baggage of the previous day.

"You were like a piece of debris when I came in here. It was difficult to get you under the covers." He finished the last button of his shirt, then ran his hand through his hair.

I climbed to my feet and joined him by the mirror. Cheddar hopped down from the wardrobe and landed on my shoulder.

"Should I comb it back?" Tristan asked me as he continued to play with his hair.

"No, I like it loose," I remarked, adjusting my own hair so it rested behind my ears.

"But does it elicit command?"

"I think your command comes from your comfort." I rested my arms around his waist and pulled him close to me. His skin smelled of the sea and burnt driftwood. I wanted to hold him there, forget everything. In my half-awake state, I almost believed the previous day had been a dream.

Tristan turned to face me. "I am speaking with Captain Lok this morning once the gangplank is secure. You do not have to come with me if you need time."

"I would welcome the distraction," I replied as I adjusted a strand of his hair. "Besides, you need a trader to assist in any negotiation."

"But are you up to it?"

"What better way to honor my mother?" I expected the tears to return, but as I spoke, my mother's pride filled me.

If there was an afterlife, and she watched me, then I hoped she might see how her teachings stayed with me.

Tristan squeezed my hands in his gloved hands. "We'll find out what happened to them, Lyam. That's a promise."

"Thank you."

He kissed me lightly, then returned to the mirror to make the final adjustments to his outfit.

I gathered myself, pulling on a fresh tunic, my tool belt, and my boots. Together, Tristan and I left the cabin. Cheddar fluttered out ahead of us, circling where Hari secured the gangplank to the ship. Beside us, the *Sanguine Tortuga* watched, like an older sibling ambling about their younger one.

My splinters prickled along my arms, pulling toward the ship.

"Plank's secure!" a man with an uneven beard shouted from the *Tortuga*.

"Thanks, Pickford!" Hari called back in his direction. "All secure here!"

Tristan approached the gangplank and turned to Hari. "Is Captain Lok ready for us?"

"Seems so. She's in her cabin, waiting," Hari said.

"Good. Stay here. Keep the ship running."

"I'll station Zo at the gangplank in case anything goes awry."

"Do you have reason to believe it will?" Tristan asked.

"It's just a precaution, sir."

"Very well," he glanced at me, "You ready?"

"Ay, Captain."

Tristan led the way across the gangplank. Despite the short distance, the narrow beam made my stomach twist. The wood groaned with each step, threatening to snap if we did not hurry our crossing.

With its last threat, I stepped onto the *Sanguine Tortuga*. My skin rippled again, this time sending quiet shockwaves across my nerves. I swallowed back the pain before Tristan took note.

Tristan didn't need a guide upon boarding the ship. While the *Tortuga* was bigger, its design mimicked the *Cobalt Hare*. The captain's cabin sat beneath the helm. Its double doors welcomed us with a smattering of gold. As we approached, the crewmates around deck watched with curiosity.

Tristan inhaled, then knocked on the door.

The door opened at once, causing Cheddar to leap from my shoulder and fly in a circle around us. I whistled for her to land, then guided her back onto my shoulder with my fingers. She pecked her beak against my ear, then took a perch on the pillar to the crow's nest.

"Be good, Cheddar-bird," I whispered, then followed Tristan into the cabin.

Captain Lok's cabin was far different from the one on the *Hare*. Gold and gems lay in piles on the floor, while the wall bore different maps from across the region. Three different swords hung from the wall. Amid all of it sat Captain Lok.

With long black hair, a dotted piercing on her round face, and an emotionless stare, she commanded the room with her presence. One hand had been replaced by a hook, tapping along the top of her desk. Her dark eyes watched us as we entered, not blinking. Beside her, Leena sat on the edge of the desk, arms crossed.

"Captain Lok…it is good to see you again," Tristan stated.

"Captain Davies. Please, take a seat."

Tristan obliged. I took to a spot against the wall, rubbing my arms to lull the continuous prickling on my skin.

"I heard from Hari that your trade did not go as we hoped?" Captain Lok did not linger on small talk.

"There were complications."

"Do elaborate."

Tristan tensed in his seat. He stole a glance in my direction, then returned to Captain Lok. "We were provided the name of a trader in the northern city of Merton. Tarek Kek is their name."

Captain Lok showed no signs of recognition.

Tristan continued, "Tarek told us that the treasure, the Divitiae as they called it, is a powerful substance that, if in the wrong hands, could lead to travesties. They provided us with a down payment of five hundred doubloons to protect the Divitiae from those who might use it for harm."

Tristan had chosen his words with care. From her spot on the desk, Leena's eyes flickered, although she did not add anything to the conversation.

Captain Lok shook her head and chuckled. "So you're expecting me to end the trade routes, is that right?"

"We must. If it gets into the wrong hands—"

"Why should *I* terminate my most profitable trade? You received five hundred doubloons as a down payment? I receive that much for just a quarter of a barrel! I thought you would do us better, Captain Davies."

"You must understand. This Divitiae has power beyond what we can understand. The trade route could damage the balance of magic," Tristan begged.

"Says some obscure trader?" Captain Lok glanced at Leena. "This is Theo all over again."

Leena nodded in agreement.

"I saw it in action. Look at Lyam," he motioned for me to join his side. He took my arm and rolled down the sleeve, revealing the silver splinters coating my skin. On my wrist, the silver scar twinkled like a mirror. "Do you see this? Tarek used the Divitiae to do this to Lyam! It tortured him!"

"And I lost my hand to a booby trap. So what?" Captain Lok scoffed.

"This could *kill* him," Tristan pleaded.

"He looks fine."

"Because Tarek hasn't had a reason yet."

Captain Lok shrugged. "I honestly couldn't care less about your boy-toy."

Tristan continued to grip my arm. "But what if something like this happened to Leena? Or someone else on your crew? Would you care then?"

"The thing is, Captain Davies, I wouldn't let something like this happen to Leena. I'd kill anyone who even tried," her eyes widened with the statement. "I am surprised a skilled pyromancer like yourself would even let it get that far."

Tristan's shoulders fell.

But I snapped. "You weren't there. Captain Davies did what he could under the circumstances."

"I am sure he could have done more. The sea is no place for cowardice," Captain Lok retorted.

"Bravery does not equal violence."

Captain Lok's eyes narrowed. She did not move, keeping me locked in her gaze. "Bravery is fighting against control. That's what it means to rule the seas. From what I can tell, this *Tarek* is doing just that to the *Cobalt Hare*…controlling it."

"She's right," Leena added as she played with the thin golden chain of her necklace.

Tristan's nostrils flared. He continued to hold my wrist as he spoke, "Maybe Tarek is controlling us…but I also agree with them. The Divitiae is powerful. We saw what it could do. I don't know about you, but I don't want to be caught in the crossfire if it gets into the wrong hands."

"You won't be, though—you're not tethered to any nation," Captain Lok replied.

"It might not be a nation."

As the two continued their discussion, a burning sensation ripped through my wrist, as though someone had cut open a curtain and peered through it. It appeared the same, with Tristan's fingers still tracing along the side of the wound. My skin hadn't stopped tingling since we boarded the *Sanguine Tortuga*.

It had to be telling me something.

I took Tristan's hand and said, "Why keep arguing? We can show them."

"Wha—what?" Tristan gawked.

"I'm sure they have some of the Divitiae on the ship. I felt it…my skin hasn't stopped tingling since we boarded."

"We don't need a repeat of Merton," he hissed.

"But maybe that will prove our point."

Captain Lok crossed her arms. "What are you two going on about?"

I spoke before Tristan could stop me. "We can show you how dangerous this is. Bring us a bit of the Divitiae and we can show you."

Captain Lok shared a brief glance with Leena. "Very well. Humor us."

Leena disappeared for a few minutes, leaving us to sit in awkward silence with Captain Lok until she returned. Captain Lok's dark eyes almost never blinked, analyzing both Tristan and me, as if reading into our souls. She tapped her hooked hand against the surface of her desk, producing a small dent in its surface that made the wood tremble. Tristan continued to rub his fingers along the side of my hand, his own gaze wide and fearful. The difference between the two captains was apparent. Captain Lok ruled her ship with determination and command; Tristan guided his with an eager ear and thoughtfulness.

Neither was wrong.

But the contrast was evident.

As the minutes passed, my splinter skin continued to ripple. First, it was a small prickle, but as each moment passed, it grew more tender, jabbing into my veins. When the door to the cabin opened again, I swore the splinters tried to leap from my body.

Leena entered with a small jug. She dropped it on the desk, then took her seat on the corner just like before, raising her eyebrow in my direction.

"Go on," Captain Lok verbalized.

I wiggled my hand loose of Tristan's grasp and took hold of the jug. My skin tugged, trying to rip from my bones. What would happen when I opened this?

I swallowed, then uncorked the jug. The splinters on my skin pulled upwards, reacting like a magnet to the Divitiae. The liquid inside rose in unison, climbing above the rim of the jug, and dripping over onto my hand and down onto my foot.

Where it stabbed me in the shape of a wooden stake.

"Merde!" I cursed and dropped the jug. It clattered to the ground, spraying more stakes in my direction as it exploded from the vessel. I knew this would happen, but I hoped, as my vision blurred from the pain, that it would be just enough to convince Captain Lok of the Divitiae's danger.

Tristan shouted as I stumbled to the floor, where I landed near the puddle of Divitiae forming on the ground. It continued to crawl to me, masking any sense of my surroundings, placing my understanding of the ship's wood into a fog. I sank into the Divitiae's embrace.

Where I dreamt of silver.

# CHAPTER THIRTY-THREE

# Bounty

My entire body ached when I awoke. I lay on a hard bench in Captain Lok's cabin, my right foot elevated and wrapped in a poor bandage. Tristan knelt on the floor, scrubbing it, while no one else occupied the room.

"Tristan…" I groaned.

He shot up, "Lyam!"

I reached for his hand as he joined my side, squeezing it tight.

"You shouldn't have done that," Tristan murmured, bringing my hand to his lips.

"Well, it proved our point."

"It was like your skin was cracking open!" He traced one of the splintered scars. Inflammation gathered around it.

"I'm more concerned that Veta will kill me over my foot," I grunted.

"Only if I don't kill you first," Tristan shook his head. "Is your wrist okay?"

I glanced at my wrist. Compared to the splinters, that appeared normal.

"I think it reacts differently. The splinters were built from the Divitiae's reaction. My wrist is Tarek's responsibility." I sat up slightly. The room spun.

Tristan helped me lean my back against the wall, continuing his grumbling, "I swear, I should punish you later."

"That sounds like a good time," I snickered.

"I don't mean like that."

"Oh, we're getting feisty now?"

"Is now really the time for flirting?"

"I'll always find a way to flirt with you, Captain," I leaned forward, but groaned as another splinter pricked me.

Tristan scoffed and returned to my wounds. I wiggled my toes as he examined my foot, relieved to see I still had motion there.

"It only cut into the top of your foot. Deep, but should heal," Tristan muttered. "Hopefully you can walk across the gangplank to the *Hare* later."

"Yeah, I think so."

"Good," Tristan joined me on the bench. We sat there silently, allowing my head to stop spinning, squeezing each other's hands as a form of communication. I pressed my lips to the side of Tristan's shoulder, away from his wound, and held him there.

"Where are Captain Lok and Leena?" I whispered.

"They wanted to talk privately. Asked me to clean up the mess we made."

"They called that a mess? We've done worse."

"Shush," Tristan nudged me, smiling.

"What? We destroyed a dock in Rosada!"

Tristan continued to smile.

I really wanted to crawl into bed with him right then, holding him close and unraveling everything of the past couple of days. But that would have to wait until we were back on the *Hare*. After all, nothing had been resolved around the trade. That still hung in the air, as it had since I first joined Tristan's crew.

"Do you think they'll agree to stop trading the Divitiae?" I asked Tristan.

"I am unsure. Leena seemed shocked by the situation, but this *is* Captain Lok's ship. Leena is loyal to her."

"I'm guessing Captain Lok didn't have a reaction?"

"She never shows what she is thinking. That's how she was a year ago, too."

"To be honest, she kind of scares me," I said.

"Same."

We fell into a silence, waiting for Captain Lok and Leena to return. Although my skin continued to itch from the splinters, it did not cloud the creaking of the wood. Compared to the *Hare*, who puttered beneath illness when I first arrived, the *Tortuga* was well maintained, its wood strong. The *Hare* still seemed weak compared to its counterpart, but at least the rot had gone.

The door opened after a few minutes. Captain Lok and Leena sauntered into the room, taking their appropriate places by the desk.

"It is good to see your boy-toy awake," Captain Lok smiled.

Tristan crossed his arms. "His name is Lyam."

"I'll call him boy-toy. No need for me to remember the name of someone so insignificant."

Tristan's hand twitched. I took hold of it.

"Anyhow," Captain Lok leaned forward, "Leena and I have formed a compromise that we think you should take."

"And what is that?"

"We have seven barrels of this so-called *Divitiae* onboard the *Tortuga* right now. You take all seven and sail your way back to this Tarek person. Offer it to them at a discount…five hundred if you must. You tell them that's all that remains. Then, we—" Captain Lok motioned to Leena and herself, "—can continue our trade as well. You get your riches, we get ours, and we sail on our merry way."

As Captain Lok finished the statement, the silver mark on my wrist started to burn. It wasn't a subtle burn, but as though someone had stuck my hand into a pit of fire, unable to quell the flame. I cursed under my breath and reached for it. The silver mark rippled. For a moment, I thought I saw Tarek's reflection inside of it.

Tristan noticed. His voice level, he said, "That will not work. Tarek will know."

"How is that?"

"Because they're using my wounds or something to listen to this conversation!" I spat through the pain.

"Well, then, we must get rid of you. Seems easy enough," Captain Lok leaned back in her chair.

"No, Lyam is crucial to my ship's operations," Tristan retorted.

She crossed her arms, "You think you can trust him? His family put a bounty on your ship."

I clenched my jaw, my mouth falling open ever so slightly. She knew?

"There were flyers all over L'Perle. I am sure they sent them across the sea, too. Clearly, Lyam Beaumont is up to no good," Captain Lok continued.

Tristan came to my rescue, unfazed by Captain Lok's accusations. "The bounty was put out under false pretenses. They were worried about their son and were given incorrect information from a mutineer. Do not try to convince me that the Beaumont family did wrong. They were just looking out for their son."

This was not the response that Captain Lok expected. Her confidence cracked, only slightly, and one side of her mouth fell into a frown. Beside her, Leena fidgeted with her fingers, similar to how Tristan pulled at his glove.

I saw only red as I looked at the two women. They knew about the bounty, the one we found in my parents' house.

"Well, you still owe us," Captain Lok tried again. "We took care of that bounty for you."

Leena's eyes widened, although she did not look Tristan or me in the face.

My vision blurred. The words escaped my lips, low and shaking, "You…killed…them…"

The other side of Captain Lok's mouth fell.

"That's why you—" I pointed at Leena, "were up there! You weren't looking for your brother! You were finishing the job! You wanted to hide the evidence!"

Leena finally spoke, monotone, "We did not know. We were just defending our sister ship."

"You slaughtered them! In their own home!" I stumbled to my feet, my body continuing to shake beneath the realization. "Who does that? My mother was just a trader…my father was a carpenter!"

"As Leena mentioned, we were just defending the *Hare*. If there isn't someone to pay a bounty, then there is no one hunting," Captain Lok said as she leaned back in her chair and glanced at Tristan. "How was I supposed to know that your boy-toy was the son of the Beaumont family?"

"You are not going to get any sympathy from me," Tristan replied.

I shook my head. This was as bad as discovering my parents' bodies. Perhaps even worse. Leaning on my good leg, I limped from the cabin, pushing the door open with my body. The wood snapped as I opened it, hanging ajar to welcome the midday sun.

The world spun as I wandered onto deck and over to the railing. I gripped it, staring across at the *Cobalt Hare*. Storm clouds gathered just above it, dipping the world into a thickening humidity. Sweat gathered on my brow. My sight blurred. There would be no negotiations. Not like this. It was all the Divitiae or nothing; otherwise, my parents' lives would be for naught.

"Lyam!?" Veta called from the stern of the *Cobalt Hare*. "You a'ight there!?"

I shook my head, unable to speak.

"What happened!?"

My vision stabilized enough to see her standing beside Hari and Rémy. They both watched me with the same wide eyes.

But I still couldn't speak.

It would be easy to destroy the *Tortuga* right here, right now. If I commanded the planks to crack, they might listen, crack in place, and let the flood gates open. As soon as they snapped, the ship would sink to its demise, all but the sea's prisoner.

Sure, my magic wasn't powerful, but breaking a piece of wood? That was simple.

I couldn't do it, though. I wouldn't.

That would make me just like Captain Lok. There were still innocent lives on board this ship.

A warm arm fell around my shoulders. "Lyam, come along, let's get back to the *Hare* before the rain starts."

I glanced at Tristan, holding back a new set of tears.

"We'll find the Divitiae another way. The *Tortuga* is not our partner in this endeavor."

"But your sister—"

"Is my blood, but she is not my crew," he motioned me to the gangplank, helping me stay on my two feet.

But not before Leena rushed out with Captain Lok behind her.

"Tristan! Wait! We can compromise," Leena begged. "Please!"

He glared at her. "No. It's all or nothing."

"We need this trade route!"

"Do you *need* it? Or do you just enjoy the riches that it provides?"

"I enjoy the freedom it will give us!"

"No, it's not freedom. It's just riches," Tristan turned from her and continued with me toward the gangplank. Thunder cracked in the distance.

Before we reached the gangplank, Captain Lok bounded forward, blocking our path, her cutlass extended. "We can't let you take our riches from us then."

"Step aside," Tristan hissed.

"Tristan, please, we don't want to hurt you!" Leena called from behind us.

He removed his first glove. Sparks flew from his fingertips.

Captain Lok took a step toward him.

My mind raced. My hammer would provide little help here. Across the gangplank, our crew watched the standoff, preparing their weapons for Tristan's command. I couldn't see Hari or Zo, but they couldn't be far.

I instinctively reached for my hammer. Just as I touched its handle, a new warmth touched the back of my neck.

"Don't move," Leena hissed behind me.

I clenched my jaw.

Tristan kept his attention locked on Captain Lok. No one moved.

Except for Cheddar, who dove from the pillar above, a tiny soldier accepting her role in war.

At full speed, she slammed her body into the side of Captain Lok's head. The captain cursed out, dropping her cutlass and stumbling to the side. Leena's fire fizzled out behind me.

In that moment, something primal came over me. Rage bubbled inside of me, and before Tristan moved, I raced over to Captain Lok and shoved her into the railing of the ship.

Which snapped as her body hit it.

As her body toppled backwards, she reached out, snagging the cloth of my shirt with her hook.

And pulling me with her down into the water.

# CHAPTER THIRTY-FOUR

# Burgundy

The waves always looked smaller from the ship. That was no exception as I plummeted into the sea with Captain Lok. Hitting the water was like falling from a roof. It came fast, with a hard thud that would leave me bruised if I ever made it back on land.

The current washed over me, dragging me beneath the surface and away from the boats. I gasped, swallowing a mouthful of saltwater, and attempted to paddle my way to the surface. Captain Lok freed her hook from my shirt as another wave washed over us.

She vanished into the sea.

The water continued to lap over me, pushing me further down with each gasp of air. While I wasn't a terrible swimmer, I was out of practice. With the storm gathering around us, the clouds heavy in the sky with thunder, the rip currents tugged me further away from my ship.

I tried to grab onto the tail of the *Hare*. But the waves acted with force, pushing me along, unable to fight their demands. It didn't help that my body seared with pain, not just from my splinters or from my fault, but from the salt stinging the swollen wounds on my foot.

Tristan would turn the ship around. I knew that much. He would find me. I just had to stay afloat, even as the currents dragged me away from the ship. I wasn't that far.

Not yet, at least.

I could see them running about on the deck.

As well as a spark of fire.

I tried to wave my arms, but another wave pushed me down.

It never occurred to me how deep the ocean might go until those moments. If I couldn't swim to the top, my body would fall to the ocean floor, far down where sea monsters lurked. No wonder Tristan feared cephalopods. I wouldn't be able to escape them if they dared to grab me!

I pummeled to the surface again, gasping. The water stung my eyes. I couldn't quite see much of anything as the waves grew stronger. Rain fell like blankets, forming a thickening wall between the ships and me.

*I'm going to die,* I accepted as the water filled my nostrils. Even if Tristan turned the ship around now, I doubted they would find me before I succumbed to the currents again.

These storms never lasted long on L'Perle. This wouldn't either. But that didn't matter. Not if I couldn't escape the water.

It thrust me down again.

Part of me wanted to give up. To stop fighting. To just let the sea take me. Not that I wanted to die, but I could only fight for so long. Sooner or later, the sea would take me. Was it worth trying to fight it?

Besides, then Tristan would be free of Tarek's demands.

I pushed myself above the water again.

"YAM!"

I glanced up. Cheddar fluttered above, fighting through the drenching rain.

"Cheddar! Go! Not safe!" I shouted, choking down another mouthful of saltwater.

"YAM!" she shrieked again.

"Ched—" The water encapsulated me again.

I sputtered, forcing my way up to the surface against the waves. Upon reaching the surface, I panted, "Cheddar…go back to the *Hare*…be with Tristan!"

I couldn't see her through the pounding rain.

What I did see was a heavy rope landing just a few feet from me. It bobbed on the surface.

I didn't know where it came from. It didn't matter. I used all my might to swim towards it. With my hands shaking, I took hold of the rope.

It pulled me forward, out of the water, and onto a wooden deck.

I sputtered, rolling over onto my back and exhaling. My breaths fell in rampant waves from my body. Wood. I was so happy to be on a piece of wood.

A familiar piece of wood, by the looks of it.

I raised my head slightly. It was the cutter boat that Tristan and I stole from Rosada! The waves rocked it, threatening to topple it with every movement. Cheddar sat perched on one of the crates aboard, her head cocked to the side.

"What…how…" I pulled myself up to look for my savior.

But a hand fell on my shoulder.

Zo held me in place, motioning for me to stay seated.

"You okay there, Lyam?" Someone called from behind the sail.

"Hari?" I called.

"You're okay. Don't move. We're trying to get out of the storm."

Zo kept their hand on my shoulder and held up a finger, telling me to be quiet. Hari needed full concentration to keep the boat moving. I'd never seen her work the sails on the *Hare* or man the helm. But I suppose her skills were her own secret. After years at sea, she was bound to pick up something.

Cheddar nestled against me, where we sat in silence, waiting for the cutter to leave behind the storm. The rain continued to block our view of the *Tortuga* and the *Hare*. We just had to keep sailing straight, where a glimmer of sunlight peeked through the clouds.

I shivered and brought my hands to the surface of the boat. *Please stay strong,* I plead with the wood. No leaks. No cracks. Just fight the waves and keep afloat. The currents could not pull us as long as we kept moving.

Despite the adrenaline leaving me in a state of exhaustion, I stayed alert, counting each of my heartbeats as the rain slowed to a crawl. With it, the waves quieted. Sunlight inched through the clouds, allowing me to see the *Sanguine Tortuga* and *Cobalt Hare* sailing in the distance, still close, but no longer together.

Zo removed a cotton blanket from a crate and handed it to me. I pulled it over my freezing body. Hari abandoned her place by the sail, removed a few bandages from the crate, and sat in front of me. She examined my foot.

I hadn't even taken a look.

The bandages from earlier had come off in the water. On the top of my foot, a deep gray blotch pulsed. Swelling gathered around it, stinging with salt.

"I'll clean this the best I can, but we'll have to get you medical attention soon," Hari said as she tended to my wound.

"What're you doing out here, Hari?" I asked her.

She frowned, not taking her eyes from her work, before saying, "I was not going to get involved with a squabble between Captain Lok and Captain Davies. The *Sanguine Tortuga* was my home for years. I know that crew. And I can't deny that Captain Lok helped me escape a horrible situation. But…" she began to wrap my foot, "Captain Davies has been an amazing captain. I've seen him grow, and I can't betray him…because I know he would not betray me."

"So…you deserted?" I asked.

"Yes," Hari stepped back from me. "Which is lucky for you."

I didn't judge Hari for leaving. It would hurt Tristan, but I knew she would be stuck trying to choose a side.

But I had my loyalties.

"You'll take me back to the *Hare*, right?" I asked.

"Once it's safe," Hari said as she turned back to the *Hare*. In the distance, I caught a glimpse of the fiery sparks passing between the two boats.

"Tristan needs my help." I tried to stand, but my legs wouldn't allow me to move.

"I know. But as captain of this little ship, I cannot risk our lives sailing into battle," Hari pulled at one of the sails. The rain had finally stopped, gusts of wind pushing us along into the strangely blue waters that had escaped the gray storm.

I pulled the blanket tight around me. Cheddar crawled underneath it for warmth.

"It'll be okay. We'll be okay," Hari said to no one but herself. Zo joined her side and placed their hand on her upper arm. They shared a single look, one that excluded me from the conversation.

And a beat passed.

Flashes of fire continued to rock the boats in the distance, catching their sails in hints of oranges, yellows, and reds.

Another beat.

Dots ran around the ship. I could only imagine what happened on board. Were Tristan and Leena locked in a duel? Were crewmates at arms? Would both ships survive?

Another beat.

We could catch the *Tortuga* and the *Hare* on this cutter, but the danger kept us back. I couldn't do anything but watch. Hope.

And listen to another beat of the waves.

When it happened.

It started with a spark shooting off the side of the *Tortuga*. Then another flare from the *Hare*.

They fell from the body of the ships like rain, scattering over the water where they came to life.

I could not tell you who ignited it first.

In a single breath, the sparks shot upwards, stretching out their tendrils, forming walls of flames. It filled the space between the two ships, escalating and encasing them in a prison of fire. The water did nothing to quell the flames. Instead, they only rose, higher and higher, hiding the sails of the ships.

"Merde," I gasped.

The *Tortuga* and the *Hare* were nothing but comets racing across the sea, their flames reflecting on those cobalt currents and turning the sea burgundy.

# Follow the story of the *Tortuga* and *the Hare* in...

# Want more stories from the Effluvium?

## Check out…

# Also by E.S. Barrison

*The Life & Death Cycle*
*The Story Collector's Almanac*
*The Unsought Fairy Tale Collection*

# Author's Note

Dear Reader,

I would like to take the time to thank you.

Thank you for taking a chance on this book.

Thank you for joining me for this adventure.

And thank you for letting me share my little world with you.

*Those Cobalt Currents* is the second-half of the story that made me chase my dreams at eleven-years-old. While the story I wrote then is far different than this pirate story, the elements remain.

Eleven-year-old me would not recognize this story. The characters have different names, with only a few aspects still the same: fire magic, an island called Janis, and two siblings hoping to make a change.

Yet, if I had never come up with the little story in sixth grade, I may never have pursued writing as I have now. Each book allows me to not only grow as a writer, but also discover more about myself.

Leena was a prime example in *These Sanguine Tides,* and now, Lyam and Tristan join her.

I hope that you found some comfort in their stories. Or if anything, that you at least had fun.

If you did, then I hope you'll consider sharing this story with others. Whether by word of mouth, or leaving an online review, every person you tell helps this story reach a larger audience.

So once again, thank you and I hope to see you on more adventures in the World of the Effluvium.

*E.S. Barrison*

# About the Author

E.S. Barrison has been writing and creating stories for as long as she can remember. After graduating from the University of Florida, she has spent the past few years wrangling her experiences to compose unique worlds with diverse characters. Currently, E.S. lives in Orlando, Florida with her family.

www.esbarrison-author.com